MW00815462

Also by Anasa Maat

A Little Bit Of Honey

Anasa Maat

To Valerie!
Best wishes
and thanks for
your support.
Sincerely,
Anasa Maat
10/30/06

'Til Death Do Us Part

A Novel

"'Til Death Us Do Part"
© Copyright 2006 Anasa Maat
ISBN 0-9754719-1-0

Book layout Design:
Martin Maishman

Printed in Canada

Nutany Publishing Company
Newark, New Jersey 07102
Tel. 973.242.1229

ACKNOWLEDGEMENTS

I read somewhere that "African-American authors write longer acknowledgements than any other group." I'm going to try to keep mine shorter this time; but I must thank the following people for their tremendous help: I want to thank my editor, Diane Raintree, for her invaluable help. Thanks, also, to my book designer, Martin Maishman for his tenacity. I also want to thank my daughter, Danielle Screven, for teaching me a few things about graphics. Thanks go to my stepdaughter, Tawana Simmons, for introducing Buffalo, NY to my first novel, *A Little Bit of Honey.*

Thanks to the rest of my family and friends who offered their support and encouragement. You have all been wonderful. Mostly I thank those thousands of readers who were so generous in their praise for *A Little Bit of Honey.* You are the ones who helped inspire me to write *'Til Death Do Us Part.*

Special thanks, of course, to my husband, Hadren W. Simmons. Hadren your encouragement and support have been the source of my inspiration. Thanks for being you.

Chapter 1

While it was not the best of all times in the city bordered on the east by the banks of the Passaic River and on the west by the valley of the South Orange mountain range, it was certainly not the worst of all times. Newark, the largest city in New Jersey had recovered from the awful uprisings of the 1960s. The century had ended with the promise of a renaissance. A new art center stood proudly downtown to attest to that promise.

The first five years of the new millennium had taken off where the old century left off. New businesses, a flourishing museum, a newly renovated public library, new public schools, and in the making a new sports arena all promised to spur even more development in the renaissance city. Yes, Newark, New Jersey was a city on the move, but not back to the years of tension that had existed before the uprising, when the racial climate was so explosive because of the unequal division of wealth, power and opportunity so prevalent under two hundred years of white dominance.

A lot had changed since the power structure changed hands in 1970. If you lived in Newark, now, you had as good a chance of making it as anyone else regardless of skin color. Jeremiah Jones was a Newarker who could attest to that. He had lived all his life in the city by the Passaic River. Concluding a phone conversation with his father, a retired musician now living in West Africa, Jeremiah could not help but gloat on his success.

"Yes, Dad, my life is going well. My marriage is on solid ground, my businesses are flourishing and my children are healthy. I am truly blessed. What more could a man ask for?" Jeremiah laughed a hearty laugh so his father could hear his happiness.

"Sometimes even solid ground can experience an earthquake, Son," his father said.

"I know that, Dad. But we don't have earthquakes in New Jersey." Jeremiah laughed again.

"Well, I'm happy for you, Son. I remember feeling blessed like that when your mother and I first married. I wasn't prepared to lose her. It devastated me."

"Nothing like that will happen to Aliyah and me, Dad. Don't worry." Jeremiah hoped to reassure his father before saying goodbye.

After hanging up the phone Jeremiah chuckled. His father was worrying needlessly. He was sure some of the concern came from his father's recollection of the demise of Jeremiah's first marriage. The divorce had devastated Jeremiah. His father had been very supportive back then. He had been able to relate to his son's loss because he had felt the same sense of loss when he lost his first wife, Jeremiah's mother. Only that loss had been due to death. Loss of a loved one by death or divorce could shatter a person, but Jeremiah was confident that he was not about to experience either. He could not imagine anything happening to interrupt his marriage. Nothing was more important to him than his family.

Jeremiah had married two Newark women and was the proud father of two children born of his second marriage to Aliyah, editor in chief of a popular woman's magazine based in Manhattan. Yes, life in Newark was good for Jeremiah. He attributed his good fortune to his strong faith. He was a spiritual man.

For the past ten years Jeremiah had been practicing Ifa, an ancient Yoruba religion still practiced in parts of Africa, Brazil, the Caribbean and in some parts of the United States. His life had improved tremendously after he had adopted Ifa and incorporated its tenets into his own life. His periodic offerings to his guardian *orisa* and ancestral spirits, along with his daily prayers to the creator, had made such a difference in his life.

After graduating from high school, Jeremiah had attended community college studying criminal justice for two years and gone to the police academy. He had spent twenty years as a

Newark policeman before going out on a disability retirement after coming close to death on two occasions. Now he was the proud owner of two successful businesses in the city. The mayor himself had vouched for him to obtain bank loans to start both of his businesses. Newark's mayor of twenty years was committed to helping young African Americans and Latinos fulfill their potential.

Jeremiah's first business, a recycling contract with the city, was pretty much run by loyal employees these days. Jeremiah spent most of his time at Oblivion, his second business, and a popular art gallery on Halsey Street in downtown Newark. Oblivion was located in a loft above a popular jazz and supper club. Jeremiah owned the building. The gallery consisted of 3000 square feet of exposed brick walls and shiny oak flooring. The gallery was exquisitely designed to make the most of the space and light that came through the skylights he had installed two years ago. His studio was located on a portion of the roof, accessible by a spiral staircase at the far end of the gallery. Jeremiah, himself, had created many of the paintings that hung in the gallery. Reviewers and art critics agreed he was a fine painter. Other than spending time with his beloved family there was no other place that he enjoyed being more than in his studio, working on another masterpiece.

Jeremiah had been at the studio since ten this morning and had stopped working only briefly to eat a sandwich that had been sent up from the supper club below at lunchtime. Although plenty of light flooded the room, clouds and showers, which had been forecast for the late spring day, made it difficult to tell what time of day it was. When he looked up at the wall clock, beautiful artwork itself, he gasped. *Where does the time go?*

He had been working on a painting of the Harriet Tubman School. The 125-year-old structure was finally being replaced. He was trying to preserve something of the old building. He had spent the past three hours studying photos he'd taken of the building and trying to bring it alive on canvas. Now it was six o'clock, and he had promised his wife he'd be home for dinner by seven. The thought of spending time with his two adorable children and his beautiful wife made him rush to close up shop.

At 7PM Jeremiah put his key in the front door and entered the foyer of his home. The three-story brownstone was over one hundred years old, with a quaint, comfortable feel about it. Aliyah had purchased it a couple of years before he met her and had decorated it to give it authentic African charm. It was one of the things that impressed him about Aliyah when he first met her. She had great taste.

"Anybody home?" he yelled out as he hung his jacket on the coat rack in the foyer.

"We're in the kitchen," he heard two voices say in unison. One was the squeal of a child.

Jeremiah entered the bright, spacious kitchen where his tall, shapely wife wearing an apron, stood at the stove stirring something. Nia, his eighteen-month-old, precocious baby girl, sat in her highchair eating finger foods, and four-year old Mandela, the spitting image of his father and just as smart, sat at the kitchen table drinking a glass of milk.

"Help me get the kids bathed and into bed," Aliyah said, putting the lid on the pot.

"I'm starving. When are we going to eat?" Jeremiah asked, helping, Mandela put his dirty glass into the dishwasher.

"I just finished working an hour ago," she said. "Jean fed the kids before she left, so I'm just whipping up something for the two of us. I have a lot to tell you over dinner. I guess we can eat in about an hour."

Over the next hour Jeremiah and Aliyah bathed their children together, playing and splashing water, then tucked them into bed and read them a story before turning out the lights in the nursery and going downstairs where Aliyah had already set the dining room table. Just as she had predicted it was exactly 8PM when they started eating their dinner. Aliyah was like that; organized to perfection, another thing that had impressed him about her.

"What is it you had to tell me?" Jeremiah asked as he put a mouthful of something delicious into his mouth. "And what is this we're eating? It's great!"

"It's turkey stroganoff. You've had it before. I want to tell you about my plan to get my writing staff to expand their horizons. We're competing with some of the most popular women's magazines in the country. I want to reach out to black women all over the Diaspora. I want to encourage my staff to look at issues facing black women in Africa and Europe as well as in Asia and the Caribbean. What do you think, Jeremiah?"

"That's great. Most African American women know so little about their sisters in other parts of the world. If you present articles in *Enigma* about some of their issues you will be helping bridge the gap created by the 18th century slave trade. Women of African descent will be so much more enlightened."

As Aliyah and Jeremiah cleared away the dinner dishes, she said "I feel a lot more confident asking my staff to go out on a limb and do something a little different now that I've talked to you about it. Why don't you relax for a while? I'm going to check on the kids and take a bath, okay?

"Okay, darling," Jeremiah said, and then smiled.. He liked it when she complimented him on his ideas or acknowledged his support of her. It showed that she appreciated his intellect. While Aliyah took her bath he would relax, maybe watch a little television.

At ten o'clock Jeremiah turned the television off, having just finished watching the second game of the subway series between the Mets and the Yankees. Pedro Martinez and Mike Piazza had come through for the Mets once again. They were looking good; good enough to win all three games this year. He smiled as he turned his attention to his wife and climbed the stairs to their bedroom.

Aliyah looked like a goddess as she lay on their bed, her braids piled on top of her head and twisted into some form of knot. She was wearing the white nightgown he liked so much to see her in. Her long bronze legs gleamed from the oil she had applied after her bath. She had lit candles standing tall in pillars on both sides of the bed. A dozen or so other scented candles glowed from the dresser, the night tables and the windowsills. She was reading an *Essence* magazine and the mellow sound of Miles Davis playing "Around Midnight" emanated from the stereo. The fragrance of lemon grass and lavender was intoxicating.

Jeremiah hurriedly undressed, took a five-minute shower, and jumped into bed. He snuggled his nose up to Aliyah's neck and nibbled her ear lobes. "You smell wonderful," he said, pulling her into his arms as they sank into the pillowed bed.

"So do you," Aliyah said, taking a whiff of his clean body before kissing his neck, face, and his lips. "Take me. I'm yours." She laughed softly before submitting to him.

Later as she lay sleeping in his arms he sighed. Their lovemaking was still as wonderful as it had been the very first time, on their first date. Their attraction for each other had been so strong from the beginning that it had kept them apart for a little while at first. But they had soon come to realize that they were meant for each other. Jeremiah went to sleep knowing that the best thing that he had ever done for himself was to marry Aliyah. He felt so blessed, yet he was consumed with disturbing dreams of loss.

At breakfast the next morning Jeremiah read the local newspaper, while Aliyah made hot cereal for him and the kids. *The Ledger* had just released the names of the ten top scholarship winners selected from among the twelve high schools in the city. There were six African Americans, three Latinos, and one Portuguese, proportionately a fair representation of the people in the city. The first place winner, an African American male, would receive an $80,000 scholarship to attend Massachusetts Institute of Technology. The other nine winners were going to Ivy League colleges across the country including Stanford, Harvard and Princeton. The article noted that although there were many more deserving students in the city only ten scholarships could be awarded each year.

"This gives me hope that by the time Manny is old enough for high school things will be even better in this city," Jeremiah said as he sipped a cup of hot Ovaltine, his favorite morning beverage. "He's only three now, but in fourteen years he'll be ready for college, and goodness knows what tuition costs will be by then. He'll certainly need a scholarship if he's going to attend one of those Ivy League schools. Tuition for four years might be close to a quarter of a million dollars by that time,"

"Don't call him Manny," Aliyah said, giving her husband an annoying look. "His name is Mandela. I want him to learn to answer to his full name and not accept nick- names from anyone, including family." She helped her son blow on his breakfast oatmeal to cool it off.

Selecting names for their children had been difficult enough. Aliyah didn't want to minimize their effort by calling their son by a shortened version of the name they had finally selected. Mandela was a good strong name. Jeremiah had been worried that giving their first born son an African name would have an adverse affect on the opportunities that could be afforded him later in life. He had read a university study revealing that job applicants with names that sounded black like Ebony, Aisha, or Kareem were discriminated against during the recruiting process. It appeared that applicants with white names like Gregory, Brett, Anne or Emily were afforded more opportunities to land an interview.

Despite the results of the study, Aliyah had won that argument, especially when she pointed out that Barack Obama had been elected to the United States Senate, and that Kweise Mfumi had been a United States Congressman. Her son stood as good a chance as either of them with his name.

"Don't forget about Nia," Aliyah said. Nia meant purpose in the Swahili language. It was also the fifth principle of Kwanzaa. "We'll have to think about her education too. She might be the one that wins the scholarship to MIT." She looked at the wall clock, wondering where Jean could be.

Jean, the children's nanny, generally arrived by 7:30 A.M.,

allowing Aliyah plenty of time to get ready and leave the house for her Manhattan office by 9 or 9:30. These days Aliyah was lucky to get to work by 10. Before the children were born she was out of the house before 7:30AM and at her desk by 8. Now she did most of her work out of her home office and went into Manhattan only two or three days a week. Today was one of those days that she needed to be at the office by 10, and it was already after 8 and Jean was not there yet.

"What time are you leaving for the gallery?" Aliyah asked. Oblivion was only a short distance from their home. Jeremiah routinely opened the gallery at 9, but Aliyah thought she might persuade him to take over with the kids while she ran upstairs to get dressed.

"I can be late," Jeremiah said, anticipating his wife's next question. Neatly folding the newspaper and placing it on the counter, he picked up the baby from the high chair, put his face in hers and giggled along with the laughing baby. "Are you going to workout before you get ready for work?" he asked, taking his son's hand and leading him into the living room where they would wait for the late nanny.

"No. I don't have time. I'm late as it is." She rushed up the stairs to get dressed, wondering why he had asked her that. She had given up trying to fit a workout into her busy schedule almost a year ago.

Jean still hadn't arrived when Aliyah finished dressing. But she

17

had called and said she was running behind and would get there within a few minutes. Jeremiah was playing with the kids in the spacious living room when Aliyah finally came downstairs. "Try to get home for dinner by seven," she said as she hastily deposited a kiss on each of her baby's foreheads and a light kiss on Jeremiah's lips. She noticed his eyes checking out her appearance as she made a dash for the front door.

Four years of marriage and two children had not only made a difference in her daily routine but also in her appearance. Always tall and thin, Aliyah had gained a few pounds. She once ran five miles before work to stay in shape, now the only exercise she got was running through their large brownstone, chasing up and down the stairs behind the kids, lifting the baby, and making love with Jeremiah. Being a wife and mother was far more demanding than she'd ever imagined, especially with all the work she had to do for *Enigma.* The demands were enormous, but she had held up and been instrumental in helping bring *Enigma* to one of the top ten women's magazines in the country.

As Aliyah walked the short distance to the train station she wondered if Jeremiah was aware that her fortieth birthday was approaching in less than two weeks. She would be reaching another milestone.

Chapter 2

It wasn't quite five when Aliyah put her key in the front door of their brownstone. In the six hours at the office her department meeting had gone well, her staff was receptive to the suggestion that they branch out and write about women of African descent from various parts of the Diaspora. She decided that she would also write a feature article focusing on motherhood in different cultures in Africa and maybe the Caribbean.

She would have to do some traveling. Perhaps Jeremiah would travel with her. Maybe they'd take the kids to West Africa for a visit. Aliyah's best friend, Claudia, lived in Ghana and perhaps they could visit Ghana and gather information for her article. Maybe they could even stop over in Senegal and visit Jeremiah's father and stepmother. Aliyah couldn't wait for Jeremiah to get home.

After hanging her jacket on the coat rack in the foyer, Aliyah went into the kitchen where Jean was feeding the children their dinner. "Hi," Aliyah said as she entered the kitchen.

"Mommy, Mommy," Mandela screamed and flung himself at her, hugging her legs.

"How's my big boy?" Aliyah laughed as she picked her son up and hugged him tightly.

"Dah dah, Dah Da," Nia chimed in, stretching out her arms wanting to be picked up too.

"Not until you say Ma Ma." Aliyah teased her daughter.

"You'll be hearing mama soon enough." Jean reminded her. "Then you'll be wishing she had never started." She laughed with Aliyah.

Jean had been with the family since Mandela was an infant. Reverend Doggett, pastor of Metropolis Baptist Church in Newark, had highly recommended her. He had married Aliyah and Jeremiah and was a trusted family friend. Jean turned out to be all he had said she would be.

Jean, in her mid-to-late sixties wore her gray tresses in a neat bun at the nape of her neck. She always wore a colorful housedress, was so efficient, and liked having the kids fed by the time Aliyah finished working, enabling her some quality time with the children before their bedtime.

"Something smells good." Aliyah looked into the pots on the stove.

"I made spaghetti for Mandela," Jean said. "There's enough left for you and Mr. Jones." She often fixed dinner for the entire family on the days Aliyah went into Manhattan to work. "I made a salad and garlic toast." She smiled.

After the kids finished dinner Aliyah took them upstairs to the playroom where she played with them on the soft pile carpeting. Mandela attended a preschool class for three hours a day, three times a week. He was learning the alphabet and Aliyah helped him at home with some colorful blocks carved in the shape of various letters. He already knew how to spell his name. She was teaching him how to spell mommy and daddy.

"Find me a "d," she said, watching her son scramble through the blocks looking for a "d".

"I found one," he squealed with delight.

"Okay find me two more." Aliyah smiled at her son. "The word daddy has three ds in it." She helped Nia stack some blocks while Mandela scrambled to find more ds.

After a hectic day at work Aliyah looked forward to the time she spent playing with her children. She knew how important it was to spend good quality time with them. After putting the blocks away she turned the stereo on, and the three of them danced to the tune of Luther Van Dross singing, "Dance With My Father."

"I never get to dance with my father," Mandela said, dancing wildly about the room.

"Well maybe Daddy will get home a little early and we can all dance until bath time." Aliyah danced slowly.

No sooner had she spoken than she heard Jeremiah from the doorway. "May I have this dance," he said looking at her.

"Yes you may." She smiled at him, stepping into his waiting arms. They danced until the song ended.

"Bath time," Jeremiah said, looking at Mandela.

"But I didn't get a chance to dance with my father," Mandela said, noticeably upset.

"Okay," Jeremiah said and picked up his son as Aliyah replayed the track.

Jeremiah holding Mandela, and Aliyah holding Nia, danced together in the middle of the floor until the song had played through again.

After bathing their children, Aliyah put the children to bed while Jeremiah tidied the bathroom. Aliyah listened while Jeremiah read a story to the children, then she and Jeremiah went downstairs for their spaghetti dinner and to talk over the events of the day.

This was their life. Quiet, loving, routine and peaceful. The only time it deviated was on the weekends. Jeremiah only worked on weekends when there was a new exhibit opening. He and Aliyah generally spent Saturdays running errands in the morning and taking the children somewhere special like the zoo or the museum in the afternoon. On Saturday evenings they sometimes got a sitter and went to the Jazz Garden or out to dinner and a movie. Sometimes they visited friends or had guests over to their house.

Sunday was reserved for family, relaxation, and meditation.

Sometimes Aliyah attended church with her mother. She practiced Yoga, meditated and made periodic offerings of honey to Osun, her guardian *orisa.* She would walk down to the river or drive to Weequahic Park Lake and pour the honey into the water asking Osun to continue to bless her with a life of pleasure.

Jeremiah used this time to strengthen his bond with the creator, his ancestral spirits, and with his guardian *orisa,* Shango. Both Aliyah and Jeremiah credited their guardian *orisas* for bringing them together. The ancestral spirits had blessed their marriage. It was a match made in heaven and nothing could shake it, or so they thought.

———————

On the Saturday morning of her fortieth birthday Aliyah woke to the sound of Stevie Wonder singing "Happy Birthday To You." When she opened her eyes Jeremiah and the children were all on the bed clasping gifts for her.

"What a wonderful way to start my birthday," Aliyah exclaimed.

"Open mine first." Mandela thrust his gift into her hands.

"What is it?" Aliyah asked, shaking the nicely wrapped box with a big yellow bow.

"It's a surprise," Mandela squealed.

Aliyah ripped off the colorful paper wrapping and opened the box. She squealed, too, when she discovered a cute little stuffed Persian cat. It was all white and fluffy with a blue ribbon around its neck. Aliyah held the cat close to her, leaning over to kiss her son.

"Thank you, darling," she said. "How did you know I wanted a cat?"

"I wanted to get a real one Mommy. But Daddy said you're lergic to real ones."

"Allergic, Mandela," Jeremiah said. That means that mommy's nose is very sensitive to things like cat fur and cigarette smoke."

"But this cat is just purr-fect," Aliyah said, hugging it closer to her.

"Okay, Jeremiah said. Time to open mine."

Excitedly Aliyah ripped open a tiny box she knew from its size contained a piece of jewelry. "Oh Jeremiah this is so beautiful," she said taking a gold bracelet out of a small, black velvet box. The gorgeous bracelet had four charms, all Adrinka symbols from West Africa, symbols representing love and peace.

"Do you like it?" he asked.

"I just love it she said, extending her arm for him to fasten the clasp around her wrist

"You have to open Nia's present," Mandela said, and giggled.

Nia's gift was a lovely scented candle. Aliyah inhaled the fragrance. "Lemongrass and lavender." She smiled at her daughter. "Thank you baby. This is my favorite scent." She picked her daughter up and held her close. "You all are so wonderful."

"We're going out to breakfast, too, Mommy," Mandela said, jumping up and down on the bed.

"I have a day of surprises for you, lady," Jeremiah said. "So get up and get dressed so we can get started."

I am so blessed, Aliyah thought. *How can things get better than this?*

After a fun-filled day with the kids, Jeremiah babysat while Aliyah took a nap so she'd be rested for an evening on the town. He wouldn't tell her what he had in store for her. She surmised that it would be a quiet dinner for two, perhaps at one of the local eateries. Jeremiah woke her at six-thirty and suggested she start getting ready. The babysitter was already downstairs, and they had dinner reservations for 8:00PM.

"Where are we going?" she asked.

"You'll find out soon enough." His smile was mischievous.

"Give me a hint so I'll know what to wear."

"Wear that black knit dress that looks so good on you. I haven't seen you wear it in a long time." He headed towards the bathroom to trim his mustache.

It was 7:00 when Aliyah came downstairs, dressed to kill in a cobalt blue dress with matching accessories. She wore her long braided hair piled on top of her head with a cobalt blue jeweled comb keeping it in place.

"You look great," Jeremiah said. "But why didn't you wear the black dress?"

"I'm not in the mood for black. I wanted to wear something electrifying to go with my hot mood." She didn't want to tell him that the black dress appeared to have shrunk since the last time she wore it.

When Jeremiah pulled the car in front of the Jazz Garden, Aliyah got a little suspicious. "Why are we stopping here? Don't you ever get enough of this place?"

"I thought we could stop in for a quick drink before going to the restaurant. I want to show off my gorgeous wife on her fortieth birthday."

Jeremiah held the door for her to enter the club. Almost immediately the music started blasting Stevie Wonder singing "Happy Birthday To You" for the second time that day. Just as her eyes became adjusted to the dimness of the room, the lights came on full blast, and everybody yelled out "Surprise," before they joined voices with Stevie. Aliyah looked around the room into the smiling faces of her brother, Jamal, and his wife, Sheniqua; Jeremiah's sister, Naomi, and her husband, Phillip; and her friends and spiritual advisors, Kanmi and Oya. Her mother was there, too, grinning from ear to ear. It was a wonderful surprise. She turned to give Jeremiah a hug and a kiss just as the bartender announced, "Let the party begin."

The party had been going full blast for about two hours when Jeremiah took over at the piano and began to play. Aliyah watched him as a jazz singer, Miss Melody, took the microphone and sidled up to the piano. She started singing "You'd Be So Nice To Come Home To," in a very seductive voice.

As she sang Miss Melody kept her eyes on Jeremiah as though she was singing directly to him. Aliyah wondered if she was imagining things but the few times Jeremiah looked up from the piano he appeared to make eye contact with Miss Melody. Aliyah recognized the glassy look in his eyes. She had seen it often enough when he was in a romantic mood. Miss Melody was a very attractive woman. And she was dressed in a black knit dress that showed off her shapely size-eight body. They seemed to be making a connection, this sexy singer and her husband.

Aliyah looked around the room to see if anyone else noticed. All eyes were focused on the two of them, but everyone was smiling and appeared to be into the music. *My imagination is running wild* Aliyah thought. *Maybe I've had too much champagne.* When the song ended Miss Melody whispered something into Jeremiah's ear and he began to play again. They performed together for almost an hour.

"Did you enjoy the surprise party?" Jeremiah asked as they drove the short distance home.

"It was okay," Aliyah said solemnly.

"Only okay? I thought it was great. Didn't you have a good time?" He pressed her for an answer.

"I guess I'm tired. It's been a long day."

Sensing her mood change Jeremiah said nothing. He knew

when something was bothering his wife, and he thought it best to leave it alone.

Throughout the night Aliyah lay awake in their bed thinking about the evening. Miss Melody had openly flirted with her husband at her fortieth birthday party. And, if that wasn't bad enough Jeremiah appeared to enjoy it. At first Aliyah thought she was imagining things. But as the party had progressed Aliyah noticed little things like how Miss Melody touched Jeremiah's arm when he introduced her to the audience. How she had grinned in his face when he asked the guests to give her another round of applause. How Jeremiah had returned her smile. How she kept whispering in his ear when she wanted him to play a particular song. *Could Jeremiah be attracted to another woman?* Miss Melody was certainly an attractive woman. She had such a cute figure.

Hmm, thought Aliyah. *Maybe that's why Jeremiah has been asking me about working out. He must think that I am getting too fat. Miss Melody certainly looked good in that black knit dress. Maybe that's why Jeremiah wanted me to wear a black knit dress. He's seen Miss Melody in that dress before. He wants me to look like her.*

Chapter
3

J eremiah slept soundly throughout the night. After getting the cold shoulder from Aliyah when he got into bed, he had rolled over and gone right to sleep. He figured that he would find out what was bothering her sooner or later; he generally did. Usually she didn't have to tell him, he knew her so well. But for the life of him he couldn't figure out what had gone wrong at the party. Everyone appeared to be having a good time. It seemed like all of a sudden Aliyah's mood changed. He had no clue as to what had happened. It was so unlike Aliyah.

He woke up early the next morning. He heard the kids stirring around in the nursery. He wanted to get them downstairs before they got too noisy. Although he had slept soundly he sensed Aliyah had not. He wanted her to sleep undisturbed now, not knowing when she had finally gotten to sleep. He was glad it was Sunday.

After splashing some water on his body and dressing hurriedly in jeans and a T-shirt Jeremiah went into the nursery to get the kids. The baby was standing up in her crib, fussing with her older brother who was busy reading a book in his toddler bed and ignoring her. They looked up when Jeremiah came in the room.

"I'm thirsty," Mandela said. "Can I have a glass of water?

"Dah da, Da, Da," the baby said, showing her toothless gums.

"Okay guys," Jeremiah said, let's get dressed and go downstairs so Mommy can get some rest.

"Is it still Mommy's birthday?" Mandela asked.

"No Mandela. Yesterday was Mommy's birthday. This is a new day, it's Sunday."

Jeremiah dressed the children and took them downstairs to fix breakfast. He hoped Aliyah would wake up in a pleasant mood. He did not want a carryover from last night.

After a mostly sleepless night Aliyah awoke to discover she was alone in the king-size bed. She looked at the alarm clock on the table beside her bed and saw that it was 11:30AM. She could hear the children laughing and running downstairs. She was grateful that her birthday had fallen on a Saturday and that she had Sunday to recuperate. She was also grateful that Jeremiah woke up first and was taking care of the children. She had awful dreams throughout the night. She dreamed that another woman was after her husband.

It wasn't until she was in the shower with hot water cascading over her body that Aliyah realized that it hadn't been a dream. Miss Melody was after her husband. Maybe Aliyah was wrong. Maybe she had misread all the signs. Maybe the champagne had made her hallucinate. Maybe she should call her mother. She would know. She had been there. Nothing escaped Betty Neal, especially when it came to her children. She always had their best interests in mind. But it was Sunday, and Betty would be in church. It would have to wait.

When Aliyah walked into the kitchen Jeremiah had a stack of pecan pancakes on the stove, a fresh pot of tea was steeping, and the kids were seated at the table waiting to be served. She felt overwhelmed with thoughts of how wonderful he was. She was so fortunate to have such a considerate husband. Never had he given her reason to suspect that he would ever be unfaithful to her. He loved her and their children. Why had she ever been concerned about him and Miss Melody? She decided then and there that she would put all thoughts of such nonsense out of her head.

"Good morning darlings," she said in her sweetest voice.

"Mommy, Mommy," Mandela said excitedly.

Aliyah gave him a big smile then hugged him. She picked up the baby and gave her a big kiss and a squeeze, deliberately avoiding her husband. She was embarrassed about her behavior the night before.

Sensing his wife's embarrassment, Jeremiah said "You must be well rested this morning, I mean afternoon," He glanced at the wall clock, which read 12:10PM.

"Yes I am," she said. I guess I overdid it yesterday."

"My fault," he apologized. "I planned too much for one day. I should have let you rest yesterday in preparation for last night. I'm sorry I wore you out."

"Oh Jeremiah, you have nothing to apologize for," Aliyah said, walking into his arms. "I acted like a bitch last night," she whispered into his ear. " I'm the one that should be apologizing. Please forgive me?" She stepped back to wait for his reaction.

"All is well that ends well. Sit down and let's eat these pancakes before they get too cold." Jeremiah smiled at her.

After brunch Aliyah sent Jeremiah and the kids up to the nursery while she cleared away the dishes. All of the doubting thoughts about the night before had disappeared from her mind, until the telephone rang.

"Hello," she answered using her sweetest voice.

"Girl that was some party last night," her sister-in-law, Sheniqua, said. "Have you recovered yet."

"Yes," Aliyah said. "I guess I drank too much champagne. I got awfully tired."

"That's not what I'm talking about. I'm talking about recovering from seeing that hoochie momma and your husband eyeing each other the way they were."

Aliyah's heart sank. *So others did notice.* She was speechless. Her brother's wife had the worst habit of saying whatever came to her mind with no consideration for other people's feelings. This was the worst yet.

"Sheniqua I don't know what you're talking about. I've got to go. The baby needs me." Aliyah hung up the telephone and within seconds her mood had returned to where it was the night before.

At 2PM, Betty, Aliyah's mother, stopped by the house after church. Aliyah was so happy to see her. Betty Neal had become a very busy lady in the last couple of years. Aliyah hardly got a chance to see her. Her husband died of a heart attack two years earlier, leaving Betty a widow at age sixty. Since her husband's death she'd become more active in her church and the community, and she had become president of the board of directors for the company her husband had founded, Nealz' Benz, an automobile dealership that sold luxury cars. She had sold the large home her children were raised in and downsized into a two-bedroom condominium not far from where the family home had been.

After greeting her mother warmly at the front door Aliyah led her into the kitchen where she had been preparing dinner. "I'm so glad you stopped by," Aliyah said. "I was waiting for you to get home from church before I called you." She went back to the chore of cutting up chicken.

"Where are the children?" Betty asked, looking around for her grandson who always liked to sneak up on her.

"They're upstairs with their father. Sit and talk with me for awhile before I let them know you're here." Aliyah knew once the kids saw her mother they would get all of her attention. "You are going to stay for dinner, right?" She looked at her mother.

"Yes indeed," Betty said. "I don't want to go home and eat alone. What are we having."

"Curried chicken and rice." Aliyah sprinkled seasoning on the chicken.

"Anything you want me to do?" Betty asked.

"No just sit and talk to me. Everything is under control."

"Did you enjoy your birthday surprise? I know I did." Betty laughed. "I haven't had that much fun in a long time." She settled into a seat at the kitchen table.

"Yeah, it was nice," Aliyah said a little somberly.

"It doesn't sound as though you had a good time." Betty looked at her daughter for a clue. "Did I miss something?"

"I don't know. Sheniqua called this morning to let me know that she didn't miss a thing. She couldn't help but notice how Jeremiah and Miss Melody seemed to connect with each other."

"Oh Aliyah now don't tell me that you're going to let something that Sheniqua said get you upset. You know how Sheniqua is. She doesn't know when to keep her mouth shut." Betty gave Aliyah a reassuring look.

"Then you must have noticed it, too." Aliyah turned back to the kitchen sink.

"There was nothing to notice. Miss Melody was performing and Jeremiah was going along with the act. That's all there is to it, Aliyah. I'm surprised at you for getting upset about something so trivial. You know how much Jeremiah loves you."

"That doesn't mean that he can't be tempted. Miss Melody is a very attractive woman, and Jeremiah is a man." Aliyah put the chicken in the oven. "All men can be tempted. Did you ever wonder if Daddy was tempted to stray?"

"Of course I did," Betty said. "Your father was a very good-looking man, and he had lots of money. I'm sure dozens of women tried to get his attention. But I knew that there was nothing that I could do to stop him if he wanted to stray. I just didn't worry about it, and I never looked for anything. I took my wedding vows seriously. I knew your father and I were married 'for better or worse, 'til death do us part.' Fortunately, nothing ever got back to me. Trust me sweetheart, you will only hurt yourself if you go around looking for something where there is nothing to find."

"You're right Mom." Aliyah gave her mother a hug and a quick kiss on the cheek. "I'm so glad that I have you to talk to. I know that I have nothing to worry about with Jeremiah. I just don't like it when other women come onto him like that."

"Well there is nothing that you can do to stop other women, so just concentrate on keeping your man happy at home and you won't have to worry about him straying."

Jeremiah smiled as he folded and lay down the sports section of the Sunday newspaper. The Mets had just won the third game in the subway series. They were doing real good. He looked at his son, still playing on the nursery floor with his little sister. They had played nicely, while he read the paper.

"Pick up your toys and put them away," he said to Mandela. "It's time to wash up for dinner. I think we have company."

"Who's our company Daddy?" Mandela asked, picking up his toy trucks, and putting them in the toy box.

"I don't know, but I think I heard the doorbell ring a while ago. Let's get ready to go downstairs."

As Jeremiah washed the children's hands he wondered what was going on with Aliyah. She seemed in a good mood when she came downstairs for brunch. But her mood had changed abruptly after she'd received a telephone call. He had come downstairs for a minute to find out what she was cooking for dinner, and she snapped at him as she hung up the telephone. These abrupt mood changes were so unlike her. He didn't know how to handle them. *This is a side of my wife that is brand new to me,* he thought.

Jeremiah was grateful to see his mother-in-law sitting in the kitchen when he and the children came downstairs. Aliyah always felt better after talking to her mother.

"Grandma," Mandela shouted when he saw Betty.

"Come here big boy," Betty said, scooping a giggling Mandela up into her arms, and giving him a big hug. "How's my number one grandson." She smiled at him.

"Fine." Mandela said, obviously happy to see his grandmother.

Betty took Nia from Jeremiah's arms and kissed and rocked her until she squealed with delight. Betty adored her grandchildren and took great care to spoil them rotten.

Finally Betty gave Jeremiah a big hug letting him know that he was loved, too. Jeremiah smiled at her wondering, *Is this how my wife is going to look in twenty years?* Betty Neal was a good-looking woman. She'd kept her figure and she looked much younger than her sixty-two years. Betty always had a smile on her face and kind words for everyone. People often mistook her and Aliyah for sisters rather than mother and daughter. Jeremiah smiled at the thought of being with Aliyah for the next twenty years.

The curried chicken was delicious, and Jeremiah made it a point to tell Aliyah just how good it was. It did not go unnoticed how her mood had switched back to happy, and he wanted to keep it that way.

"That was a marvelous meal," he said, and pushed his chair back from the table. "I should run around the block a few times to work it off. This makes two days in a row that I've overeaten."

"Why all the concern about weight and overeating all of a sudden?" Aliyah asked, wondering if Jeremiah was hinting, again, that she should work out more.

"There is nothing wrong with staying in shape, right Mom?" Jeremiah looked at Betty for confirmation. "You certainly look fit as a fiddle."

"You're absolutely right," Betty said. "I often wonder if Bill would have had a healthier heart if he had exercised more. Maybe he would have lived longer. I make it a point to exercise everyday for at least a half-hour."

"Come on, Aliyah, let's take a run around the block?" Jeremiah said. "We haven't been out all day. We could use some fresh air. You'll watch the kids for us, won't you Mom?"

"No," Aliyah said adamantly. She gave Jeremiah a look that told him to quit.

"I hope you don't mind if I go," he said, reaching for his jacket and wondering if another mood swing was coming on. *What was that all about?* He asked himself as he walked out into the brisk evening air.

Once outside Jeremiah decided to walk down to the gallery. He wanted to make sure that everything had been secured at the gallery after the 5PM closing. As he walked through the park and down to Halsey Street, he thought about Aliyah, and tried to analyze what he may have done to upset her this time. *She seemed fine until I asked her to go for a walk,* he thought. *I saw the scowl on her face when Betty was talking about exercise. Maybe that's it. Maybe she thinks I want her to lose weight.* This thought alarmed Jeremiah, especially since it was the farthest thing from his mind. He liked the way his wife looked. She was just right the way she was.

When Jeremiah got to the gallery he went directly upstairs without stopping in the nightclub. He was surprised to find the gallery still open. His staff was generally anxious to get out by quitting time, especially on Sunday. When he walked in Miss

Melody was standing towards the far end of the gallery, looking at one of his paintings.

"What are you doing up here?" Jeremiah asked as he approached her.

"I talked your attendant into letting me look around for a few minutes before she closed up, and she obliged me. Is it okay?"

"Sure," he said. "I didn't know you were interested in art." He looked at the painting she was looking at. It was a picture of Aliyah lying under "God's Tree."

"There's a lot about me that you don't know." She smiled at him. "Your wife is very beautiful. You're a lucky man."

"I know," Jeremiah said. "Blessed is what I am." He smiled back at her.

"Mr. Jones, can I leave now that you're here?" The gallery attendant asked, coming out of the storage room.

"Sure," Jeremiah said. "I'll lock up."

Jeremiah turned his attention back to Miss Melody. "How much have you seen?" he asked as they walked to the other side of the gallery.

"Just that one long wall. I haven't seen what's upstairs yet." She glanced up the spiral staircase.

"My studio is up there. I'll show it to you some other time. I just came down to check on things. I have to get back home. I have company."

As he and Miss Melody walked out, Jeremiah thought about Aliyah. *How can I let her know that I don't want her to lose any weight? I want her to exercise so that she'll stay healthy. I don't want her to get sick. Maybe I'll bring her a little something home to show her that I don't care about her weight.*

"I'm going to take you up on that offer to see your studio," Miss Melody said, bringing him out of his thoughts.

"Anytime at all, just stop by next time you're in the building and I'll give you a personal tour." He smiled at her.

When Jeremiah got home, Aliyah and her mother were still talking in the kitchen. They looked up when he walked in.

"What took you so long?" Aliyah asked, noticing that he had a package in his hand.

"I wanted to check on the gallery, make sure it was locked up," he said.

"What's this?" She reached for the package.

"It's a surprise," he said, putting the package behind him, out of her reach.

"Is it for me?" Aliyah asked, eyeing him suspiciously.

"I'll give it to you later. You're not getting ready to leave already are you?" He diverted his attention to his mother-in-law.

"Yes I am," Betty said. "I have a board meeting first thing in the morning, I need to go home and get ready for it."

"Wow, Mother," Aliyah said, and looked at her mother. "You are truly a business woman. Jamal tells me you are doing great things with Daddy's company. He says that you get a lot of respect from the other board members."

"My company, now." Betty said, correcting her daughter. I'm glad to hear that people are saying nice things about me. I really enjoy being the board president. I want to do a really good job."

"It appears that you are doing just that," Jeremiah said, helping Betty into her jacket. As he walked his mother-in-law to her car, he asked, "Does Aliyah seem all right to you?"

"You know turning forty is a milestone for a lot of women," Betty said. "They feel, for the first time, that they are getting old. It can be a very depressing time. Just give her a little extra attention, and she'll be just fine, Jeremiah." Betty smiled at him as she got into her car.

Later, after the children had been put to bed, Aliyah and Jeremiah sat on the sofa in the den listening to a Barry White CD. When the song, "Just The Way That You Are," came on Jeremiah remembered the surprise he had for his wife.

"What's this?" Aliyah asked, watching him retrieve the package from behind the sofa pillow where it had been hidden. "Haven't you given me enough birthday surprises, Jeremiah?"

"It's nothing much. I stopped at the all-night Rite-Aid to pick up some dental floss and thought you might like this." He handed her the package. It was a box of Whitman's Chocolates. *Aliyah cannot possibly think that I feel that she is fat if I give her a box of chocolates,* he had thought when he purchased it.

"Why are you giving me chocolates, Jeremiah?" Aliyah glared at him with a look of disdain after she took the box out of the plastic bag.

"I wanted you to know that I love you just the way you are, and you don't have to worry about losing my love if you gain a few pounds," he said, wondering, *Am I saying this right?*

"Where is all this "weight" talk coming from Jeremiah," Aliyah flung the box of chocolates on the sofa. "Why are you so concerned about my weight all of a sudden?" she asked, before fleeing out of the room and up the stairs in tears without waiting for a response, leaving Jeremiah staring dumbfounded at her back.

Chapter 4

A few weeks after Aliyah's birthday celebration a sense of normalcy had returned to the Jones' household. There had been a couple of tense days following the party when Jeremiah tried to be as invisible as possible. They'd made a pact shortly after their marriage that they would never go to sleep without a kiss and an embrace. Aliyah broke that pact the first few days following her birthday. Then, all of a sudden she came around.

Although things appeared to be back to normal, some things had changed permanently for both of them. Jeremiah had vowed to himself that he would never mention weight to his wife again, and definitely never buy her another box of candy. Aliyah vowed that she would make time for exercise in her life, and take her mother's advice and not look for trouble. Aliyah had recalled something she learned from her grandmother. "Before you get married keep both eyes open. After you are married close one," had been grandmother's mantra for a happy marriage. Well now was the time to close one eye.

Enigma was keeping Aliyah so busy she barely had time to think about much else. It was generally six o'clock when she closed up shop for the day and turned her attention to family matters. However, with the magazines new focus on attracting international audiences she frequently went back to her third floor office in the evenings. She'd work for a couple of hours before retiring, leaving Jeremiah in the den reading or watching television. Sometimes he would go back to the gallery to work himself.

It was 9:30 PM on a balmy Tuesday evening when Jeremiah pulled up to the gallery and parked the car. He'd left Aliyah up in her office working. He had tired of watching television all alone. His intention was to go to the gallery and open some of the mail that had been piling up on his desk. He'd been neglecting it, so engrossed in his painting. He only intended to stay for an hour at the most. He pictured Aliyah, fresh from her bath, lying on their bed with candlelight flickering off the walls, waiting to greet him when he returned home.

Jeremiah heard the music coming from the Jazz Garden as he approached the entrance to the gallery, but he ignored it. While he fished around for his key he heard a female voice behind him.

"Burning the mid-night oil, Jeremiah?"

"Something like that." Jeremiah turned to see Miss Melody standing in a shadow near the building smoking a cigarette. "What are you doing out here all by yourself?" he asked.

"You caught me smoking." She laughed. "I don't like people to see me smoking in the club." She walked up to him. "Smoking cigarettes is no longer cool, even in nightclubs," she said, and blew a puff of smoke in his direction.

"Don't do that," Jeremiah said, waving the smoke away from his face. "Smoking is bad for you, and second hand smoke is the worst."

"I'm sorry," she said in her sweetest voice. She dropped the cigarette and ground it out with one of her long black, pointy-toed shoes. "Can I come up and get a look at your studio now?" she asked.

"Now is not a good time," he said. "I just came in for a few minutes to go over some of my mail. I have to get back home."

"You promised me a private tour," she said, giving him a seductive look.

"Not tonight," Jeremiah said, ignoring the look as he opened the door.

"Okay," she said. "Will you stop in the club and play for me while I sing?" she asked.

He looked into her pleading eyes and said, "Maybe."

"Great." Her smile reflected her gratitude.

"But only one song," he said to her as she went bouncing back towards the club.

When he finished going through the stack of mail, Jeremiah gave a long sigh. He had been hoping to hear from the National Museum of American Art. He was trying to track down some of the works collected by the Harmon Foundation. The Foundation was widely known for the support and aid it extended to African-American artists during the early part of the twentieth century.

Although the Harmon Foundation had closed its doors forever in the late 1960's, Jeremiah had written a letter requesting information from the National Museum hoping it would lead him to some of their records. He hoped to arrange an exhibit of some of the work they had collected in their forty years of existence, perhaps even bring some of it to Oblivion. His dream was to pick up where the foundation had left off, extending aid to struggling African-American artists. Exhibiting some of their collection would be inspirational to many artists in the Newark area.

At 10:10PM Jeremiah entered the Jazz Garden and received the normal warm greeting from his friends. He hadn't been to the club since Aliyah's birthday party. His friends obviously missed him. Before his marriage not a day went by that he didn't stop in the club for at least a few minutes. He had once lived in the loft that was now his gallery. Miss Melody caught his eye and beckoned him to the piano. As he approached the piano Jeremiah held up his index finger indicating to Miss Melody that he was only going to play one song. She nodded and smiled back at him.

At 11:45PM Aliyah blew out the candles and crawled between

the sheets of the king size bed. She had finished her work at 9:30 and was looking forward to some quiet time with her husband. He had left the house about fifteen minutes before she stopped working saying that he would be back in an hour. That gave her time to take a hot bath and prepare for a romantic interlude.

She lit the lemongrass and lavender candles at 10:30, tuned the radio to late night WBGO, the local jazz station, then made a final check of the nursery, tightening the blankets around her sleeping babies. She lay on the bed in her red silk nightgown listening to the sexy voice of Billy Holliday singing, "The Man I Love," and waited to hear Jeremiah's footsteps on the stairs. An hour later her mood started to change. As the minutes ticked by the moodier she became. At midnight, when she finally heard his footsteps on the stairs, the romantic mood was gone. She tightened up in a ball and moved to the far side of the bed and pretended to be asleep.

The smell of freshly brewed coffee permeated the brownstone and impregnated Aliyah's nostrils as soon she awoke the next morning, letting her know that Jean was already in the house. Neither Aliyah nor Jeremiah drank coffee, but Jean always made a little for herself. A quick glance at the clock revealed that it was 7:15AM. Jeremiah was already out of the bed and in the shower. *He should have showered last night,* she thought back to the previous night when Jeremiah had tried to snuggle up to her after he had gotten into bed. His hair had smelled as though someone had blown cigarette smoke on him. She had given him the cold shoulder and went to sleep for real.

"Jean must have gotten here early," Jeremiah said, coming from the bathroom with a towel wrapped around his middle. "Do you have something special planned for the day?" He watched her lay out the business attire she planned to wear.

"I'm going to the Manhattan office today," Aliyah, said grabbing fresh underwear out of the bureau drawer, and heading to the bathroom.

Jeremiah reached for her as she passed, but Aliyah moved quickly to avoid his arms and went into the bathroom.

"Are you angry with me, Aliyah?" he asked as she turned on the shower.

"No. Just disappointed," she said, stepping into the shower stall.

Riding the train into Manhattan Aliyah wondered if her marriage might be headed for trouble. The last four years had been so wonderful, but the last five weeks were another story. She felt the distance growing between her and Jeremiah. It was true that they both had been working longer hours to meet the demands of their jobs. Jeremiah had spent the last two Sundays at the art gallery, something he rarely did in the past. Aliyah was spending more evenings in her home office trying to stay on top of things with *Enigma*. Although they both loved their work, she knew that neither of them would sacrifice work for what they had together. Getting off the train at New York's Penn Station, Aliyah walked the few blocks to her mid-town office. Her mind was still on Jeremiah and their marriage as she rode the elevator up to her office in the executive suite on the eighteenth floor. She had scheduled a staff meeting for 3PM. It wasn't quite 10AM giving her plenty of time to make final preparations for the meeting. Maybe she could get back to Newark early enough to have a special dinner with her husband. Perhaps they could go out to eat. She would call Jean to see if she could stay with the kids a little longer this evening. Her mind started racing to put her plan into action.

The staff meeting was very productive. *Enigma's* last issue had featured a story on women of African descent living in India. The caste system in India was such that the darker your skin, the lower the caste you were relegated to. Dark skinned people were called Dalits and referred to as "Untouchables." Women of African descent living in India lived such dreary lives. Readers loved the story and *Enigma* was commended as one of America's most enlightening magazines.

One of the senior editors had just come back from Guyana, and was preparing a story about women of African descent living in that South American country. Aliyah announced to her staff that she was planning to write a story about the women of Ghana. She had already made contact with the women of the December Twelfth Movement and would be making arrangements to visit their country in the next few weeks.

Following the meeting Aliyah stayed behind in the conference room, as her staff returned to their respective offices on the floor below. Thinking she was alone her thoughts quickly returned to her plan for the evening. A voice from behind startled her.

"Will you be going to Africa alone?" her assistant editor, Dotty Caprio, the only white woman in the department, asked.

"I'm hoping to take my family with me," Aliyah said, turning to face Dotty. "My best friends, Claudia and Kwame, live in Ghana, and I haven't seen them in two years. It will give us a chance to visit them while I research the story."

"How nice," Dotty said. "Oblivion must be doing pretty well if Jeremiah is going to take time off to visit Africa with you."

"We haven't really made any definite plans yet," Aliyah said. "I mentioned it to him a few weeks ago and he appeared receptive to the idea, but we haven't discussed it since. I'll explore it with him further at dinner tonight. And yes," Aliyah said. "Oblivion is doing quite well to answer your question." She smiled at Dotty who had become a friend and confidante over the past four years.

It was 6:10PM when Aliyah got off the train at Newark's Penn Station. She went outside and looked around for Jeremiah who was picking her up to take her out to dinner. She hoped he didn't want to go to the Jazz Garden. She never got a chance to have any private time with her him at that club. Patrons of the club were always approaching their table to talk to him or ask him to play the piano. She wanted him all to herself tonight.

She smiled when she saw her eight-year-old mid-night-blue Mercedes Benz sports coup parked at the curb. Jeremiah was driving the vintage car that she had kept from her single days. They kept it garaged near the gallery, rarely taking it out. Aliyah drove an SUV now with a car seat in the back for Nia, and a booster seat for Mandela. Jeremiah had a new Buick that was also large enough for the whole family. The sports car was only used when the two of them were heading out of town for a special occasion. *He has something special in mind, she thought.*

"Where are we headed?" she asked as soon as she entered the car.

"I thought we would go out of town to some nice quiet, romantic place where we can talk in private," Jeremiah said. "Is that okay with you?"

"Sure. Jean is going to bathe the kids so that we will just have to put them to bed when we get in." *This man reads me like a book,* Aliyah thought.

"Did you have any particular place in mind?" he asked, giving her a long look before turning his attention back to the road.

"How about Brenda's in South Orange? Sheniqua said it's very nice."

"Brenda's it is," Jeremiah said, bearing left after leaving Center Street and heading up Central Avenue to South Orange.

Sheniqua was right. The restaurant was very nice. The lighting was perfect for a romantic interlude. Once they were seated Jeremiah took Aliyah's hand in his, looked her in the eye and asked, "What's happening between us Aliyah? Why have you been so distant lately? You wouldn't even let me touch you last night."

"Jeremiah you told me you were only going out for an hour. You came home three hours later reeking of cigarette smoke, and wanting to cuddle up with me. I wasn't in the mood by then. It's not like you to break your word like that. I wanted to be with you and I thought you wanted to be with me." Aliyah looked up at the waiter who had come to take their orders.

Jeremiah thought about what his wife had just said. He knew he should not have stayed to play more than the one song he had promised Miss Melody. He knew Aliyah had been disappointed when he came in so late. He had noticed the lingering smell of snuffed out candles and the red nightgown she wore when she felt like being really passionate.

"Aliyah it's just that I got carried away playing the piano. I rarely get a chance to play anymore and I miss it. I'm sorry. It won't happen again."

Aliyah empathized with her husband. She knew he missed playing the piano. When he lived at the loft he had his father's baby grand piano that he had played all the time. Shortly after their marriage his father had sent for the piano, and Jeremiah had never replaced it. She decided then that she was going to get him a baby grand piano for his birthday.

"What about the cigarette smoke Jeremiah?" she asked quietly already forgiving him for coming in late. "You smelled of cigarette smoke when you came in, where did that come from?" "I guess there were people smoking at the club." He didn't think it was a good idea to tell Aliyah that the cigarette smoke came from Miss Melody.

Hmm, Aliyah thought. *That's odd.* She had never noticed people smoking at the club.

"So am I out of the doghouse?" Jeremiah gave her a pitiful smile.

"Yes." Aliyah was grateful for the chance to change the conversation to her plan for a business and family trip to Africa. When she finished telling Jeremiah about her plan, she sighed and sat back in her chair, waiting for his reaction.

"I think that might work, Aliyah," he said. "I'm anxious to go back to Africa, too. It will be great to see Claudia and Kwame again. I know they want to meet Nia, and they haven't seen Mandela since we took him to visit my Dad when he was only a year old. Maybe we can stop off in Senegal and spend a few days with him. Besides I would love to purchase some more African art for the gallery. Go ahead with your plans for the trip, Aliyah. It will be good for the whole family. Maybe we can convince Jean to come along to help out with the kids."

Aliyah squeezed Jeremiah's hand and leaned across the table to give him a kiss. "I love you, Jeremiah Jones."

"And I love you, Aliyah Jones."

Chapter
5

The institution of marriage can be so unpredictable. Things can be going so smoothly when all of a sudden an unexpected occurrence can change the whole direction. Jeremiah was certainly aware of this, after all his marriage to Aliyah was his second trip down the aisle and he knew what could happen when things went awry. He wasn't about to let anything happen that would upset his happy home with Aliyah and their children. He vowed to do whatever was necessary to keep things together. He had no desire to be single again.

"Women are so strange at times," he said to his father over the telephone one day as he worked in his studio.

"Who are you telling? Like you, I have been married twice and I still don't understand them. My father used to say, 'The ways of a woman are past coming.' I didn't figure out what he meant by that until I had been married to your mother for ten years." He gave a hearty laugh.

"I know that communication is key to resolving conflicts with women, though," Jeremiah said. "If you don't communicate with each other you'll never know what the other is thinking."

"Well that's easier said than done," Mr. Jones said. "Women feel that you should just know what they're thinking. How do you get them to communicate what they are thinking to you?"

"I usually know what Aliyah is thinking. Lately, though, I don't have a clue. I get the feeling that she is holding back sometimes. She doesn't want me to know what she is thinking. She seems so insecure lately, and I don't know why."

"Don't worry you'll work it out, Son. I can't wait to see both of you again, and my grandkids too. When do you think you'll be visiting West Africa?" he asked.

"That's the reason I called. Aliyah is in the process of planning a trip now. So we'll be visiting soon, maybe even next month. I'll let you know for sure when I call you next time, okay?" Jeremiah said.

"Wonderful," Mr. Jones said. "I look forward to hearing from you again, Son."

After hanging up the telephone Jeremiah thought about how much he missed his dad. His father was a jazz musician. In the 1960's, 70s and early 80's he had played with various bands including The Modern Jazz Quartet with Miles Davis, and the Thelonious Monk band. While Jeremiah was growing up his father frequently traveled with whatever band he was playing with at the time. Jeremiah had become used to his father's being away, but he always missed him, mainly because the time they did spend together was such good quality time.

Jeremiah's mother had died after a long illness when he was only fifteen years old. His dad stayed home with him and his younger sister, Naomi, for a whole year. He taught him a lot during that time. It had been a wonderful year despite the loss of his mother.

Jeremiah looked at the clock and saw that it was 6PM. *Time to close shop.* He got up and began to put things away. As he prepared to head home he again thought about his father. His dad and his wife, Simone, lived in Dakar, the capital of Senegal, but they also had a cottage close to a fishing village near the water. Maybe he would get a chance to do some fishing with his father. It was going to be so good to see them both again. He was so engrossed in his thoughts that he hadn't realize that someone had entered his studio until he heard a voice behind him.

"When did you put the sky lights in?" Jamal, his brother-in-law and Aliyah's younger brother asked from behind him.

Startled, Jeremiah turned around and looked into Jamal's smiling face. "Man, what are you doing here?" He walked over to greet the younger man. "This is certainly an unexpected surprise. I put the skylights in two years ago, that tells you how long it's been since you were up here."

"I was just passing through the neighborhood and thought I would drop in to say hello to my favorite brother-in-law. I haven't seen you or my sister since Aliyah's birthday party. How are you?"

"Fine," Jeremiah said, giving Jamal a handshake and a hug. "Is everything alright with you and Sheniqua?"

"I'm okay," Jamal said. "As for Sheniqua, she's okay for Sheniqua. You know how women are. There's always something going on with them."

Jeremiah laughed. "I just got off the telephone with my father and we were saying the exact same thing."

"You're so lucky to still have your father around," Jamal said sadly. "I really miss my father. We worked together in the same building for six years before he died. I got to talk to him everyday, and now I'll never be able to talk to him again."

"Well if it's any consolation you can talk to me anytime you want to," Jeremiah said. "Even though my dad is only a phone call away, I still miss seeing him." He put his arm around Jamal's shoulder. "Why don't you come home with me and we can reminisce about your dad. Aliyah misses him, too, and I know she would love to see you."

"Not tonight," Jamal said. "I just stopped in for a minute. I promised my wife I would get home early for a change. And, I promised my mother that I wouldn't work myself as hard as my father did. I'm trying to keep my promise to both of them."

"I know what you mean," Jeremiah said. "Your sister expects

me home by seven and I certainly don't want to be back in the dog house again."

"Dog house, you?" Jamal asked. "What's that all about?"

"Never mind. You don't want to know. Why don't you and Sheniqua come over Sunday? Your mother will probably stop by after church and we can make it a family affair. I'll ask Aliyah to call to confirm, okay?

"Okay," Jamal said as they left the building together.

When Sunday arrived Aliyah had prepared a scrumptious meal of grilled shrimp and vegetables, pasta salad, baked beans, and a deep-dish peach cobbler. She had to get up early that morning to start cooking, but she didn't mind. The thought of her family coming to her house for Sunday dinner filled her with anticipation. Before her father's death Sunday dinner had been a family tradition. She liked the idea of keeping up that tradition in her own home. She had been so pleased when Jeremiah told her that he had invited her brother and his wife to their home.

Her mother was the first to arrive. Betty made herself right at home in the kitchen preparing a tossed salad while Aliyah made a fresh pitcher of lemonade. Jeremiah set the dining room table with the china they had received for a wedding present, but seldom used. The kids were underfoot running here and there, but bringing such joy with their squeals of laughter.

Jamal and Sheniqua arrived just in time to sit down to dinner. Jamal looked happier than ever smiling from ear to ear and

Sheniqua had a certain glow about her. They were a good-looking couple. Jamal, tall and handsome, was looking more like his father everyday. His completely bald scalp, recently shaven, looked good on his well-sculpted head. Sheniqua, also tall and very thin, wore her hair in a long straight style that was partially her own hair but with lots of synthetic hair woven in with it. She wore tight jeans that were slung low on her slender hips revealing her belly button that was pierced. Some type of jewel, maybe even a diamond, was visibly worn in her navel.

"When was the last time you ate, Jamal?" Betty asked her son who had just fixed himself a heaping plate of food. "Don't you think you should save some for the rest of us?" She passed the platter of shrimp to Jeremiah.

Jeremiah laughed. "Let him eat, Mom. He's still growing."

"The only way he's growing is sideways," Sheniqua said. "He embarrasses me the way he eats when we're out. He behaves as though I never feed him at home." She gave Jamal an annoying look.

"Well, Sheniqua's not going to eat much so I figure I'll eat her share too," Jamal said, reaching for the rolls Aliyah had just placed on the table.

"This is so nice," Betty said, sounding a little melancholy. "I really miss Bill during times like this. I'm so busy now with my work as chairwoman of the board that it takes my mind off my loneliness for the most part, but at times like this I really miss your father."

"Maybe you should start thinking about a social life for yourself, too, Mom," Jamal said. "You need to get out and have some fun. When Daddy was alive you enjoyed traveling and going out to social functions with him. That doesn't have to stop because he's no longer here." He wolfed down a forkful of food.

"Who will I travel with or go out with?" Betty asked. "Believe me I am just fine the way I am. I have enough to keep me busy and my traveling days are over."

"As good as you look I'm sure you'll meet a man who will want to take you out and travel with you," Sheniqua said while everyone around the table gasped.

"I can't imagine Mom with another man," Aliyah said, looking at her mother, astonished at the thought of her dating. "She and Daddy were married for forty years. Have you ever dated another man, Mom?"

"Not really," Betty said, thinking back to her youth. "I talked to a few guys when I first entered East Side High School. But, your father asked me out when I was a sophomore and we were together ever since."

"That's really taking your wedding vows seriously," Sheniqua said. "I don't know many people that came together at such a young age as you and stayed together 'til death do us part' as we say in our vows."

"My parent's also stayed together 'til death do us part'," Jeremiah said. "My mother was only thirty five when she died, but she and my dad had been together since they were in high school, too."

"My parents too," Sheniqua said. "They started dating in high school and got married early. They died together in a car accident when I was just a little girl. They were together till death," she said sadly. "I hope they're still together wherever they may be. I feel like I never really got to know them." Her pretty face had a sad look on it.

"Well it appears that all of you come from parent's that took their vows seriously," Betty said. "Divorce and single parent homes are so prevalent in the black community. I pray that none of my grandchildren will ever have to be raised in a single parent home," she said, looking around the table at her children.

"Well I intend to be there for my children, with their mother, 'til death do us part'," Jamal said, looking at Sheniqua. "And I think I'm going to be a father in the very near future." He smiled, causing all eyes to turn to Sheniqua.

"Jamal you promised not to mention anything until I talked to the doctor first." Sheniqua scolded her husband. They had been trying to get pregnant for quite some time.

"We are so blessed," Betty said, bowing her head in prayer.

After everyone had left Aliyah lay snuggled up next to Jeremiah in their king size bed thinking about the dinner conversation. To be more exact she was thinking about the after dinner conversation that she, her mother, and Sheniqua had had in the kitchen while Jeremiah and Jamal watched television in the den with the children playing quietly at their feet.

"Having a soul mate is more important to women than it is to men," Betty had said while she helped Aliyah stack dirty dishes in the dishwasher.

"Why do think that is Mom?" Sheniqua had asked her mother-in-law.

"Most women want more than just a man, they want someone to share their life with, a soul mate," Betty said. "Most men want someone to cook, do the laundry, clean and share their bed with. Believe me if you ladies feel that your man is also your soul mate then you had better work at keeping them happy. There are a lot of women out there looking for a man like Jeremiah or Jamal. Men who want their women to be happy and who are willing to make the sacrifice."

"Well, any hoochie momma that tries to get Jamal away from me is setting herself up for a whole lot of trouble," Sheniqua had said in her most ghetto voice. "I did pretty well for a little orphaned girl growing up in a Newark housing project. I fell in love with a good looking, wonderful, and rich man who asked me to marry him. Jamal is my man and I will go to my grave fighting to hold onto him."

Aliyah went to sleep thinking *I hope it never comes to that with Jeremiah and me.*

"What are you doing for lunch today," Jeremiah asked his wife over the telephone. He had arrived at the gallery two hours earlier leaving Aliyah busy at work in her third floor home office, and Jean downstairs in the kitchen fixing breakfast for the children. Jean had given him a piece of whole-wheat toast to eat in the car after he had gulped down a cup of hot Ovaltine in the kitchen and made a dash for the front door.

"I thought I would take Nia out for a walk at lunchtime," Aliyah said. "It's such a beautiful day; Nia could use the fresh air. Jean already took Mandela to his preschool program for the afternoon. What did you have in mind?"

"I was thinking that we could grab a bite to eat together. But, it's more important for you and Nia to get out and get some fresh air."

"Are you sure you don't mind?"

"Yeah, I'm sure. I'll see you at home tonight, okay?"

"Try to get home by seven, okay?"

Jeremiah smiled to himself when he hung up the telephone. *Aliyah is so funny. I know that the reason that she started walking around the lake at Weequahic Park is to keep her weight under control. Yet, she wants me to think that she does it for the baby. I'll never tell.* He chuckled at the thought.

Engrossed in his work an hour later, Jeremiah did not notice that someone had entered his studio until soft sweet smelling hands covered his eyes. He recognized the smell of the lavender hand lotion that Aliyah used.

"So you decided to come anyway," he said smiling while spinning her around and into his arms. With eyes closed he kissed her passionately. A few seconds into the kiss Jeremiah realized that something was wrong. He quickly opened his eyes and looked into Miss Melody's dazed face. "I thought you were Aliyah," Jeremiah whispered, still holding Miss Melody. "What are you doing here?" He gently pushed her away.

"Cook asked me to bring you up some lunch," Miss Melody said breathlessly. "I didn't know I was going to be seduced and literally swept off my feet." She smiled seductively.

"I wasn't trying to seduce you, Melody," Jeremiah said, walking out of her space. "I thought you were my wife."

"Are you expecting her?"

"Not really. I just thought she was trying to surprise me." He looked at her with his hand on his chin and a puzzled expression on his face. "I'm sorry Melody. This is really embarrassing."

"Don't be embarrassed, Jeremiah, I'm not. As a matter fact I rather enjoyed it. I've been fantasizing about what it would be like to be kissed by you, and now I know. Believe me it was all that I thought it would be." She laughed softly.

"Why would you be fantasizing about me, Melody? You know I'm a married man."

"Being married doesn't make you any less attractive, Jeremiah. And you are a very attractive man. Aliyah doesn't know how lucky she is."

"I'm sure she does," he said. "We're both lucky." Jeremiah was beginning to feel uncomfortable with the conversation.

"Have you ever fantasized about me Jeremiah?" Miss Melody looked hopeful.

"I just finished telling you that I'm a married man. A very lucky one at that."

"Just because you're married doesn't mean that you don't find other women attractive."

"You're right, Melody. I do find you attractive. As a matter of fact you are a very attractive woman. But I don't fantasize about you. I only think of Aliyah in that way. You should spend your time fantasizing about a man that you can get," he said, giving her a look of genuine concern.

"I can fantasize about who I want to fantasize about, and there is nothing that you can do to stop me." She gave him her most seductive smile. "Until I meet someone that I want to replace you with, I will continue to fantasize about you. Who knows what the future will bring?" She laughed at the startled look on his face. "Now why don't you eat the nice sandwich Cook prepared for you?" she said, lighting a cigarette and then taking a drag before letting the smoke billow out from pursed lips.

Thinking of nothing else to say, Jeremiah unwrapped his

66

sandwich and took a bite. Miss Melody watched him eat for a while before taking a stroll around his studio.

It was seven-fifteen when Jeremiah came through his front door. He'd stopped at Washington Florist on Broad Street and picked up a bouquet of Calla Lilies for Aliyah. She loved Lilies and Calla Lilies were her favorite of all. After Miss Melody had left his studio Jeremiah had given some thought to what she had said. He felt a little sorry for her being alone and all, and fantasizing about a man that could never be hers. He felt so blessed that he and Aliyah had found each other. The flowers were intended to be a token of his love for her and just a little something that would make her happy.

Jeremiah was totally unprepared for the greeting he received when he came in. Jean was still in the house and had prepared dinner. The children were seated at the kitchen table eating when he arrived and Aliyah was nowhere in sight.

"Where is she?" Jeremiah asked Jean.

"She's upstairs lying down. I don't think she's feeling very well." Jean looked at the clock. "Do you mind if I leave now, Mr. Jones. My husband hasn't been feeling well either and I need to get home."

"Sure, I'll finish up with the kids you go home to your family."

"Thanks," Jean said, taking off her apron and giving Nia a kiss. "I'll see you in the morning." She walked out of the kitchen toward the front door.

After cleaning the kitchen Jeremiah took the children upstairs. He settled them down in the nursery, and then went to look in on Aliyah, carrying the bouquet of Lilies now nicely arranged in one of her favorite vases.

"Hi darling, are you alright?" He poked his head in the bedroom.

Aliyah said nothing. Jeremiah quietly walked up to the bed to see if she was sleeping.

"I brought you some flowers," he said, placing the vase down on her night table. When Aliyah still did not respond, he sat on the edge of the bed, leaned over and kissed her on the neck. She tightened up and withdrew from him, still not saying a word.

"What's wrong sweetheart, are you sick?"

"I have a headache, Jeremiah," Aliyah said coldly.

"Do you want me to get you some aspirin?" Her icy voice had sent chills down his spine.

"No, Jeremiah. Just leave me alone," she said even more coldly than before.

Now what's the problem? Jeremiah wondered as he left the room. Was she having another one of her mood swings? One thing for sure, her behavior was beginning to get on his nerves.

Chapter 6

A lthough there was a definite chill in the air, the cloudless sky was a beautiful blue. Aliyah thought it looked like the color blue she and Jeremiah had painted the children's nursery. Only they had added a few clouds to the nursery walls. Aliyah tightened her jacket around her and walked a little faster to the Broad Street train station. She wanted to catch the 7:45AM train into Manhattan. She had been up since six after a restless night. She'd moved about the house quietly not wanting to wake Jeremiah. She wanted to avoid him as best she could. She didn't trust herself to speak to him feeling the way that she did. She didn't want to be responsible for what she might say or do.

Aliyah had been sitting in the living room fully dressed, sipping a cup of tea when Jean came promptly at 7:30. A look of surprise was evident on Jean's face when she saw Aliyah downstairs fully dressed so early in the morning. Aliyah ignored the look, though.

Without offering Jean an explanation, she hurried upstairs to get her things. Jeremiah was in the shower and the kids were beginning to stir in the nursery. She quickly went into the nursery to kiss the children goodbye before she made a mad dash out of the house without even speaking to Jeremiah.

The walk up University Avenue to the train station in the brisk morning air helped to clear her head somewhat, but she was so melancholy it was all she could do to fight back tears. She walked slowly up the stairs to the platform. When she got to the top of the stairs Aliyah looked at the wall clock before heading out the door to the platform. It was only 7:40. She needed to sit down. She felt weak in the knees. *How am I going to get through the day? What am I going to do?*

The day before she had been so happy. The arrangements had finally been completed for the trip to West Africa, and Aliyah was looking forward to telling Jeremiah all about it. She didn't have the final itinerary when he'd called her at eleven inviting her to lunch. Fifteen minutes after his call the itinerary came by fax from the travel agency. At first she wanted to call Jeremiah, but quickly changed her mind and decided to surprise him instead.

She was so excited that she had cancelled her plan to take Nia for a walk. Instead she rushed downstairs to make a quick picnic lunch for Jeremiah and her. When Jean got back to the house, Aliyah rushed over to the gallery to bring him the good news. She had wanted to surprise him, but she was the one who had gotten the surprise.

Sitting on the New Jersey transit train heading for Manhattan Aliyah stared out the window. The train rolled pass the Riverfront Stadium, speeding by the Harrison train station across the Passaic River. She continued to look out the window but now the vision she saw was her husband holding another woman in his arms kissing her passionately. Aliyah blinked her eyes trying to make the image go away. Tears rolled down her face blurring the vision, but it wouldn't go away. *Why didn't I confront them? Why did I run away?*

Before she knew it the train was pulling into New York's Penn Station. Aliyah dabbed at her eye with a tissue as she got off the train. She walked hastily uptown to her mid-town office not paying attention to what was going on around her. She walked as though her body had been tuned to automatic pilot. She was not conscious of anything except the pain she was feeling in her heart. *Maybe once I get to the office and start working I can push this out of my mind for a little while. Maybe I can block that image out of my head for just a little while.*

The eighteenth floor was so quiet that Aliyah turned her desk radio on just for company. She tuned into 101.9fm hoping that some light jazz would help her relax. The voice of Percy Sledge singing "When A Man Loves A Woman" was more than she could bear. She lay her head down on her desk and sobbed uncontrollably. *What am I going to do?* She cried. *What am I going to do?*

The ringing of the telephone startled her out of her misery. Aliyah grabbed a tissue, wiped her eyes and blew her nose. Her secretary must have come in and picked up the telephone because it stopped ringing. The short beeps indicated that she was buzzing to see if Aliyah was in the office. Aliyah picked up the telephone.

"Mrs. Jones, is that you?" Marcia, her secretary asked.

"Who else would it be, Marcia?" Aliyah said rather harshly.

"I'm sorry Mrs. Jones. I didn't think you were in yet. Your husband is on the line, I'll connect you."

"No Marcia. Tell him I'm in a meeting. Tell him I will call him later." She wasn't ready to speak to him yet.

In the four years that Aliyah and Jeremiah had been married they had never had a real fight. Oh, there had been disagreements, but Aliyah could not recall a time when either she or Jeremiah had yelled at each other in anger, never. Now she wanted to scream at him. She wanted to call him all kinds of names and maybe hit him or scratch his eyes out. She was angry. She thought back to the day before and how she had acted like such a coward.

After her hasty departure from Jeremiah's studio she'd gotten into her Mercedes Benz SUV and driven to Weequahic Park. She'd parked the car and sat in the parking lot, in shock, for at least an hour. Then she had gotten out of the car and headed toward the jogging path that went around the lake, a two-mile trek. The clay-colored, rubberized path loomed ahead of her as she made her way through the bush and around the lake. She had made the trek a total of three times, stopping frequently and approaching the lake to speak to Osun, her guardian *orisa*. "Osun, Osun," she had said, "What did I do to deserve this?"

When she left the park, Aliyah had gone home, showered and gotten into bed. She had not responded when Jeremiah had come into their bedroom with flowers for her. He reeked of cigarette smoke and she just knew he was only being nice because he felt guilty.

The buzzing of the telephone brought Aliyah out of her thoughts. She picked up the telephone.

"Yes Marcia, what is it now?"

"Miss Caprio is here to see you, Mrs. Jones. Shall I send her in?"

Aliyah stood up flexing her shoulders to loosen up. It was time to get to work. "Give me a minute and then send her in," she said to Marcia.

"Oh, Mrs. Jones, your husband wants you to call him as soon as possible."

I'll bet he does. "Okay," she said to Marcia.

Dotty bounced into the office smiling from ear to ear. She was always smiling lately. Aliyah knew the reason for her happiness was a man. A few years earlier Dotty had been as melancholy as Aliyah was now. Dotty had been the mistress of one of the victims of the September 11, tragedy. Aliyah had witnessed the transformation of Dotty since then. She had mourned her married lover, in secret, for almost two years before she even mentioned him at the office. After two years she had started dating again. She had been dating the same man now for almost a year. She'd confided in Aliyah that not only was her new lover another married man, but he was also an African-American.

"I hear the trip to West Africa has been finalized," Dotty said, taking a seat. "You must be excited; you want to tell me about it?"

"Well, the plan is to spend a week in Ghana and then visit Cote d'Ivoire for a week. We'll stop off in Senegal to visit my father-in-law for a few days before heading home." Aliyah wondered how her discovery would affect their travel plans.

"How will you gather your data?" Dotty asked. "Will you be visiting schools to talk to mothers?"

"The women of the December Twelfth Movement and my friend Claudia set up an itinerary for me to visit some schools in Ghana, including the one that she and her husband founded. I think I will also gather information by visiting clinics where mothers bring their children for health care and checkups. I want to spend some time visiting villages where I can see for myself how young mothers spend their days."

"You're so lucky that Jeremiah and the children will be with you. I would love to go away with Derek for three weeks."

"Maybe you will one day," Aliyah said. "Is that so farfetched?"

"I doubt if his wife will let him go away without her for three weeks," Dotty shook her head doubtfully.

Aliyah stiffened; the memory of Jeremiah and Miss Melody came back, her eyes flooded with tears again. She said nothing.

"Are you alright?" Dotty asked, sensing her mood change.

Aliyah glared at Dotty with tear-filled eyes before asking, "What makes a woman go after a married man?"

"Oh, oh," Dotty said. "Don't tell me there's trouble in paradise?" She looked at Aliyah who now had tears flowing freely down her face.

Aliyah's silence was so loud that Dotty moved out of her seat and went to her, wanting to offer solace. Aliyah was not receptive to it, though. She put up her hands, stopping Dotty from touching her. "Please answer my question," Aliyah said. What makes a woman go after a married man?"

"Loneliness," Dotty said, after a few moments of complete silence. "I've been so lonely, Aliyah. Married men are the best lovers, the best companions. Their wives have broken them in, so to speak. They know how a woman wants to be treated and they oblige. Has Jeremiah succumbed to the charms of a lonely woman?" Dotty gave her a sympathetic look.

Aliyah said nothing. She moved to the window and glared out at the city. *What am I going to do?*

As if reading her thoughts Dotty said, "Fight her. Don't let her get your man."

"What can I do, if she's who he wants?"

"He wants you, Aliyah. I see the look in his eyes when he

looks at you. If he is interested in another woman there must be something more that he needs. Have you been attentive enough? I know how hard you work for *Enigma*, are you putting the magazine first."

"No." Aliyah said quickly. "I always make time for Jeremiah and the kids."

"Then find out what more he needs and give it to him," Dotty said. "Does he know that you know?"

"No," Aliyah said. I'm afraid to tell him. I don't want a confrontation. I don't want to force him to choose. He may just choose her."

"I don't know Jeremiah that well, but I am almost positive that he would not sacrifice his family for another woman." Dotty tried to reassure her.

"I'm not positive about anything at this point, Dotty."

"Then don't make any decisions now. Don't tell him what you know. Wait until you go to Africa. The three weeks away will give you plenty of time together to sort through your feelings. I know that it will all be resolved by the time you get back."

"I certainly hope so," Aliyah said, regaining some of her composure.

The train ride back to Newark wasn't nearly as difficult as the incoming ride. She had accomplished a few things at the office, confirmed the delivery of the new piano she had purchased for Jeremiah's birthday, which was quickly approaching, and finalized the itinerary for the trip to Africa. She had also decided not to mention to him what she had seen with her own eyes and try to get through the next few weeks without falling apart.

———

"Yes, Dad." Jeremiah assured his father. "Everything has been finalized. We'll be leaving for West Africa in four weeks. We plan to spend one week in Ghana, one week in Cote d' Ivoire, and the last week with you and Simone in Senegal."

"I'm so excited about this visit," Mr. Jones said into the telephone. "So is Simone. She is so fond of Aliyah you know. We can't wait to see the children again. I haven't seen Nia since Simone and I came to America when she was first born. She and Mandela must be so big by now."

"Yes, Dad. They're growing so fast that I try to relish every moment of their childhood. Before I know it they'll be all grown up."

"I only wish that I had spent more time with you and your sister while you were growing up. I wish Naomi and her family was also coming for a visit. I didn't realize until I was older how much I have wanted my children in my life. I have missed you both so much."

"I know, Dad. I don't want that to happen to me. I want my children in my life for every stage of their development. I don't want them to grow up missing me as much as I've missed you."

"Well there is nothing that I can do to undo what I have already done in my life, Son. I am only glad that you have learned from my mistakes. Please, Son, never put anything before your family, especially your work. Family is the most important thing. Don't wait until you are a lonely old man to realize that."

"I won't Dad, I promise."

After hanging up the telephone, Jeremiah looked at the stack of mail before him and shuffled through the envelopes. Finally, something had arrived from the National Museum regarding the whereabouts of the Harmon Foundation collection. Jeremiah ripped the envelope open without using a letter opener. Reading the letter he found out that the National Museum had forwarded his letter to the keepers of the Harmon Foundation collection. He was informed that he would be hearing from them shortly regarding his request to exhibit pieces of their collection in his gallery. He sat back in his chair and smiled. *Maybe my dream is about to come true.*

It was 7:10PM when Jeremiah finally put his key into his front door. He noticed as he walked through the house that the dining room table was not set for dinner. When he entered the kitchen he was greeted with the usual warm and excited grins of the children. Aliyah, busy at the stove barely spoke to him. Something he had become accustomed to in the last few days. He had been waiting patiently for this mood to pass, but it was as stubborn as a bloodstain on a white carpet. He walked over to the stove and put his arms around her waist and planted a gentle kiss on her neck. She tightened up immediately, moving out of his arms.

"Would you mind bathing the kids alone tonight?" she asked. "I have some work I need to finish up before I retire for the evening." Picking up on the cue from her, Jeremiah knew that Aliyah's latest mood change was not about to disappear anytime soon. "Do you want me to set the table for our dinner?" he asked quietly.

"No, I'm taking a plate up to my office. I'll fix one for you if you like," she said, putting the lid back on the pot she had been stirring.

"Can we eat dinner together tonight, Aliyah?"

"I really need some time to work before we leave for Africa. Do you mind?"

"I mind. But I understand," he said, heading upstairs to prepare the children's bath.

"Why is mommy so sad?" Mandela asked his father as Jeremiah washed his back.

"What makes you think mommy is sad?"

"She yells all the time, and sometimes she cries," he said.

"When?" Jeremiah asked befuddled.

"When she's cooking dinner and when she plays with me," Mandela said, in his childish, innocent manner.

"I don't know. But I will find out," Jeremiah said, hoping he had somehow alleviated Mandela's concerns.

Putting Nia to bed was also a very taxing experience for Jeremiah. For some reason she wouldn't stop crying.

"Mah Mah, Mah Ma," Nia cried as Jeremiah tried to soothe her in her crib.

"Momma will be here soon to say goodnight to you, darling," Jeremiah tried to comfort her. *My family is falling apart, and I don't know what to do about it.*

"While Aliyah worked in her third floor office, Jeremiah sat in front of the television set in the den watching the sports channel without really seeing anything. *What's happening between us. Aliyah has changed so drastically in the past few weeks that I hardly recognize her. Has she grown tired of me? Has she stopped loving me? Maybe some time away will help us pull things together,* he sighed before turning off the television and going upstairs to get ready for bed.

The digital clock on the night table read ten o'clock when Jeremiah entered the bedroom, and Aliyah was still working upstairs in her third floor office. He pulled back the bed covers and fluffed up the pillows. He checked the candles making sure there was plenty of wax left in each one. He lit the candles creating the warm glow they both loved. Finally he looked through her lingerie to find the red negligee. When he found it he laid it on the bed and went into the bathroom to take his shower.

In the shower Jeremiah whistled the tune "My Favorite Things" as he scrubbed his body. He heard Aliyah come into the bathroom and hoped she would join him in the shower. But, when he heard the faucet in the sink go on he knew she had chosen to wash up in the basin, rather than join him in the shower. When he got out of the shower she had disappeared out of the bathroom. When he entered the bedroom all the candles had been snuffed out, and she had curled up into a tight ball on her side of the bed. He looked down, and there lay the red nightgown crumbled on the floor. He turned out the light, crept over to his side of the bed and went to sleep.

Chapter
7

Two weeks after seeing another woman in the arms of her husband Aliyah had convinced herself that Jeremiah was having an affair. It was all she could do to get through each day, let alone each night. The days, however, were easier than the nights. During the day work sustained her. She was busier than ever preparing for the trip to West Africa and making arrangements for the care of things in her absence. She decided to ask her sister-in-law, Sheniqua, to check on the house while they were gone.

"Girl, you are so lucky. I wish I could go to Africa for three weeks with Jamal," Sheniqua said, while sitting in Aliyah's kitchen one day having lunch. I hope we get a chance to go to the motherland one day, but your brother doesn't seem to want to go anywhere. All he cares about is the dealership."

"Jamal is more interested in sustaining the business my father started than anything else right now," Aliyah said. "But, once he's convinced that the business is stable he'll change."

"I hope so." Sheniqua looked a little doubtful. "I don't want him to drop dead on me like your father did to your mother." She picked at her salad oblivious to the shocked look on Aliyah's face.

I don't believe she said that. "I know that Jamal wants to live his life out to the fullest," Aliyah said, giving her an incredulous look. "When is the baby due?" She deliberately changed the subject.

"In five months," Sheniqua said. "I heard it's better to wait until your fifth or sixth month to make an announcement. The time isn't supposed to be so long then. But, your brother just had to tell everybody before the doctor even confirmed it."

"He's anxious to be a father." Aliyah defended Jamal. "You've been married for four years now and he was worried that's all."

"I told him that there was nothing to worry about. It took my mother a long time to conceive me."

"Well, I'm happy for both of you. Sheniqua, while we're away I need you to look after the garden and the inside plants for me. I'll give you a key to the house."

"How come Jean isn't going to do that for you?" Sheniqua asked.

"Didn't I tell you that Jean is coming with us to look after the children while I work. Jeremiah wants to search for art for his gallery. I thought since you're not working, you wouldn't mind doing this for me. Will it be a problem?

"No problem," Sheniqua said. "I'll be glad to do it for you."

Evenings were more difficult for Aliyah. She tried to avoid Jeremiah as much as possible. She didn't want a confrontation. She feared a confrontation. What if he didn't want to be married to her any longer? What would she do?

It was 8PM when Jeremiah came home that night. Aliyah had eaten dinner with the children, bathed them and was preparing to put them into bed when he walked into the nursery.

"Daddy, Daddy," Mandela said excitedly.

"How's my little man?" Jeremiah smiled and picked up his son.

"Read me a story."

"Okay," Jeremiah said, picking up a book without acknowledging Aliyah.

After Jeremiah and Mandela had settled into the rocking chair that they used for story telling, Aliyah placed Nia next to Mandela in Jeremiah's lap. She watched the trio for a few minutes wondering if things could ever get back to normal before she turned to leave the room.

"I left you a plate in the oven," she said over her shoulder and headed up to her office to resume working.

After reviewing the line-up of stories, articles, and advertisements for the coming month's issue of *Enigma,* Aliyah sat back in her chair and reflected on her marriage. Could it be ending after four glorious years? She thought back to their brief courtship. It had been a wonderful courtship. Two weeks before Christmas

Aliyah told Jeremiah that she that she could be pregnant. He never hesitated before proposing marriage. He appeared delighted with the prospect of becoming a husband and father.

We were both so anxious to get married and start a family together. Aliyah sat and remembered. She and Jeremiah were convinced that their offerings to her guardian *orisa,* Osun, and his guardian *orisa,* Shango, had been instrumental in bringing them together. Her friend Oya had consulted their ancestral spirits to obtain their blessings and assured them that the ancestral spirits were pleased with the match. The reading of the *odu* had been so favorable. *What has gone wrong?*

Their wedding had been the most beautiful ceremony. It took place on New Years Day, the last day of Kwanza, Imani. It was such a spiritual wedding. The Swahili word, Imani, itself meant faith. She and Jeremiah had written their own vows, composed their wedding song, and planned the wedding together. The ceremony took place at her parent's home in South Orange. Only their closest friends and relatives had been invited. They had decided they did not want any negative energy present, therefore, the invited guests were only those people who had openly expressed love for the couple.

Thinking about her wedding brought tears to Aliyah's eyes. She shut down the computer and turned off the lights as she prepared to go downstairs to get ready for bed. In the darkness she noticed the moonlight coming through the office window. She walked over to the window and looked skyward. The moon was bright and full. *Exactly the way it looked on my wedding night.* She stood there looking at the moon and thinking back.

Both she and Jeremiah had worn white. She wore a white organdy dress with gold trim. Jeremiah wore white slacks and a white dashiki trimmed with gold. He wore a white and gold skullcap and she wore a white and gold flowered wreath. Her best friend, Claudia, was the maid of honor. Jeremiah's father, who just happened to be in the country for the holiday season, had been his son's best man.

The ceremony had begun shortly before midnight and by ten minutes past the hour on the first morning of the New Year she and Jeremiah were pronounced husband and wife. Aliyah smiled looking up at the moon and remembering how Jeremiah had held her and kissed her with such passion in front of all their guests.

After the ceremony everyone had gone out to her parent's backyard with fluted glasses of champagne, and toasted the happy couple in the moonlight. Aliyah and Jeremiah had prayed over a cage full of doves and sprayed the birds with champagne from their lips as an offering to the ancestors. The door of the cage was opened and the birds were set free. Suddenly the moon lit sky was full of doves flapping their wings and flying heavenward in the dark carrying Aliyah and Jeremiah's prayers to God.

With tears in her eyes Aliyah descended the stairs to her bedroom. The clock on the nightstand read 10:00 PM. Jeremiah was nowhere to be seen. Aliyah looked on the pillow and saw a handwritten note from her husband. *I got bored. Decided to go out for a walk. Be back shortly.* She put the note down, took her shower, and went to bed.

———————

After he had finished reading to the children, Jeremiah had put them to bed by himself. He tucked them in tightly then went downstairs to eat the warmed over dinner that Aliyah had left on the stove for him. Sitting alone in front of the television he used the remote to flick through 130 channels of Cablevision before coming to the realization that there was nothing on that he wanted to watch. At 9:30 he'd decided that television was just too boring. Knowing that Aliyah was still in her mood he had written her a note, left the house, and headed towards the Jazz Garden. On the short walk to Halsey Street he asked himself, *Why won't she talk to me? Why won't she tell me what is bothering her?* He didn't have a clue as to what was causing his wife to be so cold towards him.

The Jazz Garden was pretty crowded for a Thursday night. Jeremiah did not expect so many people to be out so late. It was almost 10PM and the next morning was a workday for most of the patrons in the club. He looked around trying to spot familiar faces. Making his way to the bar he spotted a couple of his buddies laughing and drinking beer.

"Hey Jay," they greeted him as he approached.

"Hey to you. What's going on?" He took a seat at the bar.

"Not much, boss," Charlie said.

Charlie was one of Jeremiah's employees. He practically ran Jeremiah's recycling business single-handedly.

"What are you guy's doing hanging out on a weeknight?" Jeremiah asked, and then ordered a gingerale from the bartender.

"We're single," Charlie answered for both men. "That's what single men do." They both laughed. "What are you doing hanging out on a weeknight? We haven't seen you in here much since you tied the knot. Where's Aliyah?"

"She's home working," Jeremiah looked around the club. "I was just taking a walk and stopped in for a little refreshment."

"You picked a good night to stop in," Malik said, joining in the conversation. "Miss Melody is about ready to do another show. This place is always packed when she's here."

Jeremiah sipped his drink with his head down listening to Miss Melody's accompanist play light jazz tunes on the piano. He only half listened as his two buddies discussed the latest sports stories. Jeremiah's mind was on his marriage. *How are we going to resolve this situation? Has Aliyah gotten bored with our marriage?* He looked up when he heard Miss Melody singing her trademark song "You'd Be So Nice To Come Home To." When his eyes rested on her she smiled directly at him.

Before Miss Melody finished her performance she coaxed

Jeremiah to the piano for her last song. He continued to play long after she finished. He played and played. Lost in the music he forgot time and troubles and before he knew it, it was midnight. When he finally looked up from the piano, he noticed the crowd had thinned out. He looked around the club and saw Miss Melody going out the side door with a piece of newspaper covering her head. Jeremiah finished his piece, graciously accepted the applause and headed for the door.

It was pouring outside. He thought about going up to the gallery to look for an umbrella, decided against it, and then headed north on Halsey Street in the rain. He had gone only a few paces when he noticed a red sports car pull up to the curb.

"Get in before you get soaked," he heard a female voice say from the car.

Recognizing Miss Melody's voice Jeremiah headed for the car. Once inside she handed him a towel and waited patiently, smoking a cigarette, while he dried his face and head.

"Thanks," Jeremiah said, returning the towel. "You're a life saver."

"No problem," she said. "I like helping gentlemen in distress," she smiled and blew a puff of smoke through her lips. She still had not moved the car.

"When are you going to drive?" Jeremiah looked curiously at Miss Melody.

"In a few minutes. I want to enjoy your company for a while. I so seldom get a chance to have you all to myself."

"Come on Melody, you know how I feel about that." Jeremiah looked at her in a scolding way.

"And you know how I feel about that." She laughed, took a couple of puffs on her cigarette, and then threw the cigarette butt out the open car window.

"Are you going to drive me home or shall I get out of the car and walk home in the rain?" Jeremiah asked, annoyance coming through in his voice.

"I'll drive you home, but first I want to talk to you about something," she said.

"What?" he asked, giving her a suspicious look.

"Don't worry I'm not going to try and seduce you, although I sure wouldn't mind doing so."

"Come on Melody," Jeremiah said.

"Okay," she smiled. "It's not my fault that you're such an attractive and sexy man."

"Out with it Melody," Jeremiah put his hand on the door handle, threateningly.

"Okay, okay." She laughed softly. "I've got an audition coming up for a part in a Broadway musical. I was wondering if you would help me prepare for it?"

"When is the audition?"

"Next month."

"I don't know. I'll be going out of the country in two weeks. I think you should find someone else."

"Can't you practice with me for the next two weeks. Just on your lunch hour, Jeremiah. Please, please. There's no one better than you. You bring out the best in me. Please, please Jeremiah," she begged.

Jeremiah looked at Miss Melody trying to decide if this was something he should do. She looked so pathetic and desperate that he didn't have the heart to say no.

"Okay," he said finally. "One half hour a day for the next two weeks at the Jazz Club. If you are late for a rehearsal the session is cancelled. And," he looked at her very sternly, "no flirting and no funny business or the sessions are cancelled."

"Thank you, thank you. I promise to be real good, too," she said halfheartedly, smiling slyly.

"You had better be."

It was 12:30AM when Jeremiah finally put his key in the lock of his front door. He quietly walked up the steps to the second floor. First he peeked in the nursery. Both of the children were sound asleep. He walked into the master bedroom as quietly as he could without putting on a light, and made his way to the adjoining bathroom. He closed the bathroom door before turning on the light. He didn't want to awaken Aliyah. Jeremiah washed his face and hands, flossed and brushed his teeth, and removed his clothing. He turned off the bathroom light then crept into the bed with his sleeping wife. Her even breathing convinced him that she was really asleep. He rolled over to his side of the large bed and went to sleep himself.

Chapter 8

A t 7AM Aliyah was sipping her second cup of tea in her home office. She'd been up since six. Jeremiah and the kids were still sleeping. She wished she were still snuggled up in the king-size bed with Jeremiah. She imagined lying in his arms, feeling his breath on her neck the way it used to be before she discovered Miss Melody in his arms.

She went back to the computer screen where she was researching day care programs in Ghana for single mothers. She thought about her own children. If there was any way possible she was not going to become a single mother. *But what can I do if he wants another woman,* she thought. Her thoughts went back to the previous night.

She had been wide-awake when Jeremiah had come creeping into her bed long after midnight. At midnight she had gotten up and walked through the house. She was looking out the bedroom window when a red sports car pulled up in front of the house. She had watched the car for a while, curious. She couldn't see who the driver was. After a few minutes Jeremiah had gotten out and ran quickly through the rain and up the front steps. After she heard the front door open she ran and jumped back into bed.

When he finally crawled into bed next to her the lingering smell of cigarette smoke in his hair had infuriated her. She pretended to be asleep, but instead she had softly cried into her pillow. What was to become of them, she had wondered? *How much longer can I keep this up?*

Aliyah's thoughts went back to her research. A half-hour later she heard Jean downstairs in the kitchen getting the kid's breakfast ready. She went downstairs to give Jean instructions for the day. The older woman looked up when Aliyah entered the kitchen. She was mildly surprised to see her employer fully dressed again so early in the morning.

"Are you going into Manhattan this morning, Ms. Aliyah," she asked.

"No," Aliyah said. "I have a lot to do today and I wanted to talk to you before Jeremiah got up. Today is his birthday, you know. The piano I ordered for him will arrive later this morning. I've been trying to decide where it should go. At first I thought it should go in the living room, then I thought maybe the library. Now I'm seriously considering making a music room on the second floor. What do you think Jean," she asked.

"I don't know, Ms. Aliyah," Jean said. "All of the rooms on the first floor are filled with furniture. And, you do have that big empty room on the second floor. Maybe Mr. Jones would like a private room of his own that he can go to, close the door, and play the piano until his heart is content."

"You've convinced me," Aliyah smiled for the first time in days. "The piano will go on the second floor."

"Is there anything else, Ms. Aliyah?" Jean asked.

"No." Aliyah said. "But I want to remind you that company is coming for Jeremiah's birthday tonight. I was wondering if you could stop off at the market after you take Mandela to his preschool. Perhaps you could make a bowl of your delicious potato salad before you go home today. I would really appreciate it."

"I'll try, Ms. Aliyah. But my husband is still sick, and I have to leave on time to get home to him." She reminded Aliyah.

"That's right." Aliyah remembered Jean telling her about her ailing husband before. "How is your husband?"

"I don't know," Jean said. "They're taking more tests this week to see if they can find out what is making him so weak. It'll be at least another week before we know anything for sure."

"Well if you can't make the potato salad pick up some at the delicatessen and I'll dress it up with hard boiled eggs and other condiments," Aliyah said. "I'm going to take Nia for a walk in the park on my lunch hour today while Mandela is in school." As she turned to leave the room she said, "I'll add your husband to my prayer list, Jean."

"Thanks Ms. Aliyah," Jean said, before going upstairs to get the children.

At 10:30AM the piano was delivered. Aliyah was so excited. *Who knows maybe this is just what is needed to make my husband more content at home.* The piano fit very nicely into the upstairs music room. The large room was at the opposite end of the house, away from the nursery and the master bedroom, giving it almost a private wing all to itself. Aliyah had invited her mother, her brother and his wife, and Jeremiah's sister and her husband and children for a private birthday celebration. She planned to have the whole bunch hidden in the music room waiting to spring out when Jeremiah came up to see his surprise. For the first time in weeks she was feeling like her old self. In another two weeks the whole family would be flying off to Africa for three weeks where, in addition to getting some work done, they would have time for some real healing.

At noon Aliyah parked her SUV in the parking lot at Weequahic Park. She took Nia's stroller out of the back door and pulled it into position. Then she climbed into the back seat and got Nia out of her car seat. As she strapped Nia into the stroller in preparation for their trek around the lake on the cushioned path, she noticed a red sports car parked two cars from her SUV. The window of the sports car was open and a woman was sitting behind the wheel of the vehicle smoking a cigarette. Even though her back was to the path,

Aliyah could tell that it was Miss Melody who was staring out at the field, oblivious to all around her.

Aliyah wheeled Nia and the stroller onto the jogging path without saying anything to Miss Melody. *So she's the owner of the red sports car, and that's where the cigarette smoke is coming from. Jeremiah has gotten involved with a woman who smokes and leaves a tell-tale smell on him every time they're together.* She hastened her pace around the track.

At 6:45PM everyone was quietly waiting in the new music room for Jeremiah to come into the house. Aliyah and Naomi were trying to keep the children quiet so as not to give away the surprise. Aliyah had asked Jeremiah to make it a point to get home by seven so that the children could have cake and ice cream with him before they went to bed. She had made very little of his approaching birthday all week.

"Where is everyone?" Jeremiah asked from the stairwell.

"We're upstairs," Mandela yelled out.

"What's going on?" Jeremiah asked as he climbed the stairs.

"I have something to show you," Aliyah said from the second floor landing.

"What are you doing in there?" Jeremiah asked, noticing that she came out of the empty second floor room. "Where are the kids?"

"I have an idea for this room that I want to bounce off you," Aliyah said ignoring his question about the kids.

"What?" Jeremiah gave her a puzzled look as he entered the room with her.

"Surprise!" Everyone shouted out as the lights came on.

Jeremiah didn't notice the piano because everyone was standing in front of it. He still had a puzzled look on his face when he asked, "Why are you all up here? What's going on?" Then everyone moved away from the piano. The look on his face was one of shock and delight at the same time. His face lit up and he smiled so broadly that everyone laughed.

"Happy birthday, Jeremiah!" Aliyah said, stepping into his arms. "I hope you like it."

"I love it!" Jeremiah said, beaming and giving his wife a big kiss.

"I know it's not as big as your father's but I thought it would be perfect for our home, and it fits beautifully in our new music room."

Jeremiah could not stop smiling. Coaxed by his guests he sat down at his new piano and started to play.

That night Aliyah went happily into her husband's arms when they lay down, exhausted from the birthday celebration. It had been weeks since she had felt so relaxed. When she finally rolled over to her side of the bed she could not remember the last time she had felt so content and satisfied. *How could Jeremiah make love to me like that and be interested in another woman?*

The Saturday morning after his birthday Jeremiah woke up with a grin on his face. He had made mad passionate love to his wife the night before. It had been the first time in weeks that Aliyah had put so much passion into their lovemaking. *Maybe things are returning to normal,* he thought as he looked at his sleeping wife. Aliyah's face looked as content as he felt. *Whatever has been bothering her I hope she has resolved it.*

Grateful for the wonderful surprise Aliyah had given him for his birthday and knowing how tired she must be from the preparation of their soon to be trip to Africa, the surprise party, and the night of exhausting lovemaking, Jeremiah sprang from their bed. After a quick shower he dressed in blue jeans and a T-shirt, his usual Saturday morning attire, and headed for the nursery. The kids were still sleeping after being allowed to stay up way past their normal bedtime the night before. Jeremiah headed to his music room.

He looked at the piano and smiled. *She couldn't have given me a better present.* He sat down at the piano and began to play the instrument softly. He played "Willow Weep for Me," "My Funny Valentine" and "Body and Soul," all of the songs his father used to play when Jeremiah was just a boy. Oh, how he had loved to listen to his father play the piano. He was playing "Summer Time," when a pajama clad Mandela came into the room and climbed onto the piano bench next to him. Mandela looked up and smiled at his daddy. Jeremiah smiled back. He was in his glory, playing the piano for his son just as his dad had done for him so many years ago.

The day following his birthday was turning into a perfect day. Jeremiah dressed the children while Aliyah showered and dressed. They got into the SUV and drove to a nearby diner on the other side of the Passaic River and had a wonderful breakfast of pancakes and eggs. Then they took the children to the movies to see an animated Disney film, and later they had pizza for dinner. When they returned home the kids were exhausted. They bathed the children together and put them to bed.

Afterwards they lay together on the sofa in the living room reading magazines, something they hadn't done together in a long time, more content then they had been in a long time.

"Thanks for the wonderful birthday surprise," Jeremiah said, again.

"Jeremiah, you have thanked me five times at least."

"I know. I don't think I can ever thank you enough, not only for the beautiful piano but the wonderful lovin' you gave me last night. I missed that kind of intimacy, Aliyah. Is it back to stay?

Aliyah said nothing causing Jeremiah to think that things were not back to normal yet. Rather than pursue the issue, though, he held her close, and kissed her lips taking full advantage of her good mood and thinking *I certainly hope it's back to stay.*

Sunday was another peaceful day for the Jones family. Aliyah got up early and got the kids ready to attend church with her mother. After they were gone Jeremiah started his own ritual of meditation and spirituality. First he prayed. He asked God for forgiveness for anything that he may have done, inadvertently, that caused God to be upset with him. Then he did a half-hour session of yoga. After that he meditated for a half-hour.

Following meditation Jeremiah prepared an offering to Shango, his guardian *orisa*. Shango, the *orisa* of thunder and lighting often referred to as the quintessential strategist. As he replaced the bowl of, now fully consumed, apples that Shango so loved on top of one of the bookcases in the library, Jeremiah asked Shango to use his strategic powers to assist him in finding the cause for Aliyah's moodiness. He reminded Shango that it was he who had helped to bring them together along with Osun, Aliyah's guardian *orisa* and Shango's second wife. "Whatever is causing her unhappiness please reveal it to me and help me to make things right again," he asked.

Finally, Jeremiah prepared his altar for his monthly ritual of making an offering to his ancestors. As he called out the names of his ancestors, three times each, requesting that their spirits join him, he felt the tension of the last few weeks' drain from his body. He felt peaceful. He believed that whatever was troubling his wife would soon be revealed to him and that the ancestral spirits would use their influence with God to make it right. He told them that he was willing to do whatever it took to bring complete harmony back to his marriage.

The weekend ended on a good and happy note. Aliyah returned from church in the same good mood, or better, than when she had left. Her mother, brother, and sister-in-law were with her. There was to be another Sunday dinner at the Jones' household. Jeremiah felt blessed. These family gatherings were not only good for his wife, but also good for him and the children.

Jeremiah and his brother-in-law retreated to the den to watch the only television set in the household, while Aliyah, her mother, and her sister-in-law went into the kitchen to prepare dinner together. Jamal could not believe that this was the only television in the Jones' household.

"Man, do you want me to buy you and Aliyah another television for Christmas?" he asked.

"No," Jeremiah said. Aliyah rarely watches television, and I watch it sporadically. This is fine for us. We don't want the children growing up thinking that watching television should be a major part of their life. Besides there are so few positive images of black people on television that we don't want the children to grow up identifying with the images they show on the screen. "

"I agree with what you're saying, man, but this twenty-five inch hunchback television is from the dark ages. Even poor people have larger sets than this. One large screen television in the house is mandatory."

"Not for us," Jeremiah said. "This is sufficient for our television viewing. Like I said we rarely watch television. We prefer reading or talking with each other whenever we have some leisure time. Although lately," he hesitated, "Aliyah has been giving me a lot more leisure time than I want."

"What do you mean?" Jamal used the remote to find the sports channel he wanted to watch.

"Your sister has been in a very strange mood for weeks now. Something is bothering her and she won't tell me what it is. This is so unlike her that I don't know what to do about it."

"Do you want me to talk to her?" Jamal asked.

"No, not yet. I want to try to figure this out myself. I am becoming quite frustrated, though. Something is definitely wrong, and I don't have a clue."

"I'll talk to Sheniqua to see if she knows anything. Sheniqua doesn't let a thing get past her. If something is bothering Aliyah she would have picked up on it."

"Don't let Sheniqua know that I talked to you about this, okay?" Jeremiah did not want his sister-in-law to alarm Aliyah.

"Don't worry," Jamal said. "Your concerns are safe with me."

Sunday dinner was scrumptious. Betty prepared a tasty lasagna made with ground turkey. Aliyah fixed a wonderful green salad with all kinds of vegetables and black olives, which Jeremiah loved. Sheniqua made fresh dressing for the salad and some crunchy garlic bread. For dessert there was plenty of leftover birthday cake and ice cream. The conversation was up-beat with

Jamal and his mother giving the rest of the family a status report on the progress of Nealz' Benz.

"I'm telling you Aliyah you should come to a board meeting and watch Mom in action. She's really great. Everyone has so much respect for her as a leader. I'm so proud of her," Jamal said.

"Well, I learned a lot just listening to your father all those years. He always said that I might have to fill his shoes one day, but I never really thought it would happen," Betty said.

"It's a good thing that Dad had the foresight to keep you informed on the happenings of his business," Aliyah said. "You were able to step up to the plate when you were needed, and you have managed to maintain the high standards that Dad set, as well as increase the profits. I'm proud of you, too, Mom."

"Bill's death was so untimely," Betty said. "I never expected him to have a massive heart attack and die at sixty-two. He had just promised me that he was going to retire at sixty-six and spend some time with his grandchildren and me. He only got to meet Mandela, though. He would have loved Nia so much. She is so adorable. And now we are going to have another little bundle of joy, another grandchild, and a Neal at that. Your father would have been so happy." Betty sighed, and then looked at her pregnant daughter-in-law.

"I'm so sorry that my son will never get to know his grandfather," Jamal said sadly.

"How do you know it's going to be a boy?" Sheniqua asked,

looking at her husband.

"Dad was such a wonderful father," Jamal said, ignoring his wife. "I know he would have been a wonderful grandfather too."

"Dad would have been so proud of you Mom," Aliyah said. "You have really held this family together and his business too. As a family we are truly blessed to have you."

The Sunday following Jeremiah's forty-seventh birthday ended on a good note. After the family left he and Aliyah put their children to bed and retired for the evening. Jeremiah went to sleep feeling satisfied and content. Aliyah had given him another night of blissful passionate lovemaking.

"A large percentage of Ghanaian mothers earn their living selling produce in the marketplaces. Most of them take their young children to work with them. The children play together under the mothers' watchful eyes." *In less than two weeks I will be able to observe this for myself.* Aliyah stared at the words on her computer screen. She pictured herself, along with Jeremiah and their children, shopping at an open market in Accra or Kumasi, Ghana.

She was looking forward to the trip. She was anxious to get her entire family away for three weeks. She felt that it would be a great time to explore Jeremiah's feelings for Miss Melody and his intentions. Although the past weekend had been nice, almost like

old times, she hadn't forgotten that she had seen Jeremiah holding
and kissing Miss Melody in his studio.

Aliyah hadn't gone back to the studio since then, but she knew
that whenever he came to bed reeking of cigarette smoke he had
been with Miss Melody. If Miss Melody was what he wanted she
would just have to deal with it. She would have to learn to live
with the loss. *Isn't that what my mother was saying yesterday?*
Aliyah remembered the conversation in her kitchen from the
previous day.

Betty was telling her daughter and her daughter-in-law, as the
three of them prepared dinner in Aliyah's spacious kitchen, how
difficult it was initially to adjust to being alone after losing her
husband to a heart attack.

"I thought I would never get past it," she'd said.

"How did you finally get past it?" Sheniqua had asked. "You
seem to be doing just fine now."

"I started getting past it when I found something else to do;
something other than sitting around grieving. When the board
approached me to help them select a new chairman to replace Bill
I said, "Why not me?" Betty had laughed. "They were so shocked.
They thought of me as this cute little bundle of fluff that Bill kept
around for show. They didn't think I could do anything but shop
and run Bill's household," Betty had said, and then laughed again.
"Well I sure fooled them."

"You're a survivor, Mom," Aliyah had said. "I've always

known that you have inner strength, and you have proven that you do."

"So do you, darling," Betty had said to her daughter. "Whatever is bothering you just remember that you have the same inner strength that I have and you, too, are a survivor."

"What makes you think that something is bothering me?" Aliyah had asked her mom.

"I know you, Aliyah. You are my daughter and I always know when something is bothering you."

"Hmm," Sheniqua had said looking from her sister-in-law to her mother-in-law.

Getting up from her computer Aliyah glanced at the desk clock. *It's noon already. I think I'll take Nia for our walk around the lake.* She started downstairs.

"I just laid the baby down for a nap," Jean said when Aliyah got downstairs. "She had been a little cranky this morning and went to sleep as soon as her little head hit the pillow. Do you want me to fix you a sandwich, Miss Aliyah."

"No. I think I'll just go for a walk by myself."

"Why don't you go and grab up Mr. Jones? I'm sure he would love a distraction about now," Jean said.

"Maybe I will," Aliyah said, grabbing a sweater off the coat rack as she headed out the door.

Aliyah walked past her SUV parked at the curb. *I think I'll just walk over to the gallery. I can't be afraid to visit my husband when*

I want to. Walking up Halsey Street Aliyah's heart began to race the closer she got to the gallery. When she was a half block from the gallery she stopped dead in her tracks. Parked in front of the Jazz Garden was the red sports car. The same red sports car that had dropped Jeremiah off at the house, the one she had seen Miss Melody sitting in smoking a cigarette at Weequahic Park.

She started to turn around and run back home like she did the last time that she had come to visit Jeremiah unannounced. Something kept her from doing that though. Jeremiah was her husband. She didn't have to announce herself. She wasn't going to run away this time. If something was going on she wanted to know.

As Aliyah started up the stairs to the gallery she heard music coming from the Jazz Garden. It was Jeremiah. She recognized his piano playing. She heard Miss Melody singing in her sexy sultry voice. Aliyah went back down the few steps she had climbed and peered through the window to the club. Jeremiah's back was to the window. Miss Melody was facing the empty tables. No one was in the club except the two of them. The Jazz Garden never opened for lunch; it was a supper club.

Aliyah watched as Miss Melody sang "Body and Soul." She sounded a lot like Sarah Vaughn. Suddenly, Jeremiah stopped playing and went up to Miss Melody. He touched her face. She laughed. He was saying something to her and she was smiling in his face. He put his hands on her waist. She moved her hips seductively. Jeremiah went back to the piano and started playing again.

Aliyah continued to watch as Miss Melody resumed singing "Body and Soul." Again Jeremiah stopped playing. He got up again and this time he swooped Miss Melody up in his arms and placed her on top of the piano. She laughed and lay across the baby grand. He resumed playing and she resumed singing, looking into his eyes and moving in a seductive manner. Aliyah couldn't see Jeremiah's eyes but she imagined that they had that glassy look in them. The one he always got when he was aroused. She turned and walked back towards the house.

"Back already from your walk?" Jean asked as Aliyah came into the kitchen. "Did Mr. Jones go with you?"

"No," Aliyah said. "He was busy." She poured herself a glass of iced tea and grabbed a piece of fruit before heading back up to her office.

Aliyah was so absorbed in her work that she looked up in surprise when Jean came into the office to let her know that she was ready to leave for the evening. It was after five o'clock and she had worked continuously since coming back from the club at 1PM. Her mother was right. If she absorbed herself in her work she wouldn't feel the pain as much. Work would have to sustain her during these difficult times. Maybe Jeremiah would get bored eventually with Miss Melody. Maybe he would come back to her 'body and soul.'

Aliyah was bathing the children when Jeremiah came in at 8PM. He joined her at the tub and began washing Mandela's back, laughing and playing with him. Together they put the children to bed and read them a story. Then they turned the lights out in the nursery and left the room. Aliyah headed upstairs to her office.

"Aren't you going to join me for dinner?" Jeremiah asked.

"No," she said. "I've already eaten. I fixed you a plate of left over lasagna. There's plenty of salad in the fridge." She continued walking upstairs.

"How long are you going to work?" he asked.

"I don't know. I have to give final approval for this month's layout tomorrow. I want to finish reviewing it tonight."

Once in her office Aliyah turned on her computer to access the layout, however, she did not look at it. Instead she dimmed the lights in the room and went over to her window and looked upward at the sky. The sky was so beautiful, midnight blue. It glimmered with starlight and a golden sliver of a moon smiled down at her. She sat down in the lounge chair near the window and continued to look at the sky. She heard Jeremiah playing the piano downstairs on the floor below her. He kept playing Body and Soul over and over again. Finally he stopped. She continued to stare out the window. She stayed that way for a long time. It was eleven-thirty when she finally crept into bed next to a sleeping Jeremiah.

Chapter 9

Jeremiah woke up and looked at the clock next to his bed, it was 7AM. Aliyah was already up. He didn't remember her coming to bed last night. After practicing the song he was rehearsing with Miss Melody for a while he had finally showered and gotten into bed. He'd read for a while before he began to doze. When he woke up again it was eleven fifteen. He'd turned the lights out and went to sleep.

When he went downstairs he discovered that Aliyah had already eaten her breakfast and retreated to her upstairs office. Jean was giving the children their breakfast. On the stove a cup of hot Ovaltine, two slices of toast, and scrambled eggs stayed warm for him. Jeremiah got his breakfast and sat down at the kitchen table with Mandela.

"Jean have you noticed any change in Aliyah lately?"

"She seems a little tired," Jean said. I think she might be

working too hard."

"You haven't noticed any mood changes? Yesterday she seemed fine when I left, but when I returned home her mood had changed. Are you sure you didn't notice anything?"

"Well, she appeared a little disappointed that you wouldn't take time out to walk with her yesterday."

"When was that?" Jeremiah stopped eating, put his fork down, and looked up at Jean. "She never asked me to walk with her."

"Well, she left the house at noon going to the gallery to ask you to go for a walk with her. When she came back she went upstairs to her office. I didn't see her anymore until it was time for me to leave."

"Hmm," Jeremiah said. "She never came by the gallery. I wonder where she went."

Sitting in his studio Jeremiah flipped through his mail and allowed his thoughts to drift back to the day before. At noon he had been in the nightclub rehearsing with Miss Melody. The role Miss Melody was auditioning for was that of Sarah Vaughn. Jeremiah had always loved Sarah's music. When he was a young boy, still in elementary school, his father took him to meet Sarah Vaughn at the Key Club that used to be on Halsey Street, actually not very far from the Jazz Garden. He got to watch Sarah rehearse with her pianist. Sarah was wonderful at creating the right mood. She knew how to hold her head and how to move her hips. She knew how to project her voice from the top of a piano while sitting on it with her legs crossed. Jeremiah was trying to get Miss Melody to imitate Sarah's style.

He began to wonder if maybe Aliyah had come by the club while he was rehearsing with Miss Melody. Suddenly his eyes spotted a letter with a familiar logo. He quickly diverted his attention to the letter. He ripped it open. Sure enough it was from the National Museum of American Art. A representative from the museum had visited Oblivion a few weeks after he received the first letter to take a look at his gallery. They were considering his request but wanted to verify certain information. This was the first he'd heard from them since the visit.

Several pieces from the Harmon Foundation collection were currently being exhibited at a gallery in Albany, New York. The exhibit was scheduled to close by the end of the month. After careful consideration The National Museum, along with the current keepers of the collection, had decided to allow a few pieces from the collection to be exhibited at Oblivion. They had been impressed with Oblivion and Jeremiah's noble ambition. The limited collection would be delivered to his gallery in two weeks for a one-week showing on its way back to Washington. Jeremiah had to assure them that he would hire the necessary security for the exhibit and obtain insurance at his expense.

Jeremiah was more excited than he had been in a long time. Something he had prayed for was finally materializing. He had so much to do in preparation for the exhibit. He certainly would need help with the promotional aspects of it. With his thoughts rushing he quickly forgot about Aliyah's mood swings and began putting a plan into place to accomplish the task that lay in front of him. While checking his calendar it dawned on him. "That's the time I'm supposed to be in Africa with Aliyah and the children," he said out loud.

There was no way that he could miss out on the opportunity to exhibit pieces from the Harmon collection at Oblivion. Aliyah would just have to understand. She knew how important this was to him. Jeremiah gave it no further thought. He turned his attention to the telephone and began making the necessary calls that would help him prepare for the most important exhibition of his life.

At exactly 12:25PM Miss Melody walked into the studio with a scowl on her face. She waited impatiently for him to get off the telephone. He was talking to one of the best promoters in the area trying to work out a deal. Jeremiah waved Miss Melody to a seat next to his desk. She ignored his gesture and stood tapping her foot impatiently puffing away on a cigarette. When he finally got off the telephone she lit into him.

"You promised that you would give me a half hour of your time everyday until the audition," she said angrily. "Well I've been waiting for a half-hour Jeremiah. My audition is coming fast, and we have a lot of work to do."

"I'm sorry, Melody," he said. "Something really important has come up and I may just have to back out of my promise to you."

"No, no, Jeremiah. A promise is a promise. This audition is very important to me. You can't back out now," she was almost in tears.

"Well something very important has come up with me, too," Jeremiah said. "But, you're right. A promise is a promise. I'll try my best to fit a half-hour a day into my schedule for you. But not today, Melody, we'll resume tomorrow, okay? I have several more calls to make now."

When Jeremiah finally got off the telephone with another prominent promoter he was smiling. *It looks like I might just be able to pull this exhibit off. I can't believe that in less than two weeks I'll have treasured pieces from the Harmon Foundation collection right here at Oblivion.* He raised his arms in triumph. *This is so wonderful.* Then his thoughts went back to Aliyah and their planned trip to Africa. *I'd better tell her before I go another step further with this,* he thought.

It was 2PM when Jeremiah slipped his key into the front door. "Where is everybody?" he yelled out as he hung his jacket on the coat rack in the foyer. The house was quiet, at least on the first floor. As he climbed the steps to the second level Jeremiah could hear the laughter of his children coming from the nursery. Jean was settling the children down for their afternoon nap. The children were delighted to see him, but he made sure he did not get them too excited to sleep.

Jeremiah spoke to the children in a low, soothing voice telling them he had only come home for a few minutes to talk to Mommy.

He told them that he would be back later to help with their bath. After kissing them both he headed up to the third level where Aliyah was working.

"I have good and bad news for you," Jeremiah said after Aliyah recovered from seeing him home so early in the day.

"What is it?" A look of alarm spread on her face. "Tell me."

"Okay," Jeremiah said. "I'll give you the good news first. The National Museum has agreed to allow me to exhibit pieces from the Harmon collection at Oblivion."

"That's wonderful!" Aliyah jumped out of her seat to give him a hug. Then she wrinkled her nose, which was sensitive to cigarette smoke. "What's the bad news?" She backed away from him, remembering that Miss Melody smoked.

"The week that the collection is available is the same week that I'm supposed to be visiting Ghana with you." He looked at her for a reaction.

Although Aliyah said nothing, the look on her face was more than Jeremiah could bear. It was a look of disappointment, but it was also a look of pain and panic. Jeremiah was completely taken aback.

"It won't be that bad, Darling," he said, gathering her into his arms. "We'll work this out, I know we will," he said, thinking his words could comfort her. Still, Aliyah said nothing. Instead she pushed his arms away and walked slowly over to the window. She stared out the window, saying nothing as tears streamed down her face. No words or sounds came from her mouth.

"I know you're upset that I won't be traveling with you, Aliyah, so am I. But, you know how important this is to me and you've traveled by yourself plenty of times before. I'll make it up to you. We'll go away on a nice vacation later this year; better yet I'll take you to West Africa for a wonderful 5th wedding anniversary celebration.

Aliyah said nothing. She continued to stare out the window, tears still flowing. Jeremiah went over to the window. He tried to take her into his arms again. Smelling the cigarette smoke that clung to the fibers of his shirt, Aliyah pushed him away. She said nothing, but her body language spoke volumes. She was in pain.

"Talk to me, Aliyah. Tell me what you're thinking."

"I want you to go to Africa with me," she said finally.

"You know I can't do that now, Aliyah. I thought you would understand. You of all people know how important this is to me. I've got to be here for the exhibit. I've waited a long time for it. I will probably never get another opportunity like this. Tell me you understand, please tell me you do."

Aliyah moved away from the window and went back to her desk. She resumed working at the computer as though Jeremiah were not even there. After a few minutes of silence, Jeremiah left the room and went downstairs and out the front door. Aliyah lay her head down on her desk and cried and cried and cried.

"Come in," Aliyah responded to the knock on her office door. Her secretary had just called to announce that Dotty was on her way into the office. Aliyah had been gathering disks she would need to take with her on the trip to Africa. Today would be her last day in the Manhattan office until her return. She was anxious to get away now. So much had happened that she was beginning to think of the trip as a reprieve from her unhappiness. It was a chance to get away and think. She would have her best friend, Claudia, to talk to. "Sit and make yourself comfortable," she said to Dotty as she came into the room.

"I just wanted to wish you a safe and productive trip," Dotty said, making herself comfortable. "I really envy you; three weeks away in a beautiful place like Ghana with the man that you love and your offspring. What could be better?"

"Jeremiah's not going," Aliyah said without looking up from the table she was bent over."

"Not going? But, I thought---"

"Well, you thought wrong," Aliyah said rather abruptly. "Mandela and I are going alone," she said a little softer.

"What happened?" Dotty asked.

"Jeremiah has something more important to do." Aliyah walked over to her desk and put more disks in her case.

"Are you alright, Aliyah?"

"I will be. I think I may just need some time alone. It may be just what I need." Aliyah appeared to be pondering a possibility.

"If you want me to I'll go with you," Dotty offered.

"No," Aliyah said. "We can't both be out of the country at the same time. I need you to be here. I'll be fine."

"Is the children's nanny still going with you?"

"No," Aliyah said. "Her husband has cancer and she has to be with him while he gets chemotherapy treatments.

"What about Nia," Dotty asked.

"I've' made arrangements to leave her with my mother. Just Mandela and I are going to Africa," Aliyah said rather nonchalantly.

"Well, okay then," Dotty said, giving Aliyah a puzzled look.

"What?" Aliyah asked. "What's that look about?"

"What about your suspicions about Jeremiah?" Dotty asked.

"They're still there. But, what can I do about them?"

"You're going off to Africa leaving him alone for three whole weeks?" Dotty was incredulous.

"What else can I do? Should I cancel the trip altogether and stay here and watch him? If she is who he wants what can I do about it? Maybe he'll come to his senses while I'm away."

"Well, I certainly hope so." Dotty got up to leave. "Have a great trip and call me if you change your mind and want me to get a flight to Africa."

"I will call you if I change my mind." Aliyah gave Dotty a quick hug.

After Dotty left Aliyah sat down in her comfortable desk chair and thought about the events of the last few days. She had been so angry with Jeremiah that her thinking was clouded for a couple of days. She had avoided him and barely spoke to him. She had noticed the pained look on his face whenever she looked at him, but she would not relent. She was determined that she would not give him the satisfaction of begging him to come with her. She was not going to beg him to stay away from Miss Melody either.

Aliyah hung onto her anger until she had a talk with her mother. Betty tried to convince her that she could be wrong about Jeremiah. Aliyah was eager to let go of some of her anger.

It was three days after Jeremiah told Aliyah that he was not going to Africa with her, and three days after giving him the silent treatment that Aliyah sought solace at her mother's condominium in a beautiful suburban development in nearby South Orange, New Jersey. She told her mother about Jeremiah's opportunity to exhibit paintings from the Harmon Collection. She told her mother how upset she was that he would not be able to accompany her.

Somehow Betty had sensed that something other than the fact that her husband was not going to accompany her to Africa was bothering Aliyah. She had sat Aliyah down on the living room sofa next to her and took her hand. Looking directly into her daughter's eyes she had convinced her to confide in her.

"Aliyah, it helps to talk to someone you trust when something is disturbing you. What is it, sweetheart?" Betty hoped she would open up.

Aliyah needed little coaxing. "Jeremiah is having an affair, Mother," she said.

"Are you sure, Aliyah?" Betty had asked, alarm showing on her face.

"I've seen him kissing and touching her. He often comes home reeking of cigarette smoke and I know that she smokes. He comes home from the gallery later now and sometimes he goes out after dinner." Aliyah bared her soul to her mother.

"That doesn't sound like Jeremiah at all," Betty had said. "Could you be mistaken?" she'd asked.

"I don't think so, Mother."

"Who is this woman? Betty had asked. "Is she someone I know?"

"Miss Melody from the Jazz Garden." Aliyah was crying softly now.

"I don't believe it," Betty had said. "She's not his type. Listen," she took her daughter's hand again, "Things are not always what they seem. There was a time when I was sure that your father was having an affair. Later I found out that he just felt sorry for the woman and was trying to help her out of a bad situation. Nothing had happened between them. I was so glad that I didn't accuse him. I suffered for months keeping it all inside. But I was so glad that I hadn't confronted him with my suspicions." Betty held her weeping daughter in her arms.

"Then why was he kissing her, Mom? Are you saying I should

just suffer in silence?" Aliyah had asked. "While I'm in Africa she will have an opportunity to take him away from me." Aliyah cried even harder. "I'll be all alone. Jean can't come now because her husband has cancer. It will be just me and the children, alone in Africa."

"Get a hold of yourself," Betty had said. "First you won't be alone. Claudia will be there. I think you should take Mandela and leave Nia with me. You can't begrudge Jeremiah this opportunity to fulfill his dream, and you can't let *Enigma* down either. It's only for three weeks, Aliyah. Maybe the time away from each other will give you and Jeremiah some much needed time to think and to miss each other," Betty had said.

"We haven't really been together in a long time. I already miss him," Aliyah confided in her mother.

"Then go home and be a wife to your husband. You'll be leaving in a few days, and you don't want to leave your husband hungering for a woman's touch," Betty had said.

Aliyah took her mother's advice. Although she didn't have much to say to Jeremiah those last few days before her departure, she had been a wife to him in the bedroom. Not one night had gone by that he didn't fall asleep satisfied. She made sure that she wasn't going to Africa leaving her husband hungering for a woman's touch.

On the day of the departure to Ghana Aliyah, Jeremiah, Mandela, and Nia rode to JFK Airport in the limousine that

Enigma sent to pick them up. They arrived two hours before the flight was scheduled to take off. Jeremiah carried Nia, while Aliyah held Mandela's hand, a little too tightly, as they escorted the luggage to a designated security checkpoint. She hated that Jeremiah and Nia would not be able to accompany them any further. Security regulations that had been in place since 9-11 did not allow for sentimental good-byes at the departure gate anymore. Once the luggage was taken from them, Aliyah kissed Nia holding her tightly.

"Mommy is going to miss you so much, sweetheart," she said to her baby.

"Ma Ma, Mama," Nia said, clinging to her mother. Somehow she sensed that something was going on.

Jeremiah said his good-byes to Mandela. "You be a good boy and listen to Mommy," he said before giving his son a final hug.

Aliyah was on the verge of tears. Jeremiah embraced her, kissing her deeply. "I'm going to miss you, Baby."

"I'm going to miss you, too. Take care of Nia and my mother while I'm gone."

"You know you didn't have to tell me that. You take care of yourself and Mandela, Darling. Call me as soon as you arrive in Ghana regardless of the time. Give my regards to Claudia and her family, and have an enjoyable and productive trip." Jeremiah held her close, reluctant to let go.

"Did you call your father and give him our change of plans?"

Aliyah remembered to ask.

"Yes," Jeremiah said. "He knows that you and Mandela are traveling alone. Call him before you leave Cote'd Ivoire." He gave her a final kiss goodbye.

Aliyah gave Nia a final kiss and then they were gone. Aliyah and her little boy were off to Africa.

Chapter 10

"I'll come by this evening to help with Nia's bath," Jeremiah said to his mother-in-law when he dropped Nia off at her house.

"You don't have to do that Jeremiah," Betty said. "I know you have a lot to do to get ready for the art exhibit. I can manage with this little one just fine." She gave the baby's leg a playful tug.

"I know you can manage, Mom, and I'm sure Nia will manage just fine, too. It's me that won't be able to manage. I miss my family already. I want to help out as much as I can with Nia. I hope you don't mind."

"Of course I don't mind. She's your baby, Jeremiah. Come by whenever you like. I'm sure Nia will be delighted to see you."

Jeremiah watched as Betty went back into the house with Nia nestled contently in her arms. Nia smiled at him over her grandmother's shoulder. He knew that visiting Nia every night would help alleviate his loneliness. He had never been separated from his family for any length of time. *Neither has Aliyah.* Oh there were the usual business trips for two or three days at the most. But, in the four years of their marriage both he and Aliyah had managed to stay pretty close to home. This was not going to be easy for any of them.

After leaving Betty's house Jeremiah got into his car and drove directly to the art gallery. He looked around trying to determine what needed to be done before the exhibit. He would have at least three of the walls painted, he had to decide which of his paintings to put away in storage during the exhibit, and make sure that the floors were polished to a high shine. He also wanted to install more lights to highlight particular pieces. The exhibit was scheduled to open in less than two weeks. Where was his staff? He was anxious to give them their assignments.

At 11:45AM Jeremiah was downstairs in the nightclub talking to Cook about catering the opening. He wasn't convinced that Cook could handle the affair. He wanted it to be elegant, black tie perhaps. The Harmon collection was worthy of the utmost attention and respect. The artists whose works were included in the collection were the most respected African-American painters of the late nineteenth and early twentieth century. Their works were finally getting the recognition they deserved "against the odds." They had gone from a state of "oblivion" to one of recognition. Cook, however, felt that he was just as capable of catering the affair as anyone else.

"You think I can't cook food for fancy dressed up people?" he asked Jeremiah after he was told that it would be a black tie affair. "Just because most of the people that come here at night prefer regular down-home style cooking don't mean that I'm not gourmet. You just tell me what you want, man, and I'll hook it up."

"Okay," Jeremiah said. The opening will be on a Sunday afternoon. I just want some fancy hors d'oeuvres and other finger foods. People will not be sitting down, and it will be difficult to manage eating utensils while standing."

"Well, what kind of hors d' oeuvres do you want?" Cook asked.

"I don't know," Jeremiah said, wishing Aliyah was here to help him decide.

"Well, you buy them and I'll fix them," Cook said, heading back into the kitchen. "When is your wife coming back?" He appeared to have read Jeremiah's mind.

"Not for three weeks."

"She left you alone for three whole weeks?" A voice came from the doorway.

Jeremiah looked up to see Miss Melody making her way into the club. He looked at the wall clock; it was already noon. *Time to practice for her audition.* He ignored her question.

"Where has the little wife gone off to?" She would not let the subject drop as he wished she would.

"On a business trip," he said, making his way to the piano.

"Let's get started, Melody." Jeremiah hoped his abruptness would end her questions.

"She's not going to be here to help you with the exhibit? How inconsiderate. I'll help you, Jeremiah." Miss Melody gave him a look of genuine sincerity.

"That won't be necessary, Melody. I can manage, besides I have my staff."

"But it will give me a chance to repay you for helping me prepare for my audition. I want to help you."

"Everything is under control for now. If I think of something that you can help me with, I'll give you a call." He hoped that would end the conversation.

"Okay," Miss Melody said with a smile as Jeremiah began to play "Body and Soul."

At 8:30PM Jeremiah was ringing the bell to his mother-in-law's condominium. He was looking forward to bathing Nia, then going home to take a nice hot shower and going to bed himself. He was exhausted from what appeared to be an unusually long day.

"Hi," Betty greeted him at the door. "You look tired."

"I am." Jeremiah glanced over her shoulder looking for Nia.

"Well, you don't have to do this every night. I can manage by myself." She led him into the spare bedroom, which had been made into a makeshift nursery.

"I know," Jeremiah said, picking up the laughing baby who was obviously delighted to see her daddy. "I live for these moments."

He hugged his giggling daughter.

"Are you hungry?"

"No. I ate dinner at the club."

"Oh," Betty said, raising her eyebrows and wondering if Miss Melody had been there. "There's no need to eat at the club every night Jeremiah. I could just as well cook for both of us." She hoped he would accept her offer.

"No thanks, Mom. I have a lot to do, and eating at the club is more convenient."

"Well everything you need is here or in the bathroom," Betty said, turning to leave the room. "I'll be in the den working on my presentation before the board tomorrow morning."

"Do you need me to come in the morning to baby-sit Nia?"

"No." Betty stopped in the doorway. "Jean is coming for a couple of hours. I talked to her tonight. Her husband got through his first chemo treatment just fine. She's willing to pitch in and help out."

"That's great." Jeremiah said, getting Nia ready for her bath. "I know this is a difficult time for her. I really appreciate her help."

After bathing Nia, Jeremiah brought the towel wrapped baby into the guestroom where he dried and powdered her before dressing her in a nightgown. He read her a story and frolicked on the bed with her. He then lay down on the bed holding Nia on his stomach and sang her to sleep. Still holding the sleeping baby Jeremiah thought about his wife. *I really, really miss her, mood swings and all.* He lay on the bed thinking about how Aliyah had passionately seduced him the last three nights before her departure. *My wife has really become an enigma to me,* was his last thought before falling asleep.

———————

Getting off the plane at Kwame Nkrumah Airport Aliyah held Mandela's hand tightly, and made her way through the crowd to claim their luggage. It had been a long flight and she was tired. Mandela slept for most of the flight so he was full of energy. He looked around at all the people. His eyes were open wide taking in all the different sights. One of the first things he noticed was that the people were dressed differently.

"Mommy, why do the men have on dresses?"

"Those are not dresses," Aliyah said, correcting her son. "In West Africa the men wear traditional clothing called bubus or caftans."

This was Aliyah's second trip to West Africa. She was intrigued herself the first time she had visited. West Africa was so different from East and South Africa. Traditional clothing in East and South Africa was rarely seen in cities and airports. It had long been replaced with the popular Western attire introduced by Europeans when they settled in those areas.

Looking around for signs that would direct her to the baggage claim section, Aliyah spotted a young man holding a sign with her name on it. The man grinned at her when he saw that she recognized her name.

"Ms. Jones," he said loudly as he approached her. "My name is Basil and I am at your service. I will be your driver throughout your stay in Ghana. First I will help you get your luggage, and then I will drive you to your villa, your residence while you are here in Ghana." His English was impeccable.

"Thank you," Aliyah said, following the young man to the baggage claim section.

As editor-in-chief she still was not accustomed to all of the courtesies the magazine provided whenever she traveled abroad. A Ghanaian photographer would be joining them in the morning. She had a feeling that this was going to be a great trip. She only wished that Jeremiah and Nia could have been there, too.

Leaving the airport and heading to the car Mandela looked into the darkness and squeezed Aliyah's hand.

"Are you all right, honey?" she asked.

"Are there any elephants or lions out there?" Mandela asked. "My teacher said that elephants live in Africa." He continued looking out into the darkness.

"There's nothing to be afraid of, Mandela. Those animals are mostly in East and South Africa. There aren't many wild animals like that here." When she saw the look of disappointment on his face, she quickly added, "There are game parks, though. Maybe we'll get to go to a game park and see elephants and lions there."

As Aliyah and Mandela got settled in the car, a late model Volvo, her driver instructed the porter to put the luggage in the trunk. Aliyah pulled her cell phone out of her purse and dialed her home number. Jeremiah had asked her to call him as soon as she arrived. Although it was early morning in Ghana it was late night in Newark. She was disappointed when the answering service picked up. She called his cell phone and got the answering service again. *Where could he be this time of night?*

The car moved smoothly over well-paved roads apparently heading east. After about forty-five minutes Aliyah could see the beginning of the sunrise over a hill. It was a spectacular sight.

"Look," she said to Mandela. "The sun is coming up."

"Where?"

"Stop the car," she said to the driver. "I want my son to see the sun rising. He has never seen this sight before."

"Further ahead you'll get a better view of the sunrise." The driver said. "I'll pull off the road, then, if that is okay with you, Ms. Jones."

Watching the sunrise with Mandela is such a beautiful way to begin our visit in Ghana, Aliyah thought, hugging her son, as they watched the sun rise over a hill lighting the way for the remainder of their journey.

As soon as they resettled into the car Aliyah's cell phone rang. *Its Jeremiah,* Aliyah smiled while searching through her purse for the cell phone.

"Are you here?" Claudia's voice came through the receiver.

"Yes, finally we are here," Aliyah said. "We are in the car heading to the villa."

"Oh, Aliyah, this is so exciting. I drove by the villa that you'll be staying in last week. It's only fifteen minutes from my house. I know its early, but if you're not too tired I can meet you there, okay?"

"I'm never to tired to see you, Claudia. Come whenever you're ready."

"Good. Ebony is dying to see you and Mandela. We'll be at the villa when your car pulls up. We'll leave right now. Oh Aliyah, I missed you so much. I can't wait to see you."

"Ditto," Aliyah said.

"We are now in Lebone," the driver said twenty minutes later. "Your villa is just around this corner."

The villa was in a lovely gated development surrounded with plush gardens and huge trees. Each villa had a curved driveway with an attached garage. The arched entranceway led to a terracotta-tiled patio. The house was sand colored with a terracotta-tiled roof, giving it a quaint look. Parked in the driveway was a green Land Rover. As soon as the driver pulled behind the Land Rover, Claudia and Ebony jumped out of the SUV, and walked towards the Volvo smiling broadly. Aliyah leaped out of the car and embraced her friend.

"I can't believe its really you," Claudia said.

"I missed you so much," Aliyah said teary-eyed.

Ebony, ten years old and very beautiful took Mandela's hand and led him to the patio. While Aliyah and Claudia were hugging and crying two people came out of the villa. The gentleman, an older man with skin the color of roasted chestnuts, went to the car to help with the luggage. The woman, about the same age and complexion, and with mixed gray hair, approached the two women.

"I'm Ama," she said. "I am the housekeeper. Zach is my husband; she pointed to the man helping with the luggage. We are here to make sure that you and your family are comfortable during your stay in Ghana." She had a soft voice and a warm smile. Her English was heavily accented.

"I'm Aliyah," Aliyah said, returning the smile and extending her hand. "This is my friend, Claudia, and that is her daughter." She pointed to Ebony. "And this is my baby, Mandela." She picked up Mandela and hugged him.

"I'm not a baby," Mandela said. "Nia is a baby."

"Where is your husband and baby?" Ama asked. "They said there would be a family of four and a nanny."

"Our plans changed at the last minute. There will be just Mandela and me."

"Oh," Ama said, raising her eyebrows. "Will your friends be staying?"

"No, no," Claudia said. "We live nearby, though, and we will be around a lot during their visit."

"Very well. Are you hungry?" Ama asked.

"Not really," Aliyah said. "We ate dinner on the plane. I can't believe it's breakfast time already. My body will have to adjust to the new time zone."

"I was preparing a little something for you in the kitchen. It will be ready shortly. My husband and I stay in the room off the kitchen. We will be at your service during your stay in Lebone."

"Breakfast in an hour will be fine." Aliyah turned to Claudia. "You will stay for breakfast won't you?" she asked.

"You know I will," Claudia said. "Just let me call Kwame and tell him that we'll be here for awhile. I left him in bed. There was a fire at our school last week and we are on recess while the repairs are being done." She took out her cell phone.

"Tell him to come, too," Aliyah said. "This will be just like old times."

The inside of the villa was just as beautiful as the outside. The living room was huge with beautiful stone and wood paneled walls. The dining room had a huge table that could easily sit a dozen people. The master bedroom had a king-size bed and there was a Jacuzzi tub in the adjoining bathroom. There were two other bedrooms; one was set-up as a nursery. In the center of the house was a staircase that led to a loft and continued to the roof. Aliyah and Claudia looked up the staircase, but did not venture up the steps.

"We'll explore later," Aliyah said. "Help me unpack before breakfast."

"This house is beautiful," Claudia said. "Too bad Jeremiah and Nia couldn't come with you."

"Yes," Aliyah said sadly. "It's too bad."

"Is everything all right, Aliyah?" Claudia sensed Aliyah's mood change.

"No. Everything is not all right." Aliyah opened a suitcase and started unpacking.

"Ebony why don't you take Mandela for a look around the house while Aunt Aliyah and mommy talk for awhile?" Claudia asked her daughter, anxious to hear the details.

While Aliyah unpacked and Claudia arranged the clothes closet, Aliyah talked about her crumbling marriage.

"I don't think Jeremiah is cheating on you, Aliyah," Claudia said, after Aliyah finished telling her what she considered to be the facts.

"Then how do explain his behavior. Coming in late smelling of cigarette smoke, concern about my weight, and don't forget I saw them together twice. He was holding her in his arms and kissing her. What else could it be, Claudia?"

"I don't know but there has got to be an explanation. I think you should talk to him about your suspicions. You never should have run away when you found him kissing her."

"I was so afraid, Claudia. I couldn't bear the thought of him telling me that he loved her and not me. I still can't bear it. I didn't know what to do. And now this. Three weeks of being separated, he may be with her right now for all I know." Aliyah sighed and lay down on the bed.

"Have you called to let him know you arrived safely?" Claudia asked.

"Yes, but he wasn't home and he's not at the gallery."

"Call him again," Claudia practically demanded.

Aliyah took out her cell phone and dialed her home number again. There was still no answer. "Where else could he be?" She looked at Claudia.

"Maybe he's at the nightclub. Why don't you call there?"

"I'm not calling him there. He should be home. It's way past midnight in Newark."

"Where's Nia?" Claudia asked.

"She's with my Mom. I'm going to call and check on her now." Aliyah dialed her mother's number.

"Hello," Betty answered the telephone sounding very chipper even though the hour was late.

"Did I wake you?" Aliyah asked, glad to hear her mother's voice.

"No, sweetheart. I'm watching a movie on television. Are you alright?"

"Yes. We're fine. We're getting settled into this lovely villa. Claudia is with me."

"Wonderful," Betty said. "I was wondering when I would hear from you. I figured you must have arrived by now."

"We've been in Ghana for a little over two hours now, Mom. I tried to call Jeremiah, but I can't seem to reach him. Have you heard from him?" Aliyah asked hopefully.

"As a matter of fact I think he's still here. He didn't come in to say goodnight. Let me look in the guestroom." Betty described the scene she saw to Aliyah. Jeremiah, sound asleep on the bed with Nia snuggled up on his chest, also sound asleep.

"Oh," Aliyah said. "How long has he been there?"

"He came to give Nia her bath and he's been with her all evening. They both fell asleep around ten. They were so quiet that I almost forgot they were here. I'll wake him now."

"No, don't wake him it's late."

"Nonsense," Betty said. "He'll be upset if I don't wake him to take your call."

Aliyah looked at Claudia and smiled sheepishly. "He's at my mother's house with Nia," she said before turning her attention back to the telephone.

"Aliyah," Jeremiah said sleepily into the telephone.

"Yes, it's me."

"Are you and Mandela alright?"

"We're just fine. What are you doing at my mother's house?"

"I miss you guys so much already. Being with Nia will help me get through the nights." He laughed quietly trying not to disturb the sleeping baby.

"I was so worried when I couldn't reach you. I tried to call you at home. Will you be spending the night at Mom's place?"

"No. I think I'll go home now. Why were you worried, Aliyah? Where did you think I was?

"I just didn't know where you were, or who you were with."

"You don't have to worry about me, Aliyah. I love you darling," Jeremiah said before hanging up the telephone.

"I knew I was right," Claudia said, looking at the happy smile on Aliyah's face after she hung up the telephone. "Jeremiah would never cheat on you."

Chapter 11

O ne week after his wife had flown off to Africa Jeremiah woke up alone and lonely in the king-size bed that they had shared for the past four years. It wasn't the first time that he had missed his wife. Aliyah made frequent trips to distant cities and sometimes abroad doing research for *Enigma*, but always with the understanding that she was leaving a loving, loyal husband behind, anxious for her return. Had something happened to change her thinking? Why would she be worried about where he was or whom he was with? That comment still concerned Jeremiah. His mind went back to his conversation with Jean on the day he had received word from the National Museum regarding his request to exhibit works from the Harmon Foundation collection at Oblivion.

As the day wore on Jeremiah kept in mind that he had intended to talk to Aliyah about her whereabouts the day before he received the good news. Jean had told him that Aliyah had walked to the gallery to invite him to join her for a walk in Weequahic Park. He remembered that it was the same time of day he had rehearsed with Miss Melody.

Had Aliyah seen them rehearsing? Could she have misconstrued what she had seen? If so, why hadn't she mentioned it to him? Was that the reason for her mood swings? Was this the reason she was worried about where he was and who he was with? He decided then that as soon as Aliyah returned from Africa they would talk about it. He would tell her about the rehearsals and find out what was on her mind.

It was 10AM when Jeremiah arrived at the gallery. He looked around, pleased with the work that had been done. The walls had been painted, the lights had been installed and everything was ready to receive the delivery that was expected later that morning. He still wasn't sure of which paintings he would be receiving from the collection, but he knew whatever works they were he would be glad to exhibit them. The reception for the opening was scheduled for the coming weekend, only three days away.

At 10:45AM Jeremiah was giving instructions to one of the gallery assistants when the delivery arrived. He was so excited that he could barely contain himself. His assistant let the deliverymen in to unload their cargo. With much anxiety and anticipation Jeremiah unwrapped the precious pieces one at a time. The first piece he unwrapped was an oil painting on canvas by Allan Rohan

Crite, painted in 1941. It was entitled *Harriet and Leon.* It was a work long admired by Jeremiah. He owned a print of this work, but seeing and touching the orignal filled him with emotion. It brought tears to his eyes. Then he unwrapped a portrait of *Anna Washington,* another oil on canvas painted in 1927 by Laura Wheeler Waring. It was beautiful and noble. Then he unwrapped a lithograph entitled *Laughter,* done in 1928 by Albert Alexander Smith.

An hour and a half-later Jeremiah sat looking at the exhibition laying at his feet. He had unwrapped a total of ten paintings that had been entrusted to his care. He marveled at the works. *How ironic,* he thought. *These artists probably died believing their works would some day be lost in oblivion. Now, here they are being exhibited in Oblivion Art Gallery.*

Jeremiah hoped that the artist's stories and their works would inspire other African Americans to continue striving to capture the spirit of their people, in unity and in struggle, vying to be recognized for their achievements. He was in awe. His dream was becoming a reality. He was going to present to the Newark artistic community such talent, such genius, such masterpieces that they could not help but be inspired.

Still overcome with emotion Jeremiah did not notice when Miss Melody entered his studio. He was wondering how he was going to display the precious pieces in the gallery when she suddenly spoke. "Did you forget about me again?" she asked.

Startled out of his thoughts, Jeremiah refocused his attention on her. "Come here, Melody," he said. "Look at these paintings. Do you recognize any of them?"

"No," she said. "Are these your paintings?"

"No, these are some of the paintings of African American artists long gone. But I intend to see that their works are never forgotten and that their drive and ambition be duplicated in the works of young African-American artists today."

"Are these the paintings you've been waiting for?"

"Yes. You don't know how long I've been waiting for them."

"Well, I'm glad they finally arrived. Maybe now you can devote some attention to my audition. It's tomorrow morning at 11AM. Are you ready to rehearse with me? It's already past noon."

"Sure," Jeremiah said. "This is our last rehearsal, right? After this I can devote my full attention to the opening. Will you be there?"

"I've been reading all the promotional stuff about this exhibit. Sounds like something I don't want to miss. Since your wife is out of town do you want me to stand in for her and be your hostess?"

"That won't be necessary," Jeremiah said quickly. "Everything is under control."

"I'll be there," Melody said. "If there's anything I can do to make it easier on you I will. I owe you for helping me with the audition."

"You don't owe me a thing, Melody," Jeremiah said, taking her arm and leading her down to the nightclub.

It was 10PM when Jeremiah put his key in the lock to the front door of the brownstone. He'd left the gallery at eight and gone to his mother-in-law's house to bathe Nia. After putting her to bed, at Betty's insistence, he had eaten a piece of peach cobbler. He'd been eating all of his meals at the Jazz Garden since Aliyah's departure, even though his mother-in-law had offered to cook for him. He didn't want to overburden her. After all she was caring for Nia most of the time. He and Jean were pitching in to help with Nia whenever Betty had to go out. The arrangement was working quite well.

It was after midnight when Aliyah called. He looked forward to the nightly calls from her, filling him in on her activities in Africa, and he enjoyed filling her in on the developments with the exhibit. All seemed well with both of them. He was happy knowing that Aliyah was happy and content. She didn't seem to have a care in the world. She told him every night how much she missed him. He missed her, too, and didn't mind letting her know it. He was anxious for her return. Jeremiah went to sleep dreaming of his wife and longing for her touch.

The following morning Jeremiah was up and raring to go at 7:15. He still had not hung any of the Harmon collection paintings in the gallery. He was meeting with a renowned curator at ten who would assist him with the placement of the precious paintings. He'd invited a few local artists to the gallery for a pre-reception the evening before the opening. He felt like a kid on Christmas Eve knowing that he would have his first bicycle under the tree when he woke up.

After showering and trimming his mustache Jeremiah headed to the kitchen where he heated water for his favorite breakfast drink, then he put a couple of slices of whole wheat bread into the toaster. He missed having Jean there in the mornings. Heck, he missed everybody. The house was so quiet and lonely. He decided then that he didn't like being in the house when Aliyah wasn't there. He was wondering what she was doing at that very moment, when the doorbell rang. *Who could be ringing my doorbell at eight o'clock in the morning?*

"Hi." Miss Melody smiled up at him when he opened the door.

"What are you doing here, Melody?" Jeremiah asked, surprise showing in his voice.

"I'm so nervous about the audition this morning, Jeremiah. I was hoping you would run through the songs with me one more time. Please, please!" She begged.

"Melody, I have a meeting at ten and I want to be at the gallery by nine."

"I won't take up much of your time, Jeremiah. I have to be in New York by eleven, myself. Please!" She said again.

Jeremiah shook his head and gave in to Miss Melody's plea. "Come on in. Let's get this over with."

"Ohh. I love your house!" Miss Melody said, taking in her

surroundings as Jeremiah led her through the living room. "This is so you, Jeremiah!"

"The credit goes to Aliyah. She's a wonderful decorator."

"I know some of the credit goes to you, too." Miss Melody followed him to the kitchen. "I'll bet I can pinpoint the places that have your personal touch."

Ignoring Miss Melody's comment, Jeremiah took a sip of his hot Ovaltine, grabbed a slice of the toast, and led the way upstairs to the music room with Miss Melody at his heels. Once in the thickly carpeted music room Jeremiah put his unfinished breakfast on a tray, and sat down at the piano, anxious to get the rehearsal over with. A minute into the first song the telephone rang. It was the security company calling to inform him of a problem securing the gallery for the days following the exhibit. He quickly turned his attention to the problem at hand.

"I have to provide twenty-four hour security at the gallery for the next eight days. What's the problem?" Jeremiah asked, looking up from the piano at Miss Melody who had kicked her shoes off and was about to light up a cigarette. "No smoking in the house," Jeremiah said, after covering the mouthpiece of the telephone. "If you have to smoke go outside on the deck while I take this call. I may have to make another call or two. Come back in fifteen minutes." He turned his attention back to the telephone call.

Twenty minutes later Jeremiah was ready to resume the rehearsal. He waited a couple of minutes for Miss Melody before opening the door of the music room to go and find her. He was surprised to see her gently opening the door to the master bedroom.

"What are you doing?" he asked angrily.

"I've been checking out the rest of your house," she said. "I absolutely love it. I hope you don't mind. I didn't disturb anything."

"Let's get on with this," Jeremiah said, looking at his watch. "I have to be out of here in fifteen minutes."

Fifteen minutes later Jeremiah escorted Miss Melody downstairs. The rehearsal had gone well, and she appeared confident. Jeremiah's mind was on his own problems, though. He had to find another security company that could provide him with the security he needed to protect the paintings entrusted to his care.

"Good luck, Melody," he said once outside. "I know you will do well. Let me know how the audition went."

"Thank you so much, Jeremiah. I owe you. You have been wonderful helping me out this way." She walked to her car with a bounce in her steps and a smile on her face.

———————————

Ghana was warm and humid this time of year. Aliyah marveled at the blueness and vastness of the sky. She hadn't realized until now how restricted her exposure to the sky was, living in the city as she did. Unencumbered by tall buildings the African sky seemed endless. In the mornings she had her breakfast served on the patio overlooking rolling hills and lush foliage. Huge birds flew freely, sometimes landing near the patio. At first she was afraid of them, not being used to such large birds in her own environment, but soon she became accustomed to them.

Aliyah was so grateful that Claudia and Ebony's school was on recess and they had the time to spend with Mandela and her. Mandela had fallen in love with Ebony and was having the time of his life. Ebony appeared just as delighted to have her little cousin, as she referred to Mandela, clinging to her as he did. Aliyah enjoyed watching them frolic about as she and Claudia visited different sites gathering information for her article, and talking about old times and what the future may have in store for them. The Ghanaian photographer followed them around taking pictures.

"Your marriage to Jeremiah was one of the most beautiful weddings I ever attended," Claudia said one day as they were reminiscing in the car while Basil drove them to a day care center in Accra, the capital of Ghana.

"It was lovely, wasn't it?" Aliyah said, remembering. "The amazing part is that we put it all together in less than three weeks."

"That's right," Claudia said. "It was only a week after Jamal and Sheniqua got married that you and Jeremiah took the plunge. They got married on Christmas day as I recall."

"Right," Aliyah said. "Remember they had a big elaborate affair with sixteen attendants and a reception for over two hundred guests. It was huge."

"Yeah, but I enjoyed your wedding more. It was small and intimate and so romantic. I loved the offerings and the part where the doves took your prayers to God. You and Jeremiah looked so beautiful and so in love."

"It's hard to believe that we'll be celebrating our fifth wedding anniversary this year. Where did the time go? Where did the love go?" Aliyah sighed.

"Are you saying that you don't love him anymore?" Claudia gave her a look that said I don't believe that.

"I love him more than ever, Claudia. He's my soul mate, but apparently he doesn't feel the same way."

"I don't believe that for a moment. Did you see the look in his eyes when he said 'til death do us part?'" Claudia said, reminding Aliyah of the moment she and Jeremiah had exchanged vows.

"I see that same look in his eyes when he's with Miss Melody, Claudia."

"We are here," Basil said, pulling up in front of a one-story building with a clay roof and fenced in yard encasing a playground for children.

The day care center founded by the December 31st Women's Movement was a cheerful place, and they were warmly greeted. The children sang a welcome song and danced a traditional dance. The children's mothers worked primarily in the offices in the Accra area. Although office workers represented only a small portion of the workingwomen in Ghana, they were the mothers who took advantage of formal day care for their children. They could afford it. The majority of workingwomen in Ghana, over seventy-percent, were vendors of some type. These were the women who took their children to work with them. The December 31st Women's Movement was trying to change that. Their mission was to provide affordable day care services for the majority of working mothers, thus giving Ghanaian children an opportunity to benefit from early childhood education.

Later that week Basil drove them to the Volta Region of Ghana. "This region is the heart of the Ewe society," Claudia said. "The Ewe people are so friendly, and their culture is fascinating."

Aliyah was impressed with the beauty of the natural landscape of the region. The lakes were beautiful and serene. There were beautiful white sandy beaches lined with palm trees. They drove through a National park and Mandela got a chance to see the wildlife. He marveled at elephants, hippos, and monkeys. Then they visited a slave castle where Aliyah tried to explain to her son the horrors of the slave trade and how it had devastated Africa and future generations of African descendants.

On Aliyah's fifth day in Ghana they visited an open-air market. The market was crowded with vendors and shoppers. Most of the shoppers were local people buying fresh produce for the week and picking up toiletries and other necessities. Aliyah stopped to look at traditional fabric being sold by a young mother whose little girl of about eighteen months clung to her dress as she showed fabric and explained, in English, but with a heavy accent, the symbols representing community values that were woven into the fabric.

"These are Adrinka Symbols," the vendor said. Aliyah, who was already familiar with the symbols, listened anyway. "The Adrinka Symbols were created by the Assante people, and some by the Gyaman people of Cote' d'Ivoire. On this piece of fabric you have the Sankofa Bird who is symbolic of 'learning from the past'; then you have the *Gye Nyame* which is symbolic of the 'omnipotence of God'; and *Tabono*, which symbolizes 'strength'," she said. Her smile reflected how proud she was of her knowledge and of her heritage.

After purchasing several yards of fabric Aliyah questioned the young woman about the availability of childcare in the region. Then, Aliyah listened intently as the woman spoke while cutting the fabric.

"Here we bring our children to work with us," she said. "If the child is too young we leave them with a relative or an elder in the village who takes care of children for a living."

"Are there any day care centers in the vicinity?" Aliyah asked.

"Not that I know of," the woman said. "Even if there are, I know I cannot afford them. I don't make much money. I must save for my children's future education."

"Do you have other children?" Aliyah asked.

"A boy of six," she pointed to a group of children playing

together in a small circle nearby. "He will be attending school when the new session begins," she said proudly.

Before leaving the market Aliyah made a point of talking to the children playing together in the circle. The age range was four to seven. Most of the children spoke English, however, only the seven-year-old knew what Aliyah meant when she asked if they knew the English alphabet. *Seven years old is quite late to start learning the alphabet, especially if these children are going to have a chance at academic success in a Western dominated society.*

The last stop on the tour of Ghana was a day care center in Ping, Ghana. It was the day before she was scheduled to leave for Cote'd' Ivoire. Ping was a very rural farming area in the Upper West Region of Ghana. Running water and electricity were foreign to the villagers. Music is what sustained them. Aliyah was so enthralled with the music that the villagers created with the *gyil*. It brought tears to her eyes. The *gyil* was a large xylophone that produced the most beautiful music that she had ever heard.

The *Dagaare* people of Ping were warm and friendly. Mandela and Ebony were at home from the moment they arrived. They danced and sang with the local children even though they could not understand the language. Basil stayed with the children while Aliyah, Claudia, and the photographer went into the fields to talk to and photograph the women. They found many young children tagging along with their parents. Aliyah spoke with one young mother who was quite proud of her English.

"Is it safe to bring children into the fields while you work?" Aliyah asked.

"Not so safe," the pretty, dark woman said. "There are snakes and scorpions that present danger, but the children get the knowledge they will need to learn about fieldwork."

"What about school?" Aliyah asked. "Do many of your children go to school."

"Education is highly desirable," the young mother said. "We are a poor village, though. We have only two schools for all of our children. I work hard to save money for my children's education. My son will go to school when he turns seven," she said proudly.

The villagers were proud of the primary and middle schools they had been able to build, but they despaired that they had not been able to build the nursery schools they needed. They were sad that older female children often had to be kept out of school to attend the younger children. The population in Ping, Aliyah was told, was less than 4% under the age of two. However, the population over sixty was only ten percent indicating a need for education to increase the life span of the people. Before leaving Ping Aliyah wrote out a check for five thousand dollars that she presented to the minister of education, who estimated it to be the cost of constructing a nursery school.

Aliyah spent her last night in Ghana with Claudia and her husband, Kwame. Kwame was a New Yorker who had repatriated Ghana. He and a few of his fellow New York teachers had built a high school near Accra. They named the school The Science Academy. The main purpose of the Academy was to provide a secondary education to Ghanaian children that were talented in science and math, but unable to afford a formal education beyond middle school.

Before Kwame and his colleagues built the school children seeking to further their education had to leave their village, pay tuition, and board in another village where there was a high school. This was much like what many African-American children living in the south before Brown v. Board of Education had to do. The mission of the Science Academy was to instill in its students a sense of duty to their country, and convince them to use the knowledge they acquired to help Ghana. Kwame was proud of his contribution to Africa. He was happier than he had ever been in his life.

While Kwame fixed a dinner for them of some of his favorite Ghanaian dishes, Aliyah and Claudia sat out on the terrace of the spacious home looking at the sunset and keeping an eye on the children playing in the yard. Aliyah lay back on her lounge chair wishing that she could bring Claudia back to New Jersey with her.

"I'm going to miss you so much," Claudia said as though she had read Aliyah's thoughts.

"Claudia, I miss you so much, too. I have no friends left. Everyone has moved on with their lives or died like my father. Sometimes I feel so alone."

"At least you have your mother and people you have known all of your life living in your immediate vicinity. I have only my husband and my child. If anything were to happen to either one of them I think I would die."

"Nothing will happen to them," Aliyah said. I've lost so many people that I love in the last few years that sometimes I just cry. My father was the biggest loss. God how I miss him. Then Teyinniwa and Morgan, my very good friends."

"What happened to them?" Claudia asked.

"Teyinniwa moved to North Carolina after Morgan moved to New York to live with an old high school boyfriend. They sold their house, you know."

"What!" Claudia said. "I thought they loved that old house too much to ever sell it."

"The last time I spoke with Teyinniwa before she moved she told me that the house in Newark was giving her a lot of trouble. It was over a hundred years old, and she couldn't find a decent contractor to fix all the things that needed fixing. She said that if she stayed there any longer she just knew she would end up killing herself a contractor."

Claudia laughed. "What's she doing now?"

"You're not going to believe this, Claudia. But, she bought a new house in Durham and fell in love with the contractor that built it."

"What?" Claudia looked surprised.

"Isn't that ironic? She also started a Durham chapter of the Daughters of Africa. It takes up a lot of her time, but she loves it."

"What about Kanmi and Oya?" Claudia asked.

"They're still around, but they are so busy. Kanmi has acquired a new store in Philadelphia, and Oya has become very much in demand as a Yoruba Priestess."

"That's wonderful. I'm very happy for them."

"Me, too," Aliyah said. "But I sure do miss them."

After their Ghanaian feast, Aliyah, Claudia, and Kwame sat in the living room talking about Africa and African-Americans. Kwame, a historian and a very scholarly person, welcomed the discussion of Africans and their descendants with a fellow African-American.

"The majority of people here are so poor, Aliyah," Kwame said. "Not as poor as in other parts of Africa like Nigeria, for instance, but poor just the same. Sixty to seventy percent of workingwomen are vendors. Some sell their wares in the marketplace and others sell on the streets. They make very little money, barely enough to sustain their families. They long to leave this beautiful continent and settle in places like America. They think they would be happier having things like DVD's and cell phones. They are so impressed with the materialism of America. They just don't understand the drawbacks to such a culture."

"I see what you mean Kwame. I noticed that a lot of Ghanaians are anxious to move to America. They want the 'good life' as they see it." Aliyah sympathized with him.

"If only they could see the difference between spiritualism and materialism," Kwame said. "I notice the difference between the different groups here. About 30% of Ghanaians are Christian; another 30% are Muslim, while 30% practice traditional values and culture. In my opinion the latter are the most happy and well-adjusted group. The Christians are so set on acquiring material wealth that they have lost focus of spiritual values, the Muslims are so set on clinging to spiritual values that they have no concept of the positive aspects of materialism, but the traditionalists see the value in both. Abandoning traditional values is the worst thing that Africans could have done. Our ancestors must be rolling over in their graves. Values and traditions that took centuries to develop with the purpose of passing down something of worth to future generations, thrown away like trash."

"That's so sad Kwame," Aliyah said. "How do you think it's affecting us globally?"

"Most of the Christians in Africa want to leave the continent and go to America or Europe where they have a better chance of obtaining material wealth. They know that in order to do so they have to obtain an education. This means that the best educated are hell bent on leaving the continent. This is creating what is referred to as a 'brain drain' on the African Continent. The most poorly educated and less likely to successfully govern the continent are left behind to preserve our history and our culture," he said sadly.

"I see that in America," Aliyah said. "I read an article in the New York Times that reported more Africans are coming to America now than during the eighteenth century slave trade. Most of them are highly educated and willing to settle for salaries that are much lower than is traditionally paid in their field, but much higher than they can get in their countries of origin."

"How sad," Kwame said. "Have you thought about the impact this is having on the status of African-Americans who have struggled to obtain equal pay status in America?"

"It's definitely creating dissension among Africans and African-Americans," Aliyah said.

The next morning Aliyah, Mandela, Claudia, and Ebony were at the Kwame Nkrumah Airport at 7AM. Aliyah and Claudia were teary eyed as they hugged and said goodbye to each other.

"This has been so wonderful, Aliyah," Claudia said, hugging her friend. "The times I spend with you are some of the best times I ever have."

"I feel the same way, Claudia," Aliyah said. "Please try to come to New Jersey soon and call me as frequently as possible."

"Aliyah talk about your suspicions to Jeremiah. You have a duty to protect your marriage. Don't forget what Kwame said about traditional values. It is traditional for Africans to enlist the help of family to settle marital problems. Talk to your mother. She has always been there for you. You waited a long time for a soul mate, Aliyah. If what you suspect is true, don't give up your husband without a fight." Claudia was still talking as Aliyah and Mandela walked to the departure gate.

The last words Aliyah heard as she and Mandela went through the doors where they would board a small jet that would take them to Cote' d 'Ivoire were "I love you, Aliyah."

Chapter 12

J eremiah checked out his well-groomed appearance in the full-length mirror in his bedroom. While he wasn't a vain man he was well aware of his strikingly good looks. His chocolate complexion was smooth and blemish free. His hair and his mustache were thick, black, and shiny, perfectly trimmed for the occasion. All of his life he had been complimented on his good looks by women, beginning with his mother. His mother would tell him "Don't let your good looks go to your head, Son." She always wanted him to know that there was much more to being a man than having women find you attractive. For the most part he had heeded his mother's advice. He was certainly more proud of the family values that his parents had instilled in him than his good looks.

Today was the day that he had been awaiting for a long time. Paintings from the Harmon collection were hanging in his gallery. The reception was scheduled for 3PM, and then a tour of the gallery would begin. Jeremiah wanted everything to be perfect. The kitchen staff from the supper club was setting up the buffet table at 2:30, and the champagne would start flowing at exactly 3PM. How he wished Aliyah could be there for the opening, but he understood. Aliyah's work was just as important to her as his own work was to him. It made her happy just as his work made him happy. He wanted for her what she wanted for herself.

At 2PM Jeremiah was at the gallery. He watched as the gallery staff ran about making sure that everything was set up properly. The back of the gallery was darkened in order to keep the guests in the front during the reception. At three-thirty the lights would go on and they could begin to move about freely. His mother-in-law was there early, as she had promised, to help with the setup. She and Sheniqua were in the back of the gallery when Miss Melody burst through the door. As soon as she saw Jeremiah she ran up to him throwing herself into his arms and giving him a big kiss on the lips.

"Thank you, thank you, thank you," she said breathlessly.

"What's this all about?" Jeremiah said, conscious that Betty and Sheniqua were in the back of the gallery and might misconstrue what they had witnessed.

"I got the part," Miss Melody said excitedly. "Thanks to you and all that you did to help me." She hugged him again.

"Congratulations," Jeremiah said, untangling himself from her grasp. "I'm so happy for you."

"They thought I was a natural for Sarah Vaughn. I think it helped that both Sarah and I were born in Newark, and that we both graduated from Arts High School. But, the biggest seller was how you taught me Sarah's style. They were really impressed. I love you Jeremiah," Miss Melody said loudly just as Betty and Sheniqua walked into the lighted section of the gallery. "Hi," she said to them rather nonchalantly and then began ordering the kitchen staff as to how to arrange the food. "I'll take care of this for you, Jay," she said grinning from ear to ear and leaving him alone with Betty and Sheniqua who looked stunned.

Jeremiah was wondering if he should explain Miss Melody's behavior to Betty and Sheniqua when the gallery door opened again. He looked up to see his guests arriving for the opening. He excused himself and went to greet them. Throughout the reception Miss Melody appeared to be floating on air. She took over the job of hostess and gave each guest such individual attention that Jeremiah could not help but smile at her each time he passed her. He knew she was only trying to compensate him for his assistance.

At 4:45 Jeremiah was talking to his brother-in-law, Jamal, who had come in a little late. He noticed that the crowd had begun to thin out and that the caterers were cleaning up. "What did you think?" he asked Jamal.

"I'm impressed," Jamal said. "This was one of the best exhibits I have ever attended. I liked the way you exhibited the Harmon works painted by African-American artists from the early part of the twentieth century along with works by African-American artist done at the end of the same century. It was a great contrast showing the difference in style and freedom."

"That's exactly the contrast I was trying to depict," Jeremiah said. "The later works were done by local artists from the New York, New Jersey and Pennsylvania areas. Some of them were here today, but I had a pre-reception last night and most of them came. It was wonderful. This is just the beginning of what I hope will become a positive exchange of ideas among talented African-American artists, Jamal. This has been a wonderful experience for me. I just wish your sister had been here to share it with me." He looked forlorn.

"Don't worry, Aliyah will be around for many future events you will give of this nature. I'm sure Mom and Sheniqua will tell her all about what she missed today," Jamal said, just as Betty and Sheniqua joined them.

"Tell who all about what?" Sheniqua asked Jamal while giving Jeremiah a disconcerted look.

"I was just telling Jermiah that you and Mom will tell Aliyah what she missed today," Jamal said.

"Oh you can count on that," Sheniqua said sarcastically.

"It was a wonderful reception and a wonderful exhibit," Betty said. "Aliyah will be sorry she missed it."

"I can't wait to talk to her tonight." Jeremiah smiled at Betty. "How's Nia?"

"She's wonderful. I started to bring her with me, but I thought you would need my help so I decided to leave her with Jean instead." Betty looked at Jeremiah.

"You both were a big help." Jeremiah gave Betty a hug. "I really appreciate all that you did." He kissed Sheniqua's hand.

"It appears that you had more help than you needed," Sheniqua said sarcastically again.

"Everybody was so wonderful." Jeremiah said, ignoring Sheniqua. "My staff, family, and friends all of you were wonderful.

At 6PM everyone had left the gallery except the staff. Jeremiah wanted to make sure that the Harmon collection pieces were intact. He went through the gallery checking each piece for damage. He was satisfied that nothing had happened to the precious collection under his watch. As he made his way to the front of the gallery, he was surprised to find that Miss Melody was still hanging around, too.

"Don't you have something better you could be doing tonight?" he asked her.

"Not really," she said. "Don't you think we're a good team?"

"What do you mean?"

"The way you helped me. I don't think I could have gotten that part without you. And the way we worked together tonight at the gallery. I just think we work well together. Don't you?" She looked up at him with hope in her eyes.

"What are you getting at, Melody? What do you want?"

"You know what I want, Jeremiah. I want you."

"That can't happen. I'm married, I love my wife and my family."

"Lots of married men---"

"Forget it Melody. I love my wife and I would never do anything to jeopardize our relationship. It's getting late. I think you'd better go."

"Okay," she said. "I'm going. But, we are a good team. Remember that."

At 11PM Jeremiah lay on his bed waiting patiently for Aliyah's call. He thought about the events of the day and wondered if he should mention to Aliyah that Miss Melody had taken over as hostess. He knew that Sheniqua was going to mention it to her if he didn't. But, he didn't want Aliyah to worry, especially if she had witnessed the rehearsal that took place before she left. He finally decided that he would wait until she got home, then they would have a long talk.

When the telephone finally rang at eleven-thirty, Jeremiah was startled. He had begun to doze off. He grabbed the telephone out of its cradle and smiled when he heard his wife's voice.

"How was the exhibit?" was the first thing out of her mouth.

"Not even a hello first?" He joked with her.

"Tell me about the exhibit," she said excitedly. "I've been thinking about it all day and wondering if everything went okay."

"It was wonderful." Jeremiah couldn't help but smile. "It could not have been more perfect."

"Not even with me there?" Aliyah asked.

"That is the only thing that could have made it more perfect." Jeremiah laughed. "Although your mother and Sheniqua tried to fill your shoes in your absence."

"Was Nia there, too?"

"No. Nia stayed with Jean. But your brother was there. He really enjoyed it. When are you coming home?" Jeremiah's tone conveyed his loneliness.

"Well, we'll be in Cote' d 'Ivoire for another day before we leave for Senegal. I wouldn't mind cutting the Senegal portion of the trip if your father wasn't looking forward to us coming. Both Mandela and I are tired, and very much looking forward to sleeping in our own beds."

"How is my son? Let me talk to him."

"He's sleeping. Don't forget it's very early in the morning here. He's been a little grouchy the last few days. I think he's home sick."

"He'll be fine when you get to Senegal. My father has a whole slew of things planned for him. We can't deprive them of this time together, although I wish you were coming home now. I wish I could join you in Senegal for the last leg of the trip."

"Why can't you?" Aliyah asked hopefully. "The exhibit is over."

"The Harmon collection will be hanging in my gallery for the next week. I wouldn't feel comfortable leaving it. I want to make sure that the paintings are shipped back, in tact, to the National Museum myself."

"Is that the only reason you won't come, Jeremiah."

"The only reason, Aliyah. There is nothing more that I want right now than to be with you."

When he hung up the telephone Jeremiah wondered about Aliyah's question. *Why would she ask me if that was the only reason I'm not meeting her in Senegal. What is she thinking?* He went to sleep determined that he would definitely have a talk with his wife when she returned. Something was bothering her and he was determined to get to the bottom of it. He knew he had to talk to her before she talked to Sheniqua.

———————

Cote' d 'Ivoire had been interesting enough, and Aliyah had managed to complete the research she needed for her article. In Senegal she was going to rest and try to relax a bit. She had certainly enjoyed herself in Ghana, but the last six days in Cote' d 'Ivoire had been hectic. The accommodations had been wonderful. She and Mandela stayed in a luxury hotel suite. Not only was she provided with a driver and a nanny for Mandela but a bodyguard as well. The country had been in chaos just months before her arrival and the magazine was not taking any chances.

Mandela had been whining since they left Ghana. He really missed Ebony. He cried for the first two days they were in Abidjan.

"Are we still in Africa, Mommy?"

"Yes, Mandela, we are still in Africa."

"Then why can't Ebony come to see us anymore? Where is she?"

"We're still in Africa but we are too far for Ebony to visit us." Aliyah tried to explain.

"I want to go home then," Mandela cried. "I want my daddy." For the next six days Aliyah listened to this cry.

The nanny that was provided seemed especially nice, but she was older and not as much fun for Mandela as Ebony had been. The bodyguard tried to entertain him whenever he could, but Mandela could not be consoled. By the time they arrived in Senegal Aliyah was at her wits end. She was so grateful to turn Mandela over to the charms of his grandfather who met them at the airport.

"So you're my grandson?" Mr. Jones asked Mandela.

Mandela looked at the man who had a striking resemblance to his own father and asked, "Who are you?"

"I'm your grandfather," he said to Mandela.

"Is he my grandfather?" Mandela asked Aliyah. He had no recollection of either of his grandfathers. He hadn't seen Mr. Jones since he was a baby and his maternal grandfather had died when he was only a year old.

"Yes Mandela, this is your daddy's father. That makes him your grandfather." Aliyah smiled at her son.

"My grandfather?" Mandela smiled at the older man and let him take his hand.

Once they got to the house, a lovely French villa close to downtown Dakar, Simone, Jeremiah's stepmother, insisted that Aliyah take a nap and rest up before dinner. Two hours later when Aliyah awakened from her nap, Mandela and his grandfather had become best friends.

"My grandfather is going to teach me to fish," he told Aliyah. "Do you know how to fish, mommy?" Not waiting for an answer he hurried on. "You put a worm on a hook and put it in the water and you catch a fish," he said excitedly. "Do you want to come with us?"

"We're all going to the village day after tomorrow," Mr. Jones said. "You'll love it there, it is so peaceful and right on the beach."

After a delicious dinner of Jollof Rice, plaintain, and fish they talked into the wee hours of the night, catching up on the happenings of their lives. Finally Mr. Jones carried his grandson to bed and they all retired for the evening.

Aliyah and Simone shopped the next day, leaving Mandela with his grandfather. Aliyah purchased gifts for her mother, brother, and Sheniqua. She found a lovely oil painting of some fishermen on a beach with their day's catch and bought it for Jeremiah. Simone took her to the post office where she wrapped it and mailed it to the gallery.

That night after dinner Mr. Jones played the piano for them and let Mandela sit on the piano stool alongside him. Mandela was so happy.

"My daddy lets me sit next to him when he plays the piano, too," he told his grandfather.

"When your daddy was a little boy like you I let him sit on the piano stool while I played the piano. Just like you and I are doing now."

"Tell me about my daddy when he was a little boy," Mandela said.

"He was a lot like you," Mr. Jones said. He played a soft melody and proceeded to tell Mandela stories about Jeremiah when he was a little boy. Aliyah was as enthralled with the stories as Mandela.

Talking to Jeremiah that night on her cell phone, Aliyah laughed when she told him how Mandela and his grandfather had become best friends. She could sense her husband's happiness when she told him how his father and son had sat at the piano just as Mandela and he sat at the piano at home.

"I miss you, Jeremiah," was the last thing she said to him that night.

"I miss you, too, Darling," Jeremiah said before hanging up the telephone.

The next day Mandela and Aliyah accompanied Mr. Jones and

Simone to the fishing village where members of Simone's family still lived. Aliyah was fascinated. Mr. Jones had built a three-bedroom cottage right on the beach. It was tastefully furnished and very comfortable. Aliyah loved hearing the ocean before she went to sleep at night and waking up to it in the morning. Mandela loved it, too. He accompanied his grandfather out in the mornings. They would stay out all day fishing and talking with the other fishermen.

Aliyah often passed them during the day as she walked the beach. Her mind was heavy. She prayed that she would not have to go home and face the same problem she had before leaving. *Maybe Miss Melody moved,* she thought. *It would be so wonderful if she would just disappear from our lives.*

The rest and relaxation made a world of difference. By the fifth day of her visit to Senegal, Aliyah was raring to go home. Whatever awaited her she was ready for it. She had spent her time praying and meditating. She made offerings to the goddess of the sea, Yemanya. Aliyah purchased a bunch of large purple grapes everyday and tossed them into the ocean asking Yemanya to protect her and her son while they were visiting the motherland. She also asked Yemanya to talk to Osun, the goddess of love and pleasure, and ask her to intervene on her behalf to save her marriage.

The night before Aliyah and Mandela were to leave for Newark, Aliyah and her father-in-law had a heart to heart talk. "Why are you so unhappy?" he asked her. "I don't see you laugh or smile anymore. What has happened to change you so?"

"I'm sorry," Aliyah said. "I wasn't aware that I was so transparent."

"You needn't apologize, my dear." He sounded so paternal. "I just want to know what is bothering you, perhaps I can help."

"I wish it were that simple. It's very complicated, and I don't want to burden you." Aliyah looked away, nervously biting her bottom lip.

"Nothing regarding my family is a burden. You are my son's wife, the mother of my grandchildren. You are very important to me, Aliyah. I want you to be happy. If you and Jeremiah are happy then my grandchildren will be happy. That is all that I want." He tried to make eye contact with Aliyah, attempting to read her face.

"I love Jeremiah so much." Aliyah looked at her father-in-law. I want to make him happy, and I want our children to be happy, but…"

"But what?" Mr. Jones coaxed her to confide in him.

"Nothing," Aliyah said. "I have to talk to Jeremiah first. I should never have left home without talking to him about my feelings."

"Listen my dear," he said reaching for her hand. "I am up in age now, seventy years old. I have had two wives in my lifetime and I know a little about marital bliss. Rule number one is to never let issues fester. When something is bothering you, get it out in the open before it gets too big. Small problems left untreated turn into big problems that cannot always be treated. Communication is the key to a happy marriage. You have to listen to your mate and let him know what you feel, things are not always what they appear." Mr. Jones nodded his head as if to emphasize his point.

"I have always been able to tell what he is feeling. I have never doubted my husband before, now, I don't know. So much has changed in such a short time. I don't know what to think anymore." Aliyah looked at her father-in-law hoping for his understanding.

"Well when you get home make a date with your husband and talk about those doubts. The longer you delay talking the worse you will feel, and the worse you feel the worse Jeremiah will feel. Trust me my dear. I speak from experience." He reached for her hand. "You will feel a lot better when everything is out in the open."

The next morning Aliyah and Mandela were on the plane, a Boeing 747, bound for Newark. In seven hours she would be home. *Communication is the key,* she thought about her father-in-laws advice. That's exactly what was lacking in her marriage, at least for the last few months. How could she have allowed things to get this far without talking to Jeremiah? She accepted full responsibility for the lack of communication. Jeremiah had tried to talk to her. It was she who had shut down. *Well things are going to be a lot different from now on,* she thought while Mandela slept in the seat next to her.

The welcome Aliyah received at the airport was overwhelming.

Jeremiah was there along with her mother, Jean and Nia. They were all delighted to see her and Mandela come out of the terminal, and Aliyah could not have been happier. Jeremiah swooped her up into his arms and kissed her passionately in front of everyone. Mandela tugged at his father's trousers until Jeremiah released his wife and picked up his son. Aliyah took a delighted Nia into her arms and squeezed until the baby squealed. It was a wonderful homecoming.

Slipping back into their usual routine seemed so easy after a three-week separation. After enjoying the wonderful meal that Jean had prepared for the family, Aliyah and Jeremiah bathed their children and read them a story before tucking them into their own beds for the first time in three weeks.

After the children were settled into bed Aliyah let her husband lead her into the master bedroom where he had replaced the old candles with fresh ones and made up the bed with their finest linen. Aliyah's red negligee lay out for her to slip on along with a new bottle of *Trésor*, his favorite scent on her. After they took a long hot shower together they lay on the king-size bed just holding each other, touching and stroking intermittently.

"Jeremiah, we have got to talk about our marriage. There is so much that I need to talk to you about," Aliyah said, so intoxicated by her husband's touch that she was practically purring.

"I know darling. I want to talk to you, too, but not tonight. Tomorrow I will leave the gallery early and we can go out to dinner, just the two of us and have a nice long talk. Right now I just want to make love to my wife," he said, pulling her into his arms, smothering her with warm kisses.

Chapter 13

"Make sure that the children don't disturb Aliyah this morning," Jeremiah said to Jean the next morning as he sipped a cup of hot Ovaltine in the kitchen. She's still sleeping and I'm sure she's probably a little jet lagged."

"Don't worry, Mr. Jones. I intend to get them up in a few minutes. I'm taking Mandela to his pre-school class later this morning. He's been away for some time now, and I know he's anxious to get back. I'm going to take Nia to the park for awhile in order to give Mrs. Jones plenty of time to herself this morning."

"Thanks." Jeremiah smiled at her. He was so glad to have his family back home. The last three weeks without them had been so lonely. He had been so busy the two weeks before the exhibit that he hadn't had much time to dwell on his loneliness. But, this last week had been the worst. Talking to Aliyah on the telephone every night had helped tremendously and spending evenings with Nia had also helped, but having his wife back in their bed, back in his arms really let him know how lonely he had been. He never wanted to be separated from his family for that long ever again.

Since the Harmon Collection exhibit, business had really picked up at the gallery. Everyday Jeremiah received requests by mail and telephone to look at some budding new artist's work. He decided to have a different exhibit every month featuring new artists as well as some of the works of more renowned artists of color from around the country. The prospect of giving young African-Americans and other people of color an opportunity to display their work at a reputable gallery such as Oblivion was exciting.

Oblivion moved into the limelight with the Harmon collection exhibit. The New York Times as well as all the local papers featured photographs as well as stories about the exhibit. Attending dignitaries had included a US congressman, the mayor of Newark, and four city council members. Jeremiah was delighted with the feedback he was receiving. Things were really looking good for Oblivion. With Aliyah home Jeremiah's life was right back on track. Right where he wanted it to be.

At ten o'clock Jeremiah decided to go by the Maize Restaurant in downtown Newark to reserve the quiet little alcove in the back of the restaurant where he and Aliyah could have their talk. The restaurant was always very busy on nights when there was an event at the nearby Performing Arts Center, but tonight there was no show and it would be quiet and cozy making it the perfect setting for their little rendezvous. Jean agreed to stay with the children a little later than usual to allow them time together.

Jeremiah wondered what had provoked Aliyah to initiate a discussion about their marriage. What was it that she wanted to talk to him about? What was really bothering her? Again his mind went back to the day that Jean told him that Aliyah had come to the gallery to ask him to go for a walk with her. It was the day that she was so agitated when he got home that she wouldn't talk to him. It was also at approximately the same time he was rehearsing with Miss Melody. *I'll tell her about it.* He decided. She might have seen us together and misunderstood. *I've got to make her understand that we were only rehearsing. I'll tell her about the exhibit too. I don't want her mother or Sheniqua telling her about Melody's behavior before I tell her.*

After reserving the alcove at the Maize for dinner that evening, Jeremiah returned to the gallery. He stopped in the nightclub to grab a sandwich for lunch. He found Miss Melody picking up her belongings and her final paycheck and bidding everyone farewell.

"I'm glad you came in," she said to Jeremiah. "My days of singing at the Jazz Garden are over. I'm off to bigger and better things." She laughed.

"I wish you the best, Melody." Jeremiah extended his hand to her.

"A handshake?" Miss Melody looked at him with disdain.

"You've got to be kidding. I want a hug." She threw her arms around him.

"I owe you a lot, Jeremiah. Promise me you'll come to the opening. Bring your lovely wife with you if you have to." She laughed. "I'll make sure that you get front row seats."

"What's your favorite color roses?" Jeremiah asked.

"Pink."

"We'll be there with a dozen pink roses just for you," he said, and then smiled.

"The cast is throwing a big party after the opening night performance, you're invited. Do you think you'll be able to come?" Her eyes were begging him. "With your lovely wife, of course," Miss Melody added and then laughed.

"I'll let you know." Jeremiah said as Miss Melody walked towards the door.

"Well, I'll see you at the opening. Goodbye Jazz Garden. Hope I won't have to sing here to make a living again." She laughed again, and then flounced out the door.

Having promised Miss Melody a dozen roses for her opening Jeremiah wished he had remembered to have a dozen roses for Aliyah on her homecoming. As soon as he got up to his studio he called the florist and ordered a dozen roses for her. "Don't send them," he said to the florist. "I'll pick them up myself on my way home."

After hanging up the telephone Jeremiah called home. It was a little after eleven and Aliyah was just getting up.

"I can't believe I slept so late," she said. "Where are the children?"

"Jean took them out. We figured you were jet lagged and needed the extra sleep. You'll be glad you got the extra rest. I plan to make a night of this evening. After dinner I thought we might go someplace to dance a little. Put on something special, okay."

"Okay," Aliyah said. What's the occasion?"

"You're back where you belong. I'm just glad you're home."

───────────

Humming to herself Aliyah showered and dressed. Every few minutes she would stop and smile to herself. *Jeremiah really missed me.* The thought put an even bigger smile on her face. After their talk she believed everything would work out fine. *I've been such a fool worrying needlessly. Jeremiah will explain everything tonight and we can get back on track.*

While making up her bed, barefooted, she stepped on something hard on the carpeted floor on her side of the bed. *What's this?* She bent down and picked up an earring. *Where did this come from?* She fingered the earring in her palm puzzling over its meaning. The ringing of the doorbell interrupted her thoughts. *Who could that be?* She slipped the earring into her pant's pocket and rushed downstairs to open the door.

"Sheniqua, what brings you here so early in the day? Aliyah asked before standing aside to let her sister-in-law enter the foyer.

"I just came by to return your key. Remember you wanted me to check on the house and water your plants while you were away?"

"Oh that's right," Aliyah said. "Turns out it wasn't necessary for you to do that. Jeremiah didn't go with me to Africa, but you know that by now."

"You've got that right."

"What?" Aliyah asked.

"Nothing. You got something hot to drink?"

"Come in the kitchen, I'll make you some tea."

"How was the trip to Africa? When did you get back?" Sheniqua asked.

"The trip was productive and wonderful. I got back last night. I'm so glad to be home. I really missed my babies." Aliyah felt the teakettle and determined the water was hot enough.

"I thought Mandela was with you."

"He was. I missed my other two babies, Nia and Jeremiah." Aliyah laughed. "Jeremiah must have really missed me, too. He's taking me out dancing tonight." Aliyah twirled around on the kitchen floor, demonstrating her happy mood.

"Hmmm, that's the least he should do," Sheniqua said.

"What do you mean by that?" Aliyah asked, putting two mugs on the kitchen table.

"Well, I don't know if I should say anything, Aliyah. I really don't want to upset you."

"If you have something to say just say it, Sheniqua." Aliyah was becoming impatient.

"Jamal told me to mind my own business, but I told him I would want to know if I was you."

"Know what?" Aliyah asked, really annoyed now. She poured hot water into the mugs.

"Well," Sheniqua said stirring some sugar into her tea. "No one told me not to check on the house so I let myself in without ringing the bell."

"And?" Aliyah asked, removing her teabag and taking a sip of her tea.

"She was here," Sheniqua said.

"She who?"

"Miss Melody. She was coming down the steps, from the bedroom, I suppose."

"What?" Aliyah jumped up from the table knocking over her tea.

"I knew you were going to get upset." Sheniqua grabbed a sponge and started drying up the spill.

"When was this?" Aliyah asked. "Tell me what happened."

"It was about a week after you left. I felt it was time to water the plants. She was coming down the steps with no shoes on and wearing only one earring. I didn't know what to think."

The silence that followed was stifling. Aliyah did not say a word, and Sheniqua, now that she had spoken, was regretful. Aliyah was visibly shaken. "Are you all right? Jamal was right, I shouldn't have said anything." Sheniqua said.

"Is this the earring that she was wearing?" Aliyah pulled the earring out of her pocket and dangled it in front of Sheniqua.

"That's it," Sheniqua said. "She had on one just like that."

"Did you see Jeremiah?" Aliyah asked with tears in her eyes.

"No. She told me that he didn't go to Africa with you. She said he was upstairs, but that he was busy. I just left, Aliyah. I didn't ask any more questions. Should I have told you this? Sheniqua wanted assurance that she had done the right thing.

"Absolutely," Aliyah said. "I can't go through life with both my eyes and ears closed. I've got a lot of thinking to do, Sheniqua. Would you mind leaving now."

"I understand," Sheniqua said. "You would have found out sooner or later anyway. The way that woman acts it's so obvious what's going on. She was ridiculous at the exhibit."

"What do you mean?" Aliyah asked.

"I mean right in front of everyone she said 'I love you Jeremiah.' She just took over at the exhibit. Mom and I went early to help Jeremiah, but then she came in and became the hostess, acting like she was you. Jeremiah didn't seem to mind at all the way he kept grinning at her. It was shameful the way they behaved."

After Sheniqua left Aliyah went into the living room and sank into the nearest chair. *What a fool I have been,* she thought for the second time that day. *Here I was thinking that he missed me so much and all along it's guilt. He's feeling guilty that he had that woman in my house and probably in my bed. Flaunting her in front of my family. How could he do this to me, to us?* She shook her head in disbelief. *I cannot continue to go on like this.*

Jean came in with the children. Mandela was all excited about his first day back to preschool. He wanted to tell Aliyah all about it.

"Mommy we learned "W" today. Come upstairs and let's play with the blocks and I'll show you "W", okay?

"Not now, Mandela. Aliyah cupped his little face with her hands. *What's going to happen to my children? Will I have to bring them up without a husband?* She had so much to think about, so much to plan for.

"Take the children upstairs for their nap," she told Jean. "I need some time alone."

"Okay. When I come down I'll fix dinner for the children. Do you want me to feed them before or after you and Mr. Jones leave to go out?"

"I won't be going out with Mr. Jones tonight, Jean. You can leave after you feed the children their dinner." Aliyah's voice denoted her sadness.

"Are you all right?" Jean asked.

"No," Aliyah answered honestly. "But don't you worry about it."

After Jean took the children upstairs Aliyah thought some more. *What went wrong with this marriage? I did everything I thought I was supposed to do. What made Jeremiah turn to Miss Melody? Maybe marriages are not supposed to last forever. Maybe monogamy is not a male thing. Maybe all men cheat.*

When Jean came downstairs to begin dinner Aliyah asked her, "Jean has your husband ever cheated on you?"

"Not to my knowledge." Jean looked up in alarm. "Why are you asking?"

"I'm just trying to understand men," Aliyah said.

"Well, I personally think it's the values of the society. In some society's faithfulness is a value, and people that are unfaithful to their spouses are condemned. In this society it is accepted, especially for men. I think if our society condemned it, there would be fewer instances of unfaithfulness." Jean started cutting up potatoes to boil.

"What should a woman do if the man she loves, is married to, is unfaithful? Does she forgive him?" Aliyah watched Jean's face.

"I can't answer for other women, but for me that's unforgivable. Marriage vows are sacred to me. My husband and I vowed to 'love, cherish, and honor each other until death do us part.' Until this day I believe my husband has been faithful to me. His illness has taken him to the brink of death, and I have been by his side the whole time. I don't think I would have wanted to be there for him if I did not believe he had been faithful to me as he promised." She washed the potatoes.

"You're right Jean. Marriage vows are sacred. I'm going out for a while. I'll be back shortly."

Before leaving the house Aliyah took a small jar of honey from the cupboard. She went outside, got into her SUV, and drove to Weequahic Park. The two-and a-half mile rubberized track loomed before her. The walk would do her good. She needed to be alone at the same time she needed someone to talk to. She would pour an offering in the lake, and talk to the spirit of Osun.

The first time around the lake Aliyah ran like someone was after her. She cleared her head of all the thoughts that were pressuring her. She ran through the heavily wooded sections, and past people fishing on the banks, she ran up the steep hills and along side the highway. She didn't stop until she saw her SUV parked in the lot facing the field used for baseball and soccer. Then she slowed down her pace and jogged around the lake noticing birds and chipmunks this time around. The third time around, Aliyah approached the lake. She took out her jar of honey and slowly poured it into the lake asking Osun to guide her through this difficult time in her life.

"I asked you for a soul mate," she said to Osun. "You gave me a soul mate. Whatever the reason for him going into the arms of another woman I will have to deal with it. Please give me the strength to get past this. I know that 'this, too, shall pass.'"

When Aliyah got back to the house the children were eating

dinner. Aliyah told Jean she could leave. She didn't want an audience to hear what she had to say to Jeremiah when he got in. She wished there was some way she could prevent the children from hearing what she had to say, but she could not think of anything to do about it. She fed Nia her mashed potatoes and spinach. Nia played with the chicken that Jean had cut into strips. After the children were fed she took them upstairs and washed them up. She put Nia in her playpen and gave Mandela his blocks to play with. "Stay in here, Mandela, and don't come downstairs unless I call you."

When Aliyah got downstairs she made herself a cup of hot chamomile tea, her favorite to relax with. She thought out carefully what she was going to say to Jeremiah and then went into the living room. She dimmed the lights and turned on the stereo. After putting in her favorite Luther Van dross CD she perched herself on the sofa to wait for her husband to come home.

Chapter 14

Jeremiah's day at Oblivion had been very productive. He loved it when he had days like this. He kept a list of things he hoped to accomplish during the course of the day hanging right in front of him as he worked at his desk. Topping the list for today had been to read all of his mail and answer all correspondence that had been on his desk for more than five days. He had invited five young and aspiring African-American artists to come to Newark over the next ten days. He would select the works of one of them to exhibit in the gallery for the coming month. He had written letters to three established artists soliciting a showing of their works as well. Most of the morning, though, he had spent painting.

The one aspect of his work that he enjoyed doing more than anything else was painting. He was working on a painting for his mother-in-law. Her birthday was approaching, and the painting would be a birthday gift to her. Jeremiah stood back and looked at the painting. It was coming along just fine. He knew that Betty was just going to love it. His only concern was finding the time to finish it before her birthday arrived.

With a new opening planned for the beginning of each month there was much to do. Jeremiah knew that if he managed his time wisely everything would work out. He had a very capable staff and his own ambitions for Oblivion motivated him to such a degree that he could not rest until he completed his to do list each and every day. With his family back home he could not be more content. He was looking forward to the time he would get to spend with his wife this evening. Once they got past this "talk" she had suggested they have, he would ask her to tell him all about her trip to Africa and if there was any time left he would tell her about his plans for the gallery. It had been quite some time since they'd had a face-to-face talk about anything.

Although the closing time for Oblivion was five o'clock, Jeremiah generally spent another hour or so at his studio going over the books, checking on upcoming exhibits, or painting a little. But tonight he left before his staff at exactly 4:30. He planned to drop by the florist and pick up the flowers for Aliyah before going home. He wanted to be out of the house no later than 5:00 to give them a good three hours together before they had to get home. He knew that Jean did not like leaving her husband alone in the evening, and he wanted to make sure that she left by eight.

Although Jean's husband was responding well to chemotherapy, Jeremiah knew that she still worried about him.

It was 4:50PM when Jeremiah put his key in the door. The house was quiet but he could hear Luther Van Dross singing, "A House is not A Home" in the background. It was still light outside, but because there were few windows in the brownstone the house looked dark. There was a dim light coming from the living room that shone into the foyer. "Hi. I'm home," Jeremiah called out as he walked into the living room. He was a little taken back when he saw Aliyah sitting in the living room all alone. She was dressed casually in slacks and a white man-tailored shirt that hung outside her pants. Her braided hair was pulled high on her head in a ponytail.

"You're not ready yet?" he asked.

"I'm not going." Aliyah gave him a look that made him shudder.

"What's wrong?" Jeremiah asked alarmed. "Has something happened to the kids?" The look she had given him let him know that something was wrong.

"The kids are fine," she said icily.

"Then what is it, Aliyah? Tell me what's wrong?"

"No, you tell me." She said, demandingly.

"Tell you what?" He stared back at her incredulously.

"Tell me why you brought that bitch into our home?"

"What are you talking about, Aliyah?"

"Why did you bring her into our home, Jeremiah; into our bed?"

"I don't know what you're talking about," Jeremiah said. "I would never do that."

"Liar." Aliyah screamed at him.

"Aliyah, I am not lying. I have never lied to you. I don't know what you're talking about.

"Are you denying that you had Miss Melody in our home while I was in Africa? Are you denying that you had her in our bed?" Aliyah pulled out the earring and dangled it in front of his face. "Does this look familiar to you?" she asked. Her face was twisted with rage and anger. "I found it on the floor in our bedroom on my side of the bed."

"Aliyah, I can explain. Believe me I have never touched Miss Melody."

"Liar. I saw you with my own eyes." Tears were streaming down Aliyah's face now.

"When?" Jeremiah tried to reach out to her, dropping the bouquet of flowers in the process.

"Don't touch me." Aliyah screamed. "I saw you holding her and kissing her in your studio. I know you had her in our home, in our bed. I hate you."

"Please don't say that, Aliyah. I can explain. It was a mistake."

"The only mistake was that I trusted you she screamed. Get out! Get out, Jeremiah."

"I'm not going anywhere, Aliyah. You've got to listen to me."

"I don't want to listen to you. I don't want to see you. Get out of my house!"

"I thought this was our home."

"It was until you violated it. Now get the hell out," she said harshly.

With all the anger, screaming, and tension that was happening neither Jeremiah nor Aliyah saw Mandela creep down the stairs and into the room until he suddenly flung himself at his mother. He was crying hysterically. He had never heard his parents talk so harshly to each other before. He was frightened. "Stop, stop!" he cried. "Mommy, please don't make Daddy leave."

Jeremiah, moved by passion for his son, picked him up and held him tightly. "Don't worry son, Daddy's not going anywhere." He tried to soothe the trembling child.

"Then I will," Aliyah shouted at Jeremiah. "I'm out of here." She ran pass Jeremiah, trampling the flowers, grabbing her purse off the credenza in the foyer, and fled out the door before she could be stopped.

After Aliyah left the house Jeremiah took a sobbing Mandela upstairs only to find a crying Nia in the playpen. Nia, too, had heard the loud talking and had become frightened. She wanted her mommy. Jeremiah felt sorry for Nia. Her mommy had only been home for one night and now she was off again. He picked up his crying daughter in his free arm and tried to comfort both children even though he felt like crying right along with them. *What the hell has happened?* He held his children tightly.

After quieting both children down with a warm bath, Jeremiah put them to bed. He sat in the nursery reading a story to them trying to remain calm. His nerves were shattered. He was worried about Aliyah being alone in the car when she was so distressed. He wondered where she had gone. When the children finally went to sleep he went back downstairs and sat in the living room waiting for his wife to come home. So many thoughts went through his mind. *How could she believe that I had Miss Melody in our bed? Doesn't she know me better than that?*

Flashbacks of the preceding months caused Jeremiah to worry even more. Aliyah had seen the mistaken kiss in his studio. *Why hadn't she mentioned it?* The earring she had dangled in front of his face. *Could that earring belong to Miss Melody?* If so, how did it get in his bedroom? *How could Aliyah know that Miss Melody had been in the house?* He wasn't trying to hide this information from her; it was just that he hadn't had an opportunity to talk to her in a long time. He missed the time they had spent talking to each other and informing each other of the daily happenings of their lives. *Why had this stopped?*

Jeremiah sat on the couch thinking for a long time. Then he got up and went to the stereo. He put on a Miles Davis Compact Disc. The soothing sound of "Around Midnight" flowed into the room. He went back to the couch and lay down. He listened to the music wondering where his wife could be, and what was going to happen next. Before long, Jeremiah drifted off to sleep. It was dark in the house when he woke up. He looked at the clock on the stereo and saw that it was after midnight. *Where could she be?* He asked himself. He got up and went upstairs. He looked in the nursery and saw that the children were sleeping soundly.

Jeremiah went into the music room and sat at the piano. *Such a nice thoughtful gift,* he thought. *H*e ran his fingers over the keyboard. Aliyah was like that, thoughtful. Why would he ever want to cheat on her? What would make her think that he would? He thought she knew him better than that. He had professed his love for her over and over again. *Why is she so insecure?* He looked at the clock, 1AM. Nothing like this had ever happened to them before. What should he do? He called her cell phone; the recorded greeting came on. He left a message, "Aliyah come home, please. I can explain all of this; just listen to me. I need you, darling; the children need you. I love you, Aliyah. Come home, please." Then he lay down on the bed and waited for her to come home.

Aliyah checked the time on her cell phone for the tenth time in less than an hour wondering where her mother could be. It was getting late. Betty rarely stayed out after dark unless she was with her family. Aliyah was beginning to get concerned. The SUV had been parked in the parking lot directly in front of Betty's condominium now for almost three hours. Aliyah had backed the car into the parking space giving her a clear view of the townhouse. She sat in the car and thought back to her encounter with Jeremiah.

After hastily running out of the brownstone she had driven around the city frantically seeking refuge. She'd left her husband and didn't know where to go. She called her mother, but Betty wasn't home. She drove to Livingston Mall and walked around trying to clear her head, all the while praying, asking God to help her with the situation she found herself in. *What should I do?* She had prayed. *Help me through this please, Lord.*

After spending a couple of hours at the mall Aliyah felt more composed. She knew she wasn't going back home, not as long as Jeremiah was there. She did not want another confrontation with him. She could not bear to hear him lie to her again, and she certainly didn't want to upset the children again. She called her mother for the fourth time. Betty was still not home. Aliyah returned to her car and drove the short distance to her mother's house. When she arrived, her mother's car was parked in the usual spot. She stood on the front stoop ringing the doorbell wondering where her mother could be. The house was dark. Aliyah tried to peer through the window for a clue as to her mother's whereabouts. She wished she had thought to take the key to her mother's house before she had left so hastily. Now she would just have to sit in her car and wait for her mother to get home.

During the next three hours Aliyah was consumed with thoughts about the changes her life had undertaken in the last four years. Before she met Jeremiah she had been yearning to get married. She had started making offerings to her guardian *orisa,* Osun, hoping to meet her soul mate, and it had worked. *What went wrong?*

She wished her friends were still around for her to talk to. Over the last four years she had been so busy with her job and family that she hadn't realized how much she missed her friendships. They had been such a comfort to her during her periods of loneliness when she was single. The time she had spent with Claudia in Ghana had reminded her of the closeness they had before she got married. *Gone now, all of them,* she thought. Except for occasional phone calls, a holiday card, birthday card or e-mail she rarely heard from Teyinniwa or Morgan.

Kanmi and Oya are still around, Aliyah remembered. They were so busy, though, she rarely saw them. Months would go by and she wouldn't hear from them. Aliyah still called them occasionally, especially when she needed spiritual guidance. She certainly needed some guidance now.

Oya was a fully initiated Yoruba priestess. She and Kanmi had introduced Aliyah to the Yoruba culture and the religion of Ifa. It was through them that she had learned to make offerings to her guardian *orisa.* She always credited them with helping to bring Jeremiah and her together. How could she tell them, now, that they had broken up?

It was almost eleven o'clock when Aliyah saw her mother strolling up the walkway to the condo. But, her mother was not alone. A man was with her. Aliyah watched them walk up the steps, oblivious to her presence. Her mother was grinning up at the man, who was quite tall. He looked to be about six feet. The porch light, sensitive to movement, came on as they approached the door. Aliyah could see the man's face. It was Dr. Gordon, her mother's gynecologist. *What's she doing with him?* Aliyah stared at them.

Aliyah was shocked when she saw Dr. Gordon embrace her mother and give her a passionate kiss on the lips. She shrunk in her seat, feeling guilty, as though she was spying. When he finally released her, Betty smiled at him. He took her key and opened the door for her. Aliyah could tell by the way her mother was gesturing that she was inviting him into the townhouse. Dr. Gordon refused, though. Aliyah could tell by the way that he was backing down the steps. Betty waved goodbye to him as he walked to his car, passing Aliyah. Betty watched him get into the car and then she disappeared into the house. The lights came on in the condo. Aliyah sat there dumbfounded for a few minutes waiting for Dr. Gordon to drive off.

For whatever reason, Aliyah felt betrayed again. She wanted to drive off and seek refuge somewhere else, but couldn't think of anywhere else to go. How could her mother get involved with Dr. Gordon without even mentioning it to her? She waited in the SUV for another ten minutes before she got out of the car and walked slowly up to her mother's house.

The look on Betty's face when she answered the doorbell and saw Aliyah standing on her stoop was one of complete surprise. When the doorbell rang she had thought maybe Dr. Gordon had changed his mind and come back for the nightcap she had offered him.

"What a surprise this is." Betty gave Aliyah a quick hug. "What are you doing here so late in the evening all by yourself?" she said as an afterthought, after peeking out the door to see if Jeremiah or the kids were behind her.

"I left Jeremiah," Aliyah said, brushing past her mother and entering the spacious, beautifully furnished townhouse.

"What?" Betty's face registered the shock she had felt.

"You heard right, Mother. I've left him," Aliyah said, bursting into tears.

"Come in and tell me all about it." Betty gathered her crying daughter into her arms.

They went into the living room and sat down on the plush beige sofa. Betty listened as Aliyah spilled out the months of anguish she had been experiencing, every since her birthday party, wondering if her husband was interested in another woman. She told her mother about seeing Jeremiah with Miss Melody in his arms at his studio. She told her about the late evenings when he came home reeking of cigarette smoke. She told her about seeing him in the club touching Miss Melody's face and lifting her onto the piano.

Finally, she told her mother about the earring in her bedroom and, Sheniqua discovering Miss Melody coming down the stairs of her home.

By the time Aliyah finished telling her story she was crying hysterically. Betty rubbed her shoulders trying to soothe her. Betty said nothing for a long time. She let Aliyah get all the tears out first. While she held her sobbing daughter she thought about the exhibit opening a little less than two weeks ago when Miss Melody had exclaimed, "I love you Jeremiah" for everyone within earshot to hear. Betty wondered if there could be some truth to what Aliyah was feeling; knowing that she, too, had become somewhat suspicious after seeing Jeremiah smile each time he had passed Miss Melody that evening.

Leaving Aliyah sobbing softly on the sofa Betty went into the kitchen and brewed two cups of strong chamomile tea. When she came back Aliyah was stretched out on the sofa staring at the ceiling. Betty placed the tea on the coffee table, took her cup and sat in the adjacent chair. She took a sip or two from the cup and then said, "What does Jeremiah have to say about all of this?"

"He tried to deny it at first," Aliyah said. "But, when I showed him the earring he tried to tell me that it was all a mistake."

"A mistake?" Betty asked. "What kind of mistake?"

"I didn't wait around to hear anymore. I grabbed my purse and left. I couldn't take any more. Besides Mandela was there. He was so upset, Mom. My baby was crying and begging me not to make his daddy leave." Fresh tears began to stream down Aliyah's face.

"I don't know what to say, Aliyah. I never would have thought that Jeremiah was capable of such a thing. He's always been so honest and caring. I love that man. He has been a wonderful son-in-law, and from what I could see a wonderful father and husband." She shook her head in total disbelief. "There must be some explanation for his behavior."

"I don't know what it could be," Aliyah said. "I do know that I can't live with a man that cheats on me and brings another woman into my bed. I don't want to ever see him again," she cried harder.

"Give it some time, Aliyah. I'm going to take this problem to the altar at church on Sunday. I still don't believe that Jeremiah is capable of such behavior."

"I don't want to believe it either, Mom. But lately everybody seems to be shocking me with their behavior. Even my own mother."

"What do you mean, dear?" Betty looked up from her tea.

"I saw you and Dr. Gordon tonight. How long has this been going on?"

"Nothing is going on, as you put it. We're just friends."

"He didn't kiss you like a friend." Aliyah looked at her mother.

"Were you spying on me?" Betty asked.

"Mom, I was parked in front of your house for three hours. I couldn't help but see you. It didn't appear that you were trying to be discreet. I'm sure some of your neighbors saw you too."

"I don't care," Betty said. "I'm over sixty years old and I've been a widow for almost three years. He's over sixty-five and he has been a widower for over five years. What we do together is no one else's business."

"You're right, of course," Aliyah said, sincerely. "I just thought you would have told me. I feel like everybody is keeping things from me, lately."

"There was nothing to tell. I've had a few dates with him and I like him. I have always considered him a friend as well as my doctor. I planned to tell you about us when you got back from Africa, but I haven't had a chance. It's just as well that you found out about our friendship."

"He didn't kiss you like he was just a friend." Aliyah said for the second time.

"No he didn't," Betty said, and then smiled. "Maybe he likes me, too. I certainly hope so."

Seeing the happiness on her mother's face caused a new wave of tears to flood Aliyah's eyes.

"Don't cry darling," Betty embraced her daughter. "Everything is going to be all right."

"I just feel that I am losing everyone I love to other people." Aliyah sobbed and sobbed.

Chapter 15

At 7AM Jeremiah woke up alone in the king-size bed. For a moment he had forgotten about the occurrences of the previous evening. He lay in the bed listening for the sounds of his family. All he heard was the sound of raindrops hitting the windowpanes. Then it dawned on him; Aliyah had not come home. For the first time since their wedding, four years ago, he felt abandoned. He remembered this feeling of abandonment from his first marriage. His former wife, Kathy, had left him pretty much the same way that Aliyah had. They had never gotten back together again.

How could this be happening again? Jeremiah lay in bed thinking. Kathy had left him when he was Newark policeman. She had left a note saying she couldn't be a policeman's wife anymore. It was just too stressful for her worrying each morning if she would be a widow at the end of the day. She wanted children, but was fearful that she would have to raise them alone if something happened to him. He had been injured severely, and had promised her, under duress, that he would quit the police force when he recovered. When he didn't keep that promise she had left. He came home one evening and she was gone, leaving him feeling completely abandoned.

But things were different with him and Aliyah. They didn't meet until after that part of his life was over. He remembered Aliyah saying when they first started dating that she was glad that he was no longer a policeman. He was glad, too. He didn't think that anything could come between them. It was fate that brought them together. Aliyah had been making offerings of honey to her guardian *orisa,* Osun. And he had been making offerings to his guardian *orisa,* Shango. Osun and Shango had brought them together. *Why tear us apart now?*

In the shower Jeremiah lathered his tall, lean, brown body with his favorite hand made soap. He had purchased it from a friend who made special blends of soap in his kitchen and sold it at open market places. It had Egyptian musk oil in it, giving it a nice exotic smell. Aliyah loved that smell. It was one of the things that first attracted him to her. Jeremiah remembered how she had blushed when he first told her that Egyptian musk oil was his favorite oil to bathe in.

Sitting on the side of the bed putting on his socks, Jeremiah wondered if he needed to make an appointment with his *babalowa.*

He always consulted his *babalowa* when he had a difficult choice
to make. But this situation was not about making a choice. He
knew what he had to do. He had to talk to his wife and convince
her that he loved only her and that there was no one else. *How
could she possibly think there could have been?* No he didn't need
a *babalowa,* not yet anyway. He would make an offering to Shango
and ask for assistance getting Aliyah back. But first and above all
he was going to pray to God.

It was 7:30 when Jeremiah went downstairs. Jean was in
the kitchen making herself a cup of coffee. The teakettle was
whistling. Jeremiah went to the stove to fix himself a cup of hot
Ovaltine.

"Good morning," he said to Jean solemnly.

"Good morning, Mr. Jones." She cheerfully greeted him. Is
Mrs. Jones up and about?" she asked. Aliyah was generally the first
one downstairs in the morning.

"No Jean. She's not here. She left last night."

"Oh," Jean said, raising her eyebrows. "I know she was upset.
Is she all right?"

"I don't know," Jeremiah said. "Did she say anything to you?"

"Not really," Jean said apprehensively.

"If there is anything that you can tell me to help me figure this
out I would really appreciate it, Jean." Jeremiah looked pleadingly
at her.

"Well, I don't know if I should say anything, but Aliyah did ask me if my husband ever cheated on me."

"When was this?" Jeremiah asked.

"It was after I came back with the children yesterday. She seemed fine when I left, but when I returned she had changed her mind about going out to dinner with you, and that's when she asked me about the cheating."

"Umm," Jeremiah said. "What could have happened during the time you left here and the time you returned?" he asked, almost to himself.

"Well, I don't know if it has anything to do with it, but as I was driving the kids home I noticed Miss Sheniqua's car pulling away just as I approached the intersection."

"Umm," Jeremiah said again. *Could Sheniqua have something to do with this?* "Thanks, Jean. I'll call you later." He got up to leave. He thought about asking Jean to call him if Aliyah came home, but he didn't want her to feel mixed loyalties. Besides, he didn't want to involve her in his domestic problems.

At his studio Jeremiah worked on the birthday present for his mother-in-law. Painting always helped to clear his mind. He became so engrossed in his work that the pressures of life escaped him. He needed the relief. He was so worried about his wife and their marriage, yet there was nothing he could do unless she talked to him. He had left at least a dozen messages on her cell phone requesting that she call him, and she had not called yet. *Could something have happened to her?* By noon he decided to call home.

No one answered the telephone at the house. *Jean probably took the children out.* Jeremiah listened as the telephone rang and rang. *Maybe Jean took Mandela and Nia to the park.* He hung up the telephone before the answering machine picked up. Then he called his mother-in-law. Betty picked up on the second ring.

"Hello," she said very cordially.

"Hi," Jeremiah said. "I'm trying to reach Aliyah, Betty. Do you have any idea where she might be?"

"Not at the moment, Jeremiah. She spent the night here, but she left early this morning."

"Did she say where she was going? I'm at the studio and I've called the house. No one answers the phone." He sounded exasperated.

"She said she was going by the house to see the children and she planned to go into Manhattan to her office later this morning." Betty sounded weary.

"I guess she told you that we are having some problems," Jeremiah said.

"Yes she did," Betty said without revealing a word that Aliyah had told her.

"I need to talk to her, Betty." Jeremiah was in anguish.

"She's quite upset," Betty said.

"I know. Betty I love Aliyah. I would never do anything to hurt her. Please try to get her to talk to me. I can make this all right. I just need for her to listen to me."

"I certainly hope so." Betty sighed. "I'll do what I can to get her to talk to you, Jeremiah." She hung up the telephone.

Jeremiah sat back in his chair and looked heavenward. "Please God let Aliyah call me." He prayed.

At five o'clock Jeremiah began to close down shop for the day. He cleaned his brushes and put them away. He hung the painting on an easel and then went into the small lavatory and washed his face and hands. Then he put on his jacket and left the studio. He wanted to get home early. If Aliyah didn't come home he wanted to relieve Jean of the children to allow her to get home to her husband.

As he approached the house Jeremiah's eyes began to search the street for Aliyah's car. He didn't see it, but he didn't see Jean's car either. He parked in front of the house and walked up the steps slowly. As soon as he put his key in the front door an uneasy feeling spread over his entire body. He sensed that something was wrong, but he couldn't put his finger on it. He walked into the foyer and listened. Silence. He walked into the kitchen; no one was there. The lights were out although rays of light from a descending sun were streaming through the kitchen window.

The house was empty of his family. He knew they were gone. He had this same feeling of their absence for the entire time Aliyah and Mandela were in Africa. He was so happy when they returned home just two nights ago and now emptiness again. He went upstairs and looked in the master bedroom. The still packed suitcase Aliyah had left on the bedroom floor last night was gone. The bureau drawers that usually held her clean lingerie were open. When he looked he saw that they were empty. He looked in the bathroom. Her toothbrush was gone. It had been there this morning right next to his.

Jeremiah opened the door to the nursery. Nia's favorite stuffed toy, a soft cuddly bunny, that was there last night was gone. Her favorite blanket that she couldn't sleep without was gone. Mandela's pajamas that hung on a clothes rack tacked to the back of the nursery door were gone. Jeremiah hung his head and slowly walked out of the nursery. *What had he done to deserve this?* He walked to the far end of the second floor and went into the music room. He sat down at his piano and started playing "Broken Hearted Melody." He played and played sad love songs well into the night.

As the New Jersey Transit train sped toward Manhattan's Penn Station Aliyah stared out of the window. Just a few months earlier she was riding this same train when she had wondered if her marriage were crumbling, now it had crumbled. She had made the decision to leave Jeremiah. She could not live with a man that cheated on her. Her mother had tried to convince her to give it more time. "Talk to Jeremiah," she had said. But Aliyah had made up her mind. There was nothing to talk about. How could he explain bringing another woman into their home and into their bed? No. There was no way he could explain that.

The morning after she had ran out of their home, Aliyah returned to the house. She had waited until she was sure that Jeremiah had left for his studio. She wanted to get her kids, grab some of their things and get out as quickly as possible. She told Jean that she was moving out with the children. She let Jean know that she needed her more than ever now. She wanted Jean to stay with the children at her mother's house while she went to work in Manhattan each day. She decided she would not return to the house until Jeremiah moved out.

"This is only a temporary arrangement," Aliyah had told Jean. "But I do need your help with this. Will you help me?" she had asked.

"I'll do whatever you want me to," Jean said to her. "But are you sure you're doing the right thing? Mr. Jones doesn't appear to be the type of man that would do anything to hurt his family. He looked so sad this morning before he left for work."

"No, I'm not sure that I'm doing the right thing. But this is the only thing I can do right now." *I can never sleep in that bed with him again after he made love to another woman in it.* That thought had brought tears to Aliyah's eyes.

After Jean agreed to the arrangement, Aliyah rushed frantically through the house grabbing what she felt she needed from her office, the master bedroom, and the nursery. Then she had piled everything into the SUV and drove to her mother's house. Jean followed in her car with the children. After getting everybody settled into her mother's house, Aliyah took off again in the SUV and drove to the train station in South Orange where she searched for a place to park her car. She needed to get to Manhattan. Despite all of her personal problems she had a deadline to meet for *Enigma*.

Aliyah barely spoke to anyone at the office that day. She hadn't seen her staff for close to a month, but she was just not in the mood to talk about the trip to Africa. She barricaded herself in her office and worked for eight straight hours without taking a break. Work was the medicine she always used for loneliness and depression. She hadn't had to use it for a long time. Now, once again, it was proving useful.

When Aliyah returned to her mother's condo at seven that evening Jean had gone home. Betty had fed the children and they were playing in the living room. Her mother gave her a concerned look, but Aliyah went directly to the bathroom and ran a tub of warm water for the kids. By the time she finished bathing them and reading a story to them she was exhausted. She ate the light meal that either Jean or her mother had prepared for her before she showered and went to bed herself. She never checked the messages on her cell phone.

The next morning Aliyah took the train into Manhattan again. She looked up as the train approached the New York station. She grabbed her leather briefcase and headed for the exit. Walking to her office she looked up at the sky. In Africa the sky had been so exquisite, unobstructed by tall buildings, bluer than she had ever seen it. It had been so peaceful and beautiful. Aliyah thought back to the day that she and Claudia had taken the children to Aburi Gardens in Ghana.

At Aburi Gardens Aliyah got a chance to see God's tree; the tree that Jeremiah had told her so much about before they got married; the tree that was larger than any other tree in Ghana. It's branches extended into the clouds. Jeremiah had painted a picture of her lying under that tree. She had dreamed about dancing with him under the tree. She had hoped that he would be with her when she first laid eyes on the tree. *Well it will never happen now,* she thought making her way up to 47th Street.

Aliyah left instructions with her secretary to put all calls through to her except calls from Mr. Jones. Her secretary gave her a strange look, but Aliyah ignored it. She went into her office, but she did not lock the door. It was time for her to rejoin the world. She could not remain barricaded from the world forever. The first call that came through was from Dotty.

"Hi girlfriend. I heard you were back. I tried to see you yesterday but you were unavailable. Is everything all right?"

"Hi Dotty, everything is fine," Aliyah said.

"How about lunch today? I'm dying to hear about Africa."

"Okay. How about the Rooftop Café?"

"Good. Is noon okay?"

"See you at noon," Aliyah said and hung up the telephone.

She heard her cell phone ringing, looked at it and shut it off. It was Jeremiah. There were a dozen or more messages on her voice mail from him. She erased all of them without listening. *What could he possibly have to say to me? That he loves me? Yeah, right!* Aliyah put the phone in her purse and the purse in her desk drawer.

She spent the morning responding to her e-mails, and giving instructions to her secretary regarding the large batch of mail that had accumulated in her absence. She made an appointment to meet with the publishers, two very charming African-American women who were the founders of *Enigma Magazine.* When she looked at her clock it was 11:50AM. Aliyah hurried to meet Dotty for lunch.

Telling Dotty about the trip to West Africa relaxed Aliyah and helped her to relive some of the excitement of the trip. She found herself laughing out loud when she told Dotty about the antics of the some of the children she had visited in day care centers. The children did everything imaginable to get her attention in order to get rewarded with a piece of the candy that she kept in her purse.

"It was a wonderful trip," she said, and smiled for the first time in two days.

"I'm glad you had a good time," Dotty said. "Now tell me

Aliyah how do you cook collared greens?"

"What?" Aliyah asked astonished. "Why are you asking me that?"

"Derek loves them and I want to know how to fix them."

At the mention of Derek's name Aliyah remembered that Dotty was dating an African-American man, a married one at that. Her mood changed to reflect her feelings.

"Why do you have to cook them for him?" Aliyah asked. "There are plenty of good soul food restaurants in Manhattan."

"Derek could eat them everyday, and we can't eat out everyday." Dotty smiled slyly.

"Since when did you start eating with Derek everyday? I thought you had a designated day of the week to see him," Aliyah said sarcastically.

"That was before his wife threw him out." Dotty smiled. "Now I get to see him everyday and cook for him in my own kitchen."

"Are you saying that he has moved in with you?" Aliyah was incredulous.

"Of course he moved in with me," Dotty said. "Where else was he supposed to go?"

Aliyah said nothing; she just stared at Dotty with her mouth open. She couldn't believe that Dotty had caused someone's marriage to break up. Seeing the look on Aliyah's face, Dotty stopped smiling. She looked at Aliyah then reached over and took her hand.

"I have never been happier in my whole life," she said. "Be happy for me Aliyah. Don't you think I deserve some happiness, too?"

Aliyah said nothing. She started eating her soup and kept her head down. She didn't want Dotty to see the tears that were forming in her eyes. Finally she looked up.

"Jeremiah and I just broke up, Dotty. I found out he's been cheating on me." A tear ran down her face and into her soup bowl.

Dotty reached over and took Aliyah's hand, again. "I'm sorry about you and Jeremiah, Aliyah. I really am. But this is not about you and Jeremiah. This is about Derek and me. His wife drove him away. I know you didn't do that with Jeremiah. You were a wonderful wife to him. I don't know why he cheated, but it certainly wasn't your fault. Be happy for me Aliyah." Dotty pleaded with her.

"I'll try, Dotty," Aliyah said, wondering if Jeremiah would move in with Miss Melody now that he was free to do so. The thought made her shudder.

Chapter 16

It was almost a week since Jeremiah had come home to find that his family had moved out. He hadn't talked to anyone about it. He was too depressed. He still got up in the morning and went to the gallery every day. Work was the only relief he got from the pain he was feeling. He missed his family. He'd been working since nine that morning. When he stood up he felt a little dazed. It was almost 8PM. He thought about going downstairs to the Jazz Garden and ordering something to eat. He hadn't been eating well at all.

Last night he got home late, much later than usual and walked through the house picking up and fondling things that reminded him of better times. Aliyah had left her red nightgown in the drawer. He slept with it, holding it close to him, smelling the lavender and lemongrass scent that she kept in the bureau drawers to keep things fresh. He went to bed hungry because he couldn't bring himself to go into the kitchen to fix some food.

Jeremiah awakened hungry, too. The bed looked huge without Aliyah. Nothing was the same. He dreaded going downstairs. He knew that Jean would not be in the kitchen, and the kettle would not be hot. He couldn't wait to get out of the house it was too empty. He arrived at work hungry and worked throughout the day never leaving the studio. Cook sent him a sandwich from the kitchen downstairs at lunchtime. Jeremiah gobbled it up and washed it down with a half gallon of water. Now it was quitting time and he didn't want to go home to an empty house.

It was 8PM when Jeremiah made his way to the bar at the Jazz Garden. He didn't sit at a table, thinking he would look too conspicuous. He didn't really want to be there, but he didn't want to go home either. For the first time in a very long time he was lonely. He remembered that it had taken him a long time to get used to that feeling after Kathy had left him. He didn't like it, but he got used to it. Then Aliyah came along and he believed he would never be lonely again. *Well what the hell happened?*

His buddies, Charlie and Malik, came in and spotted him. They joined him at the bar. "What are you drinking?" Charlie asked.

"I don't know," Jeremiah said. He wasn't really a drinking man. "Maybe I'll have a beer.

"Make that three beers," Charlie said to the bartender.

"Bring me something to eat, too," Jeremiah said to the bartender.

"What do you want to eat?" the bartender asked, putting a chilled glass of beer in front of Jeremiah.

"I don't know, vegetables, rice, fish," Jeremiah said.

"What are you doing eating all by yourself at the bar?" Charlie asked. "I thought Aliyah was back from Africa. Did she kick you out?" he said, jokingly.

Jeremiah said nothing. He stared into his beer. Charlie looked at him and shook his head, understanding Jeremiah's silence.

"Women," Malik said, picking up on what was happening. "Can't live with them and can't live without them." He took a long swig from his glass of beer.

Jeremiah continued to stare into his beer. *It wasn't like that with Aliyah and me,* he thought. But he said nothing. He didn't want to discuss his marriage with anyone right now. He had to figure things out for himself. He sat silently eating his dinner, never looking up. When he finished eating he ordered another round of beers. He sipped his slowly, in silence, and then he got up and walked out of the bar.

It was ten o'clock when Jeremiah put his key into his front door. He entered the house without turning on any lights. He walked up the stairs in the dark. Only a tiny glow from the nightlight in the kitchen lit the way for him. He went directly to his music room and sat at the piano bench. A little moonlight shone through the window. He felt the piano keys and softly played the melody, "Willow Weep for Me." Jeremiah played one sad love song after another before he finally went into the master bedroom, lay down on the king size bed, and drifted off to sleep.

Day after day, this became his routine. Work is what sustained him. Although his marriage was at an all time low, Jeremiah's business was at an all time high. The Harmon Foundation exhibit was having such a rippling affect. Interest in Oblivion had increased to such a level that he found himself busier than ever. Young men and women of color were calling him everyday asking for a chance to exhibit their work at Oblivion. Jeremiah found himself interviewing a different artist everyday. Two weeks after Aliyah left he was interviewing a young man from Texas.

"Why are you so interested in an exhibit at Oblivion?" Jeremiah asked the young man.

"I've been trying to get an exhibit at a New York City Gallery for three years now. Newark is only a jump away from New York City. I know if I can show my work here New York will be next."

"Your work is impressive," Jeremiah said. "But I can't guarantee that having a showing at Oblivion will get you into the Guggenheim or the Shomberg." He laughed softly.

"I know that." The young man smiled. "But I feel it will help get my foot in the door. That's all most new artist's ask for, a chance. People don't realize how much time and effort we put into our paintings. Many people are amazed that we ask so much for our work. We rarely get what they are worth, and even with what we get we barely eke out a decent living," he said.

"I know," Jeremiah said. "Painting is what I have always wanted to do, but I never could make a living doing it. I've had several jobs that had to sustain me while I painted. But now painting is what I spend most of my time doing. It took a long time though. I know a lot of artists that are members of SAG. They are all waiting for that one break."

"What's SAG?"

"Starving Artist's Group." Jeremiah laughed at the expression on the young man's face. "African-Americans and other people of color can have a chapter all by themselves. That's mainly because so few of our people are accustomed to buying artwork, that costs thousands of dollars, to hang in their homes. They don't consider the paintings of African-American artists to be an investment."

"Why do you think that is?" The young man appeared curious.

"African-Americans only recently took an interest in hanging the works of black artists in their homes. The Cosby TV Show helped to promote this practice by featuring famous paintings hanging on the walls of their home. Still most of our people can only afford to buy cheap prints; rarely do they invest in original paintings that will increase in value. It's a new concept for our people, but it's a growing concept," Jeremiah said confidently.

Jeremiah felt good that he had been able to give the young man some real hope, and boost his confidence. As he watched the young man leave he was surprised to see Miss Melody entering the gallery.

"What are you doing here?" he asked. "Aren't you supposed to be rehearsing now?"

"Rehearsals are just about over. I wanted to remind you that
I am getting front row tickets for you for the opening. I heard
through the grapevine that you would only need one ticket now. Is
that right?"

"Word sure gets around," Jeremiah said solemnly.

"I'm sorry," Miss Melody said, but her look let Jeremiah know
that she wasn't really sorry. "Is there anything I can do to help?"

"No!" Jeremiah said quickly.

"Will you come to the opening." She had that pleading look on
her face again.

"When is it?"

"On the fifteen of next month, that's a Wednesday night.
Jeremiah you've got to come. I am doing everything that you
taught me and the rest of the cast says that I am doing a great job.
I want you to come and see what a great job you did coaching me.
Can I count on you?"

"I'll be there," Jeremiah said. "Now if you don't mind I have to
get back to work."

"I'm going." She smiled, then turned to leave.

"By the way, Melody," Jeremiah said. "Just how did your
earring get into my bedroom?"

"You found it?" Miss Melody turned around beaming. "I knew I
had it on when I came to your house."

"I didn't find it, Aliyah did." Jeremiah gave her an angry scowl.

"Oh, oh! Don't tell me that's why Aliyah left you?" Melody looked surprised.

"How did it get in my bedroom, Melody?" Jeremiah asked again, ignoring her question.

"I told you I was being nosy and that I wanted to take a peek at your house. I loved the coverlet on your bed and wanted to look at the tag to see who designed it. It must have fallen off when I leaned over the bed. Your maid noticed that it was missing when I went downstairs. I was going to look for it when I came back upstairs but you discovered me trying to go back into the bedroom and I forgot about it."

"What maid?" Jeremiah asked surprised.

"She was downstairs when I got there. She was getting ready to water your plants. She seemed surprised when I told her you hadn't gone to Africa with Aliyah. I told her you were upstairs. She said no one told her that you would be there, and then she left."

"Umm," Jeremiah said. "We don't have a maid. What did she look like?"

"She was young, late twenties or early thirties; dark and very pretty. She looked like she may have been pregnant."

Sheniqua, Jeremiah said to himself. *So that's how Aliyah knew Melody was in the house.*

"I hope Aliyah didn't leave you because of that. She's a fool if she lets you go. I know a lot of women that would just love to have you put your shoes under their bed every night." She gave him a seductive look that let him know that she was one of those women.

"I'll see you at the opening, Melody." Jeremiah said, turning to go back up to his studio.

When Jeremiah got home that night he'd made up his mind that he was going to see Aliyah and talk to her "by any means necessary." *This has gone on long enough,* he thought. *Aliyah has got to come to her senses.* He had done nothing wrong. As soon as he got settled and ate the take-out-dinner that Cook had prepared for him he picked up the telephone to call Aliyah for the hundredth time since her departure. She didn't answer her cell phone again. He left a message. He called his mother-in-law's number. Again she told him that Aliyah would not come to the phone.

"Tell Aliyah that unless she comes to the telephone I will come up there and make a disturbance until she sees me. She cannot keep my children away from me like this." He appealed to Betty.

"Let me talk to her before you come, Jeremiah," Betty said. "I don't want a scene in front of the children again. I will try to get Aliyah to call you. If she doesn't, I will call you back in a half hour, okay?"

"Okay," Jeremiah said before hanging up the telephone. He went into the living room, put on a George Benson CD and lay on the sofa waiting, hoping that Aliyah would call him. Exactly one-half-hour later the telephone rang. Jeremiah picked it up on the first ring hoping it was Aliyah.

"I'm sorry, Jeremiah," Betty said. "I couldn't get her to talk to you, but she came up with a plan for you to see the children."

"Oh!" Jeremiah said sadly. "Betty what does she want me to do? I miss her and the kids. I love her. What does she want me to do?" he asked again.

"She's hurting, Jeremiah," Betty said. "She doesn't know what she wants right now. She's feeling so betrayed."

"If she'd give me a chance I know I can explain everything to her satisfaction. I know I can make her understand what happened."

"Can you, Jeremiah?"

"Believe me, Betty, it was just a silly misunderstanding. I can make things all right," he said desperately.

"I'll talk to her some more, Jeremiah. I'll try to convince her to talk to you. In the meantime she has agreed to let Jean keep the children at the house during the day where you can visit them as you wish. Jean will bring the children back here in the evenings."

"Will they be here tomorrow?" he asked.

"Yes, they'll be there in the morning."

Jeremiah went upstairs to bed thinking that at least he would get to see his children. But hell, he missed his wife.

The drive from South Orange NJ to Manhattan could be rough in the mornings. Aliyah discovered that it took her almost a half-hour longer to drive from South Orange to Manhattan than it took her to drive from Newark to Manhattan. The only reason she drove was because she rarely found a parking space at the South Orange train station. She missed being able to walk to the train station. The whole commute by car was at least an hour when the traffic was good. She hated the traffic jams but she hated the time she had to spend in the car alone even worse. She had too much time to think. By the time she arrived at her Manhattan office she was often confused and upset. This morning had been one of the worst.

The night before had been upsetting enough. Jeremiah called demanding to see the children. Her mother convinced her that he had every right to see his children. She knew her mother was right. Mandela had been asking every night where was his daddy. Last night when she gave him his bath, he'd asked, "Does Daddy still love us, Mommy?"

"Of course Daddy loves us," Aliyah had said, surprised at the cognition of a four-year-old.

"Then why doesn't he want to see us anymore?" Mandela had asked.

"Oh, he wants to see us, baby," she'd said.

"Then why doesn't he come to see us?" He looked so hurt and sad.

"You miss your daddy?" Aliyah had asked.

"Yes." Mandela had said. "I love my daddy."

After Aliyah had put the kids to bed her mother had a talk with her. "Aliyah you can't keep Jeremiah away from his kids," she had said. He's a wonderful father to those kids and he has as much right to them as you do."

"I know, Mom, but what am I supposed to do? I'm just so confused now." She looked to her mother for guidance and understanding.

"All I know is that those kids need their father as much as they need you. You need to talk to Jeremiah and see if you can resolve this situation. Jeremiah says that he can explain this to you, he says that he can make it all right."

"What can he possibly say?" Aliyah had asked her mother. "He had another woman in our home, in our bed. How can he possibly explain that?"

"I don't know," Betty had said exasperated. "But you should give him a chance. Just think about it sweetheart."

Speed was picking up a little after Aliyah got through the mid-town tunnel. It was nine-thirty when she eased her car into the parking lot that was a block away from her office building. *Jeremiah is probably with the children right now.* She had decided the night before to let Jean keep the children at their house during the day to give Jeremiah an opportunity to visit them at his leisure. Besides the children would be home, in familiar surroundings, with all of their things. Jean would pick them up in the morning and deliver them back to her mother's townhouse in South Orange in the evenings. Aliyah knew it wasn't the best solution, but it was the best she could come up with for now.

At nine forty five Aliyah was in the conference room. She'd called for a ten o'clock meeting with all of the particulars necessary to pull the next edition of *Enigma* together before it went to press. Dotty was there as well as the two senior editors, and the two junior editors. Staff and feature writers were there as well. The layout was on display in all of its different formats. The Ghanaian photographer had done a wonderful job of taking pictures, reassuring Aliyah that she had made a good choice going with a Ghanaian rather than taking one of *Enigma's* photographers along with her.

"It looks like we have successfully pulled together another edition of *Enigma,*" Aliyah said smiling.

"This looks really great." Dotty gave Aliyah a look of triumph. "Your article on 'Motherhood' is wonderful," she said. "It was a marvelous idea devoting one article each month to an issue relating to women of African decent all over the Diaspora."

"For next month's edition we have the article about African women's hairstyles in Zimbabwe," Aliyah said referring to a work in progress by one of the senior editors.

"And then we'll run the article that I'm going to do about West African fashions, right?" Dotty asked smiling. "I'm really looking forward to going to Africa to research that article. Derek may go with me." She was smiling from ear to ear. Dotty had been a fashion writer for a Canadian magazine before coming to *Enigma.*

"That's right," Aliyah said. "Make sure you get great pictures. The pictures accompanying my article are really excellent. That Ghanaian photographer was really good. I'm very happy with the complete issue."

"Speaking of pictures," Dotty said, "What do you think of these?" She reached into her purse and passed Aliyah some pictures of Derek and her taken around Manhattan."

After looking at the photographs for a few minutes Aliyah smiled at Dotty and said, "They're nice Dotty." She handed the photographs back to her. Surprisingly, Dotty passed them to another staff member. As the photos were passing around the room Aliyah watched Dotty move from person to person, explaining each picture, and grinning the whole time.

After the meeting, when everyone had returned to their respective offices except the two of them, Dotty explored Aliyah's feelings some more. "So what did you think of the photos?"

"They were nice. I already said that." Aliyah looked Dotty in the eye. "But he's still a married man, Dotty, remember that.

"When a man starts to take his mistress out in public that's a sure indication that his marriage is over. Derek has no qualms about people seeing the two of us in public together. He was the one with the camera. I know he's ready for a divorce, Aliyah." She looked so happy, smiling broadly.

Aliyah said nothing as she went about the task of pulling together the different layouts. She moved about the room, methodically, gathering pictures and other material that she wanted to keep together. Dotty followed her around the room with her eyes.

"So, you still find this relationship troublesome, Aliyah?" she asked after a few minutes had gone by.

"Yes I do, Dotty."

"What is it that you find so troubling, Aliyah? Is it the fact that he is married or the fact that he is black and I'm white? Which is it?"

Aliyah hesitated before speaking. "If you must know, it's both." She knew what difficulty she could encounter bringing up a racial issue, but she plunged on. "Everyone knows how difficult it is for black women to find decent black men; men that are educated and working. So many black men get lost in the prison system, in the military, and in the streets. Some of the best black men, few as there are, are being lured away by white women. Yes, that bothers me, Dotty."

"That's not my fault, Aliyah," Dotty said. "I'm just looking for a decent man, too. I want to find happiness. If I find that with a black man why should I feel guilty? It's not my fault that black men are looking beyond their race for soul mates. Maybe black women should do more introspection, maybe they are doing or not doing something to push their men away." She gave Aliyah a look that asked for understanding.

"What about the fact that Derek is married. Married means

committed, taken, hands off," Aliyah said emphatically. "He has children for God's sake, Dotty."

"He came on to me." Dotty became defensive.

"That's no excuse. A married man is just that, married, off limits." Aliyah stared at her. The silence was making her uncomfortable.

"You're right," Dotty said finally. "I'll have to live with that. Please don't judge me, Aliyah. Our friendship is really important to me."

"I'm still your friend, Dotty. I just don't approve of what you're doing. I won't speak of it again, though. I don't want this to come between us."

The drive back to South Orange gave Aliyah plenty of time for introspection. Could she have done something to drive Jeremiah into Miss Melody's arms? Aliyah checked herself out in the rear view mirror. Her pretty bronze face looked back at her. She still looked good. She had gained a few extra pounds after Nia was born, but she had worked off the extra weight. She now maintained a body mass index of 22.5. Maybe it was something else.

She had been spending a lot of time working lately, staying in her home office until late in the evening. After her first suspicions of Jeremiah and Miss Melody she had changed their nightly routine. *Was she trying to punish him?* she wondered. Maybe she had been wrong. Even her mother had said that there was no real evidence that anything was going on at that time. Maybe she had pushed Jeremiah into Miss Melody's arms.

What about the times Jeremiah came in late after she had gone to bed. Wasn't she guilty of being unavailable? Was she the reason he went out late and came in late? She thought about those nights she stayed up in her office working. The nights she had left him downstairs by himself. *Could it have been my fault? Yes*, was her resounding answer. She had to take some of the blame for the failure of her marriage.

Returning to her mother's condominium Aliyah let out a long sigh before she entered. Her mother had asked her to think about what she was doing to her family by denying Jeremiah access to his children and his wife. Well she had thought about it and decided to make his children accessible to him, but access to his wife that was another story. She was still in pain from his betrayal. She was not ready to forgive him for that. She didn't know if she would ever be able to forgive him for that.

While Aliyah bathed Mandela he couldn't stop chattering about spending the day with his daddy. He was so delighted that he could barely contain himself.

"My daddy said I should eat all of my vegetables so I can grow up to be a strong man," he said, flexing his little muscles. "My daddy said I can learn to play the piano just like him. My daddy taught me the middle C on the piano today." My daddy, my daddy, my daddy, he rambled on and on.

"I'm glad you had such a good time with your daddy today."

Aliyah dried him off with a fluffy blue towel.

"Can I sleep at our house tomorrow, Mommy? I don't want to sleep at Grandma's house anymore. I want to go home."

"We'll see." Aliyah knew that she had to do something about the situation soon.

After the children were bathed and tucked in, Aliyah showered and put on her favorite lounging pajamas and went into the living room to wait for her mother. Betty and Dr. Gordon were dating pretty regularly now. At least twice a week they had dinner together or went to see a movie or show.

Betty had finally eked out a life for herself. She was busier than ever with her board work. From what Jamal was telling Aliyah their mother ran Nealz' Benz as well or better than her father had done. She was committed to making it one of the best-run automobile dealerships in the country. She loved researching what the competition was doing and introducing new ideas to the other board members. She had become a very busy lady, and she relished every minute of it.

It was ten o'clock when Betty and Dr. Gordon came in. It was the first time that Dr. Gordon had come into the house since Aliyah had moved in. He was a very handsome man. He had a dark chestnut complexion, silver hair, and a mustache. He had a nice physique giving the appearance that he worked out regularly. He wore dark slacks and a tan sports jacket with a well-coordinated tie. Betty looked chic standing next to him. She wore a well fitting navy blue suit and matching navy pumps. She had on a white silk shirt with a dazzling silver and navy blue scarf to accent it.

"My, don't you two look dapper," Aliyah said, staring at the handsome couple. "Where are you coming from?"

"We went to the Paper Mill Playhouse to see a musical." Dr. Gordon smiled at her revealing sparkling white teeth.

"It was wonderful," Betty said. "I invited Gordon in for a nightcap." She looked at him and then at Aliyah.

"I'll leave and give you two some space." Aliyah grabbed the magazine she had been thumbing through, and got up from the couch.

"No," Dr. Gordon said. "I really just wanted to come in and say hello to you, Aliyah. Betty, I'll take a raincheck on the nightcap. I have an early morning call anyway." He moved toward the front door. Betty followed.

"I don't mean to cramp your space," Aliyah said to her mother when she returned from saying goodnight to her date. "I know it's time for me and the kids to make other arrangements. I'm just not sure as to what I want to do yet."

"I'm not rushing you out, sweetheart," Betty said. "But it's time for you to make some decisions. The way I see it you have only two choices. Talk to Jeremiah and see if you can work things out so that you can live together as a family again or---"

"Or what?" Aliyah asked.

"What do you think, Aliyah?" Betty looked at her daughter.

"Maybe I should think about seeing a lawyer."

"Is that what you want Aliyah? Do you want some fast talking lawyer to convince you that you should divorce your husband?"

The word divorce made Aliyah cringe. She had waited a long time to find a husband. She had been blessed with more than just a husband she had found her soul mate. Was she ready to let him go now after only four years? Was she ready for a divorce? "No, Mom." Aliyah looked at Betty. "I don't want a divorce. But I don't want to live with a man that cheats on me. How will I know when he might do it again? I don't want to live with the uncertainty."

"Give Jeremiah a chance to ask for your forgiveness. Give him a chance to prove that he really loves you, Aliyah. If you don't give him a chance you will live with the uncertainty of whether your marriage was salvageable, that maybe you could have made it work. Think about it, sweetheart." Betty put her arms around Aliyah to comfort her. "You have a lot to think about, Aliyah. Make up your mind what you are going to do and then do it, and do it soon."

Aliyah lay in the bed with Mandela stirring next to her. Nia was sleeping soundly in the crib near the window. She thought about what Dotty had said to her. "When a man flaunts his mistress for all to see that's a clear indication that the marriage is over." What woman would tolerate having her husband flaunt his relationship in front of family and friends? A man wouldn't do this unless he knew it was over. *Isn't this what Jeremiah did at the exhibit in front of my family and friends? So what does he want to talk to me about? Maybe he wants to rub his affair in my face. Why does he want to hurt me like this?* Aliyah wondered before drifting off to sleep holding a restless Mandela in her arms.

Chapter 17

Jeremiah smiled to himself as he lathered his body with soap. For the first time in weeks he was able to sing in the shower again. Things were not where he wanted them to be, but they were better. It was 8:30AM and there was laughter in the house. He had heard Jean enter the house just as he was entering the shower. He heard Mandela's squeal of delight because he was back home again. He couldn't wait to get downstairs where his children were waiting for him.

This was the second week that this new routine had started. The first day Jean came by in the morning with the kids Jeremiah had spent the whole morning at home. He didn't want to go to work. He played the piano for Mandela and frolicked on the floor in the nursery with Nia. His kids were so wonderful.

Jeremiah had taken Mandela to nursery school after Jean lay Nia down for a nap. He didn't get to the gallery that first day until early afternoon. He had stayed at the gallery until almost eight that night before going downstairs to eat dinner at the nightclub. After dinner he had gone home to the lonely brownstone, but he felt better. He had spent the day with his kids.

When Jeremiah entered the kitchen Jean was feeding Nia some oatmeal and Mandela was eating from a bowl. The teakettle had just begun to whistle and the jar of Ovaltine sat on the counter waiting for him to pour his breakfast drink. A little bit of normalcy had returned to his life.

"Hi Daddy," Mandela said quite routinely.

"Dah Da, Da Da," Nia chimed in.

"Good morning." Jeremiah had a smile for everyone.

"Good morning, Mr. Jones," Jean said. "Would you like a bowl of oatmeal, too?"

"Yes, I think I will have a bowl of oatmeal." Jeremiah sat down next to Mandela.

"Daddy will you teach me some more of the piano after I finish my oatmeal?"

"Not this morning, Son. I have an early appointment, but I will come back later this afternoon to spend some more time with you and Nia before you go back to grandma's house."

"I don't want to go back to grandma's house," Mandela said with tears forming in his eyes. "I want to stay home."

"Don't cry, Son. When I come back I'll teach you some more piano, okay?" Jeremiah reached over to give Mandela a hug.

Before he left the house Jeremiah took the children upstairs where they ran about checking to make sure that all of their stuff was still where they left it. Nia peeked under Mandela's bed and pulled out one of her favorite rag dolls. Mandela took his guitar from the toy box and demonstrated that he could duplicate a sound that Jeremiah had taught him.

Watching the children frolic in the house helped to convince Jeremiah that this was where they belonged. If Aliyah would not come back to their home while he was there, then he would just have to leave. *After all it's her house.* Jeremiah told himself. *She had it before she even met me.*

He had been praying and hoping that she would come back to resume their marriage, but the longer she stayed away the more doubtful he became. He hadn't spoken to his wife in close to a month. He had only made love to her once in almost two months considering the time she had been away in Africa.

When Jeremiah left the house that morning he did not drive to the gallery as usual. He drove instead to Nealz' Benz to have a talk with his brother-in-law. He had not talked about his marital problems with anyone. Well maybe it was high time that he did. Jamal was the closest thing he had to a brother. Maybe they could have a man-to-man talk and maybe, just maybe he could get his brother-in-law on his side.

Nealz' Benz was located in a small suburban community, near Newark. The two-story building was on a busy corner on the main street. It was a very impressive looking business. Jamal escorted Jeremiah up to the second floor suite of offices. As they made their way to Jamal's private office Jeremiah stopped to take a peek into the boardroom where Betty conducted monthly board meetings. *Her birthday present would look nice in here*, he thought.

"How do you like the changes we've made?" Jamal asked.

"Great," Jeremiah said, walking around the boardroom. "Your father would be so proud of you and your mother. You've done a great job maintaining this business, even making it grow. I'm proud of you." Jeremiah looked around in awe at the elegance of the décor.

Jamal went to work for his father right out of technical school. He started out as a mechanic and worked his way up to master mechanic. Three years before his death Bill moved Jamal into the sales office. After a year of selling he moved him into management. Jamal was well prepared to take over when his father suffered his first heart attack. A few months later Bill Neal died of a massive heart attack.

"We have to keep up the image." Jamal laughed. "Appearance counts a lot when you're selling luxury cars. You have to impress your clients. Have you finally decided to let us put you behind the wheel of a Mercedes and get you out of that Buick?"

"No," Jeremiah said. "I'm just not into that kind of materialism. My Buick meets my needs just fine. Besides we have Aliyah's Mercedes whenever we want that kind of luxury." Jeremiah realized what he was saying and looked down at the floor. "Maybe I shouldn't be using 'we' anymore. I know you're aware that Aliyah and I are separated." He looked into Jamal's face.

"Of course I've heard about it," Jamal stared back. "Its all Sheniqua wants to talk about. Everybody's upset about it, my mother, Sheniqua, and me. But Aliyah is devastated. I don't know what to say, man."

"It's all a mistake," Jeremiah said. "I didn't do anything wrong."

"Man, I don't want to get into your business. Aliyah is the one that you need to convince, not me."

"How can I convince her if she won't talk to me?"

"I don't know, Jeremiah. Aliyah only talks to my mother. She hasn't mentioned it to me. Everything I know I heard from Sheniqua, and I don't know how reliable that is. I want you and Aliyah to get back together, but I don't know what I can do about it." Jamal gave Jeremiah a helpless look.

"Talk to your sister for me, please." Jeremiah was not beyond begging. "Just ask her to talk to me."

"Okay," Jamal said. "I'll try. I'll try to get her to talk to you."

"Thanks," Jeremiah said, grasping Jamal's hand for a firm handshake. "Tell her that I want us back together. But if I don't hear from her I will be out of the house by the weekend. She and the children should be there even if I can't be. My kids miss their house. They want to come home."

After Jeremiah left the dealership he went straight to the gallery. He was surprised to find Miss Melody waiting for him.

"Don't worry I'm not going to take you from your precious work," she said. "I just wanted to drop off your ticket for Wednesday night. You have a front row center seat. Don't forget that you promised pink roses."

Jeremiah could not help smiling. Miss Melody was like a little child in some ways. She was so excitable. "Don't worry I'll be there," he said. "And you'd better be good." He kidded her.

"Don't worry," she said. "You're in for the treat of your life. This show is the best. Just be there." She sashayed out of the gallery.

It was ten o'clock when Jeremiah got home. He'd worked right through dinner. He was well prepared for the next new exhibit that was coming to Oblivion. Work kept him so occupied during the day that he barely had time to think about Aliyah. Oh how he missed her at night, though. He tried to wear himself out during the day so that he would be too tired to do anything else but fall asleep as soon as his head hit the pillow. This seldom worked. He knew that he would spend at least an hour thinking about his wife before falling asleep.

He went into the kitchen. Jean had left a bowl of split pea soup on the stove for him to heat up. *Jean is such a thoughtful person,* Jeremiah thought as he placed the bowl of soup in the microwave. While eating his soup alone in the kitchen he wondered what

Aliyah was thinking about. *Should I call her again? No,* he decided. Since she left he had called her at least a hundred times and she had not returned one of his phone calls. He never believed it would go on this long.

The first few days after Aliyah left, Jeremiah would smile to himself when he thought about how foolish she would feel after he explained everything to her. The thought of making up with her was enough to arouse him. So many nights had gone by, though, and now he was having doubts if they would ever make up. *Not without help,* he concluded. Jeremiah decided that he was going to have to enlist the help of his *babalowa.* All of the praying he had done, all of the offerings to his guardian *orisa,* Shango, and to the ancestral spirits had not brought Aliyah home. He knew something more was needed.

Lying on the king size bed that he and Aliyah had purchased together, Jeremiah thought about their courtship. He had noticed the tall, shapely woman with the gorgeous legs and long braided hair long before he first met her. He was spending his mornings picking up cans and bottles in downtown Newark for recycling. He'd noticed Aliyah running in the early morning hours along McCarter Highway and the Passaic riverbank. For a long time he wondered about her, especially after he saw her pour a thick liquid substance into the river on a few occasions. Jeremiah had wondered what she could be doing until it dawned on him that she must have been making an offering of honey to the river goddess, Osun.

The first time he spoke to her he'd looked deep into her eyes, Jeremiah knew that there was something special about this lady. He knew they were destined to come together. He had captured her beauty on canvas and waited patiently for the *orisas* to work their magic. The second time an opportunity arose for him to speak to her she had fallen near the river and needed his assistance. Several weeks after that, he finally got an opportunity to ask her out on a date.

Jeremiah smiled at the memory of that first date. After a wonderful night of dining and dancing he took Aliyah home. Although neither of them had expected it to happen they had made mad passionate love, and Mandela was conceived. The thought of that night aroused him and Jeremiah lay there looking at the ceiling, holding himself, and wanting his wife.

Aliyah walked briskly down Broadway returning to her office. She'd had a 10AM appointment and had decided to walk the ten or so blocks up to 61st Street. She missed the noontime walks around the lake at Weequahic Park, pushing Nia in her stroller. It had been the only form of exercise that she got on a regular basis. Since she'd moved in with her mother nothing was the same for her or the kids.

She hated not being able to work out of her home anymore. She hated that she had to drive into Manhattan at least two days a week because she couldn't find a parking space in South Orange. She could walk to the train station from her Newark home, and it was only a twenty-minute commute to Manhattan by train. The extra time she now spent commuting took away from the quality time she normally spent with the children. More than anything she hated the time she lay in bed at night lonely for her husband, knowing that he was probably in bed with Miss Melody.

So many nights she had been tempted to pick up the telephone and call Jeremiah just to hear his voice. Then the image of him holding Miss Melody in his arms would appear, and she would bury her face in the pillow and cry softly so as not to disturb the children. What they had together was so perfect, or at least she had thought so. How could Jeremiah have ruined everything by having an affair? She didn't deserve this and neither did their children. At the very least she and the children should have the house. Yes, she and the children should live in the brownstone. Last night, before she went to sleep, Aliyah decided that it was time she paid a visit to her lawyer.

The visit to the lawyer's office was painful to say the least. The lawyer, Matthew Miller, was one of the attorneys her father had used from time to time. He was well aware of Aliyah's financial status. He knew of the Neal family's financial success, besides he knew that Aliyah was drawing a large salary from *Enigma Magazine.* If it were up to him he would drag this case out, and milk it for all it was worth. Fortunately, Aliyah knew a little about the law too. She told Matthew right up front that divorce was not what she was seeking at this time. All she wanted was for Jeremiah to relinquish the house to her and the children.

Twenty minutes after she had returned to her office, Matthew Miller called to tell her that Jeremiah was not going to cooperate.

"What?" Aliyah was shocked. She had asked Matthew to speak to Jeremiah about leaving the house willingly before taking any legal action.

"He said that he's not going to cooperate with any requests. I'm going to court tomorrow and get a court order to have him thrown out, Aliyah. Trust me I know what I'm doing."

"I can't believe that Jeremiah said that. It doesn't sound like him at all."

"He sounded angry to me, Aliyah. I think he's going to be difficult. But don't worry, there's not a court in the country that would give him the house. The deed is in your name; it's your house. Be patient," he said. "I'll have him thrown out on his butt in less than a week."

The view from the window of her eighteenth floor office was spectacular. Aliyah could see over the roofs of some of the lower buildings providing a tiny glimpse of Central Park. Standing at the window she wondered what was in store for her and her children. She hadn't wanted to get a lawyer involved in her domestic situation, yet, but what else could she do? She wanted to move back into her house. Why was Jeremiah being so difficult? *Why is he angry?* she wondered. After all she was the injured party.

The ringing of the telephone jolted Aliyah out of her thoughts. She didn't feel like talking to anyone, but accepted the call when she learned it was her mother.

"What's up, Mother?"

"Honey, Gordon just called to tell me that he has an emergency at the hospital and that he won't be able to take me to the theater tonight. He purchased the tickets already and suggested that the two of us use the tickets. Let's go Aliyah, it will do you good to get out and take your mind off of your troubles." Betty tried to persuade Aliyah.

"I don't think so, Mom. I have a terrible headache and I'm just not in the mood."

"Take something for your headache. I want you to go with me. It's a new musical and tonight is opening night. Gordon wants to send us in style. He's sending a limo for me and I can pick you up early enough so we can get a bite to eat before the show. Aliyah, I won't take no for an answer."

"What about the children? I don't want to impose on Jean any more than I have to." Aliyah thought that would get her off the hook.

"Don't worry about the children. I already made arrangements for Sheniqua and Jamal to baby-sit them tonight. The kids are excited about spending the night with Uncle Jamal. Aliyah you have no excuse. I'll pick you up at your office at five. It'll be fun. You'll see."

"Oh all right, Mother, if you insist. Don't expect me to be good company, though. I've had a rough day already. By the way what are we going to see?"

"Sassy," Betty said. "It's a new musical that's opening tonight. It's about the life of Sarah Vaughn. It should be good."

The Rooftop Café in Aliyah's office building was a quaint little gathering place for small luncheon groups or singles grabbing a quick bite while they reviewed files. Aliyah often had her morning tea there and sometimes lunch, either alone or with a friend or colleague. She had skipped breakfast in order to visit the lawyer, by noon she was starving. She grabbed the folder that she had been reviewing and headed for the roof where she made herself comfortable at her favorite table seated directly in the noontime sun.

After ordering a Caesar salad with a glass of lemonade Aliyah settled back and opened the folder again. One of her senior editors had submitted an article on current fashion trends in South Africa. Aliyah was looking at a photograph of a well-dressed South African woman when a familiar voice spoke to her.

"You feel like company or do you want to be alone?" Dotty asked.

"Sit," Aliyah said, motioning to the chair directly across from her. "I know you don't like it but I'm glad you're spending more time at the office. It's good running into you again at the Rooftop. Reminds me of old times before you got married."

"Unfortunately it reminds me of old times, too. And you're right, I don't like it." They were silent for a few minutes before Dotty spoke again.

"Are you and Jeremiah still separated?"

"Yes." Aliyah did not elaborate.

Taking the hint that Aliyah did not want to discuss her marital situation, Dotty changed the subject. "Have you heard about the new musical opening tonight on Broadway?"

"Yes. As a matter of fact my mother has tickets. She's picking me up this evening for the show."

"Derek and I are going, too." Dotty appeared excited. "He loves the music of Sarah Vaughn." She waited for the waitress to put Aliyah's salad on the table. "Maybe I'll bump into you tonight."

"Maybe," Aliyah said, diving into her salad.

At five-thirty Aliyah climbed into the limousine with her mother. It was a luxurious vehicle, black and shiny with exquisite black leather upholstery and shiny chrome trim.

"Nice," Aliyah said after she was seated.

"Gordon likes to make an impression." Betty smiled. "Where would you like to go. There's a 7PM curtain call but we have plenty of time."

"I hear there's a really good Ethiopian restaurant on 48th Street and Broadway. Let's try it."

"Sounds good to me." Betty leaned up to give the driver instructions.

The restaurant was all that Aliyah had heard it was. She hadn't felt so relaxed in quite a while. A delicious palm wine was served with the meal that came on one large platter. There were stacks of paper-thin bread used to grab the morsels of food with your fingers. There were no eating utensils; reminding Aliyah of the many meals she had eaten in West Africa where the only eating utensils were her fingers. It was six-forty when they stepped outside and re-entered the limo. By six-fifty five they were seated in box seats directly above and to the left of the stage.

"These are wonderful seats," Aliyah said. "We have an excellent view of the stage."

"I told you Gordon will spare no expense to impress me." Betty gave Aliyah a look that let her know that the relationship was getting serious.

The show had barely started when Aliyah got an uneasy feeling in her stomach. Something was unsettling and she couldn't put her finger on it. It was the voice of one of the singers. It sounded so familiar. Both Betty and Aliyah realized at the same time that the lead role, Sassy, was being played by none other than Miss Melody. Betty reached over and put her hand on Aliyah's arm as if to calm her. Aliyah did not move. She was speechless and spellbound.

"Are you all right?" Betty whispered in Aliyah's ear. "I didn't know she was starring in the show. I'm sorry."

Aliyah squeezed her mother's hand, not saying anything for a few seconds. She waited until she felt her body relax a little. "I'm okay," she finally whispered back to Betty.

"I'll understand if you want to leave." Betty had her arm around Aliyah's shoulder now.

"No mother. I don't want to leave. Let's just watch the show."

Throughout the show Aliyah was mesmerized. She couldn't take her eyes off Miss Melody. The woman was really good. One of the scenes was vaguely familiar to Aliyah. Miss Melody's accompanist lifted her unto the piano, and she sang "Body and Soul" so seductively. Aliyah felt as though she had watched the scene before, but she couldn't figure out when or where. *Maybe it was in a dream,* she thought. At intermission, Aliyah jumped up and fled to the ladies room, Betty directly behind her.

In the ladies room Aliyah stayed in the stall for a long time prompting Betty to ask if she was all right. When she came out she had regained her composure. She looked in the mirror and put on fresh lipstick with her mother hovering over her. In the mirror she spotted Dotty, also applying fresh lipstick. Both women stopped when they spotted each other.

"Isn't this a wonderful show?" Dotty asked after Aliyah introduced her to Betty.

"Yes," Betty said, nervously, still worried about Aliyah's reaction.

"I'm enjoying it," Aliyah said fully composed now. "Let's get back before the curtain goes up."

Derek joined Dotty as they were leaving the ladies room. He was a handsome man. He had smooth dark skin, was clean-shaven, and impeccably dressed. He was courteous and smiled at Aliyah who politely introduced him to her mother. Dotty was smiling from ear to ear and hanging onto Derek's arm for dear life. Aliyah smiled politely and excused herself, taking her mother's arm and leading the way back to their seats.

Throughout the remainder of the show Aliyah continued to watch Miss Melody. She was sexy and seductive. She had a beautiful voice and a perfect figure. Aliyah could not help but notice what Jeremiah or any other man would see in her. By the time the show was over she wanted to cry, but she didn't. She stood up with the rest of the audience that gave the performance a resounding round of applause for three curtain calls. It was at the last curtain call when she saw a familiar figure come up to the stage from the front row clutching a bouquet of pink roses.

When the roses were handed up to Miss Melody, she practically leaped off the stage into the arms of the gentleman who dropped the roses in order to catch her. The audience roared in response. The applause was deafening. Aliyah stared unbelievably at Miss Melody, wonderfully happy in the arms of her man. The scene became unbearable and Aliyah ran from the box followed by her mother. They quickly got into the limousine and drove back to New Jersey, Betty holding a sobbing Aliyah all the way home.

Chapter 18

Maybe they're not coming, Jeremiah thought as he sat at the kitchen table, staring into his cup of hot Ovaltine, waiting for his children to come. No one had called to let him know that the children would not be there this morning. He had gotten up as usual, taken his shower, dressed, and come downstairs expecting to find Jean feeding the children their breakfast. *Has something happened?* he wondered.

Jeremiah had been worried every since he received a phone call the morning before from a man identifying himself as the attorney representing Aliyah Jones in the case Jones vs. Jones. *The man was cold and distant,* Jeremiah thought back to the conversation.

"Do you have an attorney representing you in this matter, Mr. Jones?" he had asked.

"What matter might you be referring to?" Jeremiah had asked, becoming agitated.

"The matter of Jones vs. Jones. If you don't have an attorney I suggest that you acquire the services of one as soon as possible."

"Why do I need an attorney? What is Aliyah asking for?"

"It would be better for me to speak to your attorney, Mr. Jones. I hope we can count on your cooperation in this matter."

"I'm not cooperating with anything until I talk to my wife and I don't want to talk through an attorney," Jeremiah had said angrily before slamming the phone down.

At eight-thirty Jeremiah decided to call his mother-in-law's house to find out what was going on. He was really becoming annoyed with the whole situation. He was finally at his wit's end.

"What's going on Betty?" he asked into the telephone as soon as she answered.

"What do you mean?" Betty asked, annoyed now herself.

"Well, I'm waiting for the kids and they haven't shown up yet. No one called to let me know they would be late. Are they coming or not? I have to go to work."

"The kids spent the night with their uncle last night. He dropped them off this morning. They won't be coming to Newark today. They'll be there tomorrow." Betty was courteous but distant.

"Look Betty, you know that I am a very patient man. But I'm at my wit's end now. I haven't spoken to my wife in weeks. I have done nothing wrong, and now I don't even get a call to tell me that the kids are not coming. I'm losing my patience. Tell Aliyah that I'm tired of waiting for her to talk to me."

"I think she knows that, Jeremiah. It appears to me that you haven't been waiting at all."

"What does that mean?" Jeremiah was becoming really agitated.

"Nothing." Betty spoke more harshly than Jeremiah ever remembered hearing her sound. "Goodbye, Jeremiah," she said coldly before hanging up the telephone.

Jeremiah stared at the telephone for a long time before he replaced the receiver in the base. He sensed that something new was happening, but he didn't know what. It was certainly out of his hands, though. He needed help. He picked up the telephone again, this time to call his spiritual advisor. He breathed a sign of relief when he hung up the telephone. He had made an appointment to meet with his *babalowa* on Saturday evening.

At lunchtime Jeremiah got another surprise visit from his brother-in-law. Jamal was a very busy man and rarely made social visits during the course of the day. So Jeremiah was surprised, but glad to see him walking through the doors of the gallery, he hoped he would be able to shed some light on the situation.

"Man it's good to see you." He walked toward Jamal with his hand extended to the younger man.

"I don't know if you'll feel that way when the visit is over," Jamal said, putting a newspaper under his left arm to grasp his brother-in-law's hand.

"Why wouldn't I?" Jeremiah asked. "What's up?"

"That's what I've been wondering myself. Have you seen today's newspaper?" Jamal handed him the paper that was already turned to the entertainment section of *The New York Times*.

"What's this? Jeremiah glanced at the first page he saw. The blown up picture caught his eye immediately. It was a picture of him holding a smiling Miss Melody in mid-air. The look on his face was one of astonishment, but it could easily have been misconstrued. He looked as happy as she did. It was the caption over the picture that really floored him. "Sassy and her Man," it read.

"Wow," Jeremiah said alarmed. "Has Aliyah seen this?"

"She didn't have to see the paper. She and my mother were there to see it in person."

"Oh my! I can explain this," Jeremiah said.

"It appears that you are full of explanations. Man, you don't need to explain anything to me. You need to talk to my sister before her lawyer talks her into divorce court. I saw her this morning, and she was upset to say the least. I could say nothing in your defense. Even my mother is upset about this last episode. Man, I don't think there's anything I can do to help you out of this. All I can do is pray for you and your family."

After Jamal left Jeremiah took the newspaper article up to his studio to read. The article acclaimed Miss Melody for her performance in "Sassy." It referred to him as the mystery man who had so excited her that she had leaped off the stage into his waiting arms. *Aliyah and her mother were there to see that.* Jeremiah shook his head bewildered. *How was I to know that Miss Melody would do something so impulsive? What will happen next?* he wondered.

The Jazz Garden was packed for a Thursday night. As Jeremiah made his way to the bar to order his dinner he felt that all eyes were on him.

"What's going on?" he asked the bartender.

"Everybody's excited about Miss Melody's debut as an actress. I couldn't make the opening last night, but a lot of folks were there to witness it." He smiled at Jeremiah with a sly look in his eye.

When the waitress came out of the kitchen with his dinner, Jeremiah made the mistake of looking at her. The grin on her face told him that she, too, had either heard of the opening night or perhaps witnessed it herself.

"I guess dreams do come true," she said still smiling.

"What do you mean?" he asked her.

"Miss Melody's dream of starring in a Broadway musical for one. And her dream of getting you appears to have come true, too." She strolled back into the kitchen.

Jeremiah ate his dinner of black-eyed peas and rice with a side order of collared greens and cornbread in silence. His mind was heavy. For the first time in a long time he felt helpless. He was in a real mess and didn't know what to do. His life appeared to be spinning out of control right before his eyes, and he was helpless to stop it. Perhaps his *babalowa* could offer him some suggestions.

Until then he just had to ride out the storm.

It was 9PM when Jeremiah arrived home. He sat on the sofa in the dark for what seemed like a long time. Finally he turned on the lights and picked up the book he had been trying to read for over a month. He was a prolific reader and generally read a book a week when his life was in order. Lately he had been unable to concentrate. Walter Mosley's *What Next, A Memoir Toward World Peace,* was a book he had received as a birthday gift. He had read the first three chapters before Aliyah left. He found the book interesting and was enjoying it, but after Aliyah left he couldn't get interested in it again. He had read and reread the next chapter or two but he couldn't seem to concentrate. Nothing could take his mind off of his troubled marriage.

After experiencing the same frustrating attempt to read, Jeremiah put the book aside. He'd asked Jamal to tell Aliyah that he intended to move out of the brownstone by the weekend if she wasn't back home by then. *Well, it doesn't look like that's going to happen,* he thought. The weekend was here. Tomorrow was Friday *I might as well go upstairs and start packing.* Jeremiah turned the lights out and went upstairs.

On Friday morning he woke up earlier than usual. He pushed the covers back and looked at the clock. It was only six-thirty. His packed bags, sitting near the bedroom door, reminded him that this was his last morning to wake up in this room alone. If he ever came back it would be at Aliyah's request and she would be sharing the bed with him. Jeremiah hurried to shower and dress. He had plans for the day and he needed to get started.

It was eight o'clock when Jean came in with the children. "Daddy, Daddy Mandela called out as soon as he came in the door. Jeremiah heard the pitter patter of little feet running through the house looking for him. He hid behind the doorway waiting to spring out as they ran into the kitchen.

"Gotcha," he bellowed out as Mandela ran into the kitchen followed by his little sister.

"Hi Dad." Mandela laughed as Jeremiah swung him up and gave him a big hug.

"Come here," Jeremiah said to Nia, scooping her up with his other arm. Hugging his children closely he greeted Jean as she came into the kitchen.

"Good morning," Jean said, looking exasperated. "This is some ordeal going to South Orange and getting the kids ready to come down here each morning before you leave for work," she said. "Not that I'm complaining," she quickly added.

"It's okay, Jean. This will be the last day you'll have to do this. I'm moving out of the house today. Aliyah can move back in, and the kids won't have to be shuffled around like this any longer."

"Oh!" Jean said surprised. "Miss Aliyah didn't mention it to me this morning."

"Well, when you talk to her again let her know that I have moved out. She probably wanted to make sure that I was gone before she told you."

"I want you to know that I'm really sorry to see your family break up like this, Mr. Jones. I never believed something like this could happen to you. You all seemed so happy together." Jean gave Jeremiah a look of genuine sorrow.

"Thanks Jean. I thought we were happy, too."

"I thought so, too." Mandela said to their surprise.

Picking up on his son's sadness, Jeremiah said, "What would you like to do today? Daddy is taking the morning off from work and we can spend it together."

"Can we go to Turtleback Zoo again, Daddy?" Mandela asked excitedly.

"Jean, why don't you call Aliyah? She'll take a call from you. Let her know that I plan to take the kids to the zoo today. I'll have them back by one this afternoon. She may just want you to come back to South Orange to pack the children's things to move back into the house," he said before giving his full attention to the children.

Aliyah was glad to get the call from Jean telling her that Jeremiah was moving out of the house. *That attorney is really good,* she thought. *Or maybe Jeremiah is just anxious to move in with Miss Melody.* Two days after the Times' announcement to the whole world that Miss Melody and Jeremiah's were a couple, Aliyah was just getting a handle on the situation. She had taken Thursday off from work. She had felt so humiliated. *How could Jeremiah have done such a thing in front of a New York audience? How many of my colleagues and acquaintances saw that spectacle? How much more humiliation will I have to endure?*

She worked fervently throughout the morning. The prestigious Omni awards, given out yearly to the best magazines in the country, were being presented in Atlanta in just four days. *Enigma Magazine* was one of the nominees. Aliyah was scheduled to attend the ceremony along with *Enigma's* publishers and key members of her staff. If she was to be out of town for a couple of days she needed to make sure that everything was ready for the next edition before she left.

At two o'clock Aliyah went up to the Rooftop Café to grab a quick sandwich and a glass of iced tea. She took a late lunch hoping to avoid running into anyone she knew. She was still a little shaky from the "Sassy" thing. Apparently she didn't go late enough. The café was still packed with the lunch crowd. Aliyah thought she heard snickering from a table of women as she made her way to a table in the back. *How embarrassing,* she thought. Everyone at the office knew Jeremiah. He had been to all of their office Christmas parties. *How many of these people were at the performance?* she wondered.

Halfway through her sandwich she looked up and saw Dotty

making her way to the table. *Just my luck, I should have taken an early lunch.*

"Hi girlfriend," Dotty said plopping herself down in the chair across from Aliyah. "How are you?" She had a slight smirk on her face that Aliyah didn't like.

"I'm fine." Aliyah took another bite of her sandwich.

"I was worried about you. I started to call you at home yesterday when you didn't come in, but then I remembered that you're not living at home anymore. Are you sure you're okay?"

"I'm going to be fine, Dotty. I just need to put this whole thing behind me and get on with my life."

"Are we talking about divorce, Aliyah?" Dotty had a shocked look on her face.

"I don't know what else I can do. He's chosen to flaunt his affair in front of the whole world. I'm sure you know by now that he made the *New York Times*."

"I saw that." Dotty gave her a sympathetic look. "What has he said about all of this?"

"I haven't spoken to him. I don't see any need to. He's agreed to move out of the house, though."

"Not a good sign." Dotty looked concerned.

"Look, I've got to go," Aliyah said getting up. She really didn't want to talk to Dotty about her marriage anymore.

"Have a nice weekend," Dotty said, as if she could. "I'll see you on Monday."

"No," Aliyah said. "I'll be moving back into my house over the weekend. I need Monday to get situated. I'll be working out of the house on Monday and I'll be flying into Atlanta on Tuesday morning."

"Okay then, I'll see you in Atlanta on Tuesday. I'm looking forward to the award ceremony. Derek is coming with me."

Jean moved the children's things back into the house Friday morning after Jeremiah and the kids went out. Aliyah spent Saturday morning moving her own things back into the house. By Saturday afternoon she was resettled. It felt good to be home. She had only been in the house once since she had fled that awful day when she discovered the earring in her bedroom. Before she left her mother's house they talked about her plans.

"Take your problem to the altar and let God help you," Betty said.

"Don't you think I've been praying about this, Mother?" Aliyah asked.

"Sometimes you need more than a solitary prayer. It won't hurt for you to come to church with me. You haven't been in a long time. If you take your problem to the altar, you'll have the support of the whole church. You know what God said about two or more gathering in his name."

Aliyah knew her mother was right. She hadn't been to church in a long time. She had been only a few times since her marriage. The added responsibilities of being a mother and a wife consumed all of her time. Besides, although Jeremiah was a very spiritual man, he was not a churchgoing man. Following the tenets of the Yoruba religion of Ifa seemed to be all that he needed. He prayed daily and made offerings to the *orisa* and to his ancestors. For a long time Aliyah felt that Jeremiah's strong faith and his devotion to Ifa was enough to carry the whole family. *Maybe I was wrong,* she thought.

"It's too late now, Mom," she had said to her mother. "The marriage is over. It can't be saved."

"How do you know that, Aliyah? You haven't talked to Jeremiah yet. I refuse to believe that he has stopped loving you. Remember 'the family that prays together stays together.'" Betty gave Aliyah a pleading look.

"What can I do, Mother?" Aliyah had asked.

"Before you go to see that lawyer again and let him talk you into a divorce, promise me you will go to the altar and take this problem to the Lord."

"Okay, Mom. I'll go to church with you." Aliyah had promised.

Thinking back to her promise, Aliyah wondered had she done all that she could to save her marriage. Not only would she go to church with her mother, but she also decided that she would call her friend, Oya, and arrange for a consultation.

Oya was the wife of one of Aliyah's best friends, Kanmi Olajide. She and Kanmi had been friends since her undergraduate days at Rutgers. Over the years Aliyah and Oya also became friends. Aliyah was grateful when Oya told her it was all right for her to come to their home in Plainfield, New Jersey later that same evening.

Oya and Kanmi's home was warm and inviting. Aliyah and her family were always made to feel welcome there. It was a spacious Victorian home with a large backyard. The Olajide's had two sons. Mwangi, the eldest son, was eleven years old. His younger brother, Yori, was almost six. Mandela loved being in their company. Even Nia was delighted to be there. Aliyah could tell by her squeals of delight and demands to be put down on the floor where she could get closer to the other children.

Kanmi, a very wise man beyond his forty years, took charge of the children and ushered them all into the yard, leaving Aliyah alone with Oya. He knew they had lots to talk about.

"Tell me Aliyah, what is it that you want to happen in your life now?" Oya asked as soon as Kanmi and the children were out of hearing range.

"I really don't know, Oya." Aliyah looked puzzled. "I guess I want this whole situation to disappear and for my marriage to resume as though it had never happened."

"Just what is it that you think has happened to interrupt your marriage?" Oya's voice was soft and calm.

"My husband has been unfaithful to me, Oya. We took a vow to be faithful to each other 'til death do us part.' He has violated that vow. I don't see how I can ever trust him again. If I can't trust him then I don't think I can ever live with him again as his wife."

"Do you want a divorce?" Oya asked.

"No, I don't want that. I want things to be like they were with Jeremiah and me before he had the affair. I still love him so much, but his infidelity has changed everything. I have prayed and made offerings to Osun, my guardian *orisa*, but nothing has happened to make it any better. I don't know what else to do."

"Sometimes you need more than the *orisas* to help you," Oya said. "You need the help of the ancestors. The ancestors know what their children need. They take a special interest in their descendants. Like the *orisa* they dwell in the spirit world, therefore they are closer to God. They can use their influence with God to help you with your earthly problems."

"How do I communicate my earthly problems to the ancestors?" Aliyah asked.

"Come, I will show you." Oya led the way upstairs.

In a small, sparsely furnished room in the attic of the home Oya lit a candle. The glow from the candle revealed an altar that Oya said was dedicated to her ancestral spirits.

"Our ancestors like to know that we remember them. As long as someone remembers them they are never dead. They continue to need our love and acknowledgement even though they have departed this earth," Oya said.

"What is the glass of water for?" Aliyah asked, observing the things on the altar.

"The ancestral spirits love offerings of cool water for their thirst and comfort. The candle gives them light and energy. This is a picture of my grandmother." She picked up a beautifully framed photograph of an older woman, small with gray hair and sparkling eyes. "This is my grandfather." She handed Aliyah another beautifully framed photograph of a smiling man that appeared to be in his seventies. "They both died in the nineteen-eighties," she said.

"They were a very handsome couple," Aliyah said, replacing the photographs on the altar. "Who are the people in the other photographs?"

"Aunts, uncles, and cousins who have preceded me in death."

"What are these other objects that are on your altar?" Aliyah asked.

"Just objects that I connect with my ancestors. This was my grandmother's favorite cup." Oya held up a white porcelain cup with a red rose painted on it. "Here is my grandfather's pipe," she said. "This vase once belonged to my cousin."

"Having the altar is the way that you acknowledge your ancestral spirits?" Aliyah asked.

"Having the altar is only a part of it," Oya said. "Each week I change the water and first offer it to Olodumare, one of our names for God, for his blessings. After lighting the candle I call out the name of each of my ancestors three times and then offer them the candle light and the cool water."

"Jeremiah makes a similar offering to his ancestors once a

month," Aliyah said. He has an altar in the basement."

"Kanmi keeps his altar in the basement also. I like mine at the top of the house. It makes me feel closer to God," Oya said. "The offerings vary with different groups of people. Some people do it for seven consecutive days in every month. I do it every Monday. I think the translation changed with the migration through the middle passage." Oya held the glass of water up to the sky asking Olodumare to bless it.

The flickering candle created dancing patterns of light that bounced off the walls. Aliyah watched as Oya called out the names of her ancestors, repeating each one three times. "My loving ancestors," she said, "Please accept this offering of cool water for your thirst and comfort and let this candle provide you with light and energy." And then she said, "Ancestors please use your influence with God to help my friend, Aliyah, save her marriage."

When Aliyah returned to Newark, the first thing that she did after putting the children to bed was search for a spot to create an ancestral altar. She decided on a small room on the third floor near her office. She began to visualize the things that she would put on her altar.

Chapter 19

Jeremiah spent most of Friday afternoon and evening moving into his studio. He took most of his clothes and other personal belongings. He didn't take anything else from the house except a portrait of his mother. He had painted the portrait twenty-five years after his mother died. He progressed the years on her so that she looked older. When he painted the portrait he had felt that his mother's eyes looked like they were smiling at him. Through the years he discovered that the look in his mother's eyes appeared to change from time to time. They looked sad, now, as he prepared to hang the picture in his studio. He securely hung the portrait on a wall directly across from the divan that he would now be sleeping on.

When Jeremiah awoke on Saturday morning he felt disoriented. Sleeping on the divan in his studio was a lot different than the king size bed he had grown accustomed to. One advantage to living in the studio, though, was that he could work from home like Aliyah did. The biggest disadvantage, though, was that there wasn't a shower in the studio, only a toilet and a small basin.

Searching through the gallery storeroom Jeremiah found a small cabinet that he could use for storing some basic kitchen supplies. He also found a small hot plate and a teakettle that he carried upstairs to the studio. At least he could continue to have his hot Ovaltine in the morning. After rearranging the closet in his studio, allowing him to hang up his clothes, he sat down at his desk and sipped the cup of hot Ovaltine he had prepared. *What am I doing living in my studio? I haven't done anything wrong. I certainly deserve better than this,* he thought.

At five o'clock Jeremiah was down at the Jazz Garden eating a bowl of gumbo. He had a seven o'clock appointment with his *babalowa* and he didn't want to be late. Gumbo was one of his favorite meals, and he didn't want to rush his dinner. Only a few people were sitting at the bar. Everyone was conversing about the events relating to the flooding and evacuation of New Orleans. Jeremiah ate slowly and listened to the conversation.

"You know it was racist," the bartender was saying. "If they had been white people they wouldn't have waited so long to send in help."

"Genocide! That's what it was." A female patron yelled out.

"They wanted blacks out of New Orleans and decided to do it 'by any means necessary.'" A male patron said.

"They destroyed a lot of our history along with that city," Cook said, coming out of the kitchen. "Where do you think I learned how to make gumbo like this?" He placed another helping in front of Jeremiah. "I loved that city." Tears welled in his eyes.

"Calling black people looters because they took things they needed to survive while referring to white people doing the same thing as "commandeering necessities for survival." The woman patron snickered.

"Yeah!" the bartender said. "They wanted to halt the rescue efforts to protect white peoples things. Putting things above people is sinful." He shook his head in disbelief.

"They'll rebuild the city all right, but to live there you will have to be rich. No more poor black people living in New Orleans," Cook said, on his way back to the kitchen.

"Such a pity," the woman patron said sadly. "All those lives lost because of greed and racism.

Jeremiah was glad that people were still talking about Katrina. He was afraid that if people stopped talking about what had happened in New Orleans the matter would be forgotten much like slavery and Jim Crow; the destruction of black neighborhoods in Tulsa, Oklahoma and Philadelphia, Pennsylvania; the syphilis experiments in Tuskegee Alabama; and the lynchings that took place in the South during the early part of the twentieth century and following World War II. What happened in New Orleans was a big part of African-American history and it had to remain alive.

"If they can rid New Orleans of poor black people like that, then they can rid any city in America of black people," Cook said from the kitchen.

"Black people have been saying for years that whites want to take Newark back. I wonder how they will do it?" The female patron asked.

Jeremiah listened without saying a word. The events following hurricane Katrina had a profound impact on him as well as every African-American. He had been so affected by the tragic event that he couldn't speak about it to anyone for a long time without getting emotional. So many had expressed the same views that he was feeling that he had made up his mind not to say anything for fear of exploding. He thought about what Walter Mosley had written about "universal rules of fair treatment." *It wasn't fair that New Orleans' poor people were overwhelmingly black, and that they were the ones who were sacrificed for a New World Order.*

At 7PM Jeremiah was ringing the doorbell to the home of his babalowa. He had left the Jazz Garden at exactly 6:45 and driven across Halsey Street to Williams Street. He turned right on Williams Street and left on Martin Luther King Boulevard to Clinton Avenue, one of the main streets joining the Central Ward to the South Ward. His babalowa lived in the South Ward.

"Welcome to my humble abode." He was greeted at the front door by Oscar, a renowned African-American babalowa. Oscar was American born but his roots were in Nigeria. His grandfather was a Nigerian babalowa. Oscar's father, who had come to the United States in the 1940's, tried desperately to forget his Nigerian roots. Curious about the culture his father had tried so desperately to abandon, Oscar had researched the Yoruba culture on his own.

Oscar's fascination with the way of his ancestors had intrigued him and sent him on a mission to Nigeria when he was a freshman at Stanford University. His research and study had led him to adopt Ifa, the religion of his ancestors, which he believed to be the only true religion of African people.

Oscar's home was by no means humble. It lacked the ostentatious trappings of many wealthy people's homes, but it was a beautiful home nonetheless. The entrance hall was huge. The floors were laid with imported marble, and the woodwork was authentic early twentieth century. The ceilings were high and the windows were beautifully stained. Sparsely furnished, the living room had jumbo pillows on the floor with accommodating low tables that enabled one to sit on pillows to enjoy tea or cast kola nuts or cowry shells for the reading of an odu.

Jeremiah was invited to sit on one of the pillows, which he obliged. He looked at the mantle above a large fireplace. The mantle was covered with framed pictures of Oscar's ancestors, glasses of water, white candles and other objects of distinction. Leaning against the fireplace was a staff, or walking stick decorated with beautifully colored ribbons and bells.

Following his gaze Oscar said, "That's my ancestral stick. I

use it during certain rituals or just to lean on when I feel like it."
He smiled a pleasant smile. Oscar was a rather small man, only a
little over five feet tall. He couldn't have weighed more than one
hundred and thirty pounds. He wore a rather scraggly beard, and
his receding hairline made him look to be about fifty years old. He
spoke in a soft voice and was quick to smile. By profession he was
a doctor, a neurologist. He had maintained a practice in Newark for
over twenty years.

"Thank you for taking the time to see me on such short notice."
Jeremiah said.

"I am only too happy to assist a brother in need." Oscar poured
tea, from a beautiful china teapot, into two matching china cups
that sat on the table. "Tell me what is troubling you?" His gaze
looked serious.

"Aliyah has left me." Jeremiah followed suit and got right to the
point.

Oscar raised his eyebrows a little in surprise. It was he who
had helped to perform their marriage ceremony. He had given
them a reading before the ceremony and called on the spirits of the
ancestors seeking their blessings. "What reason has she given for
this act?" he asked.

"She believes that I have been unfaithful to her." Jeremiah took
a sip from his teacup.

"And have you?" Oscar raised his cup to his lips, but did not
drink. He stared at Jeremiah instead.

"No," Jeremiah said. "I love her and I want our family back together." He held the gaze of the babalowa.

"Have you consulted the ancestors?" Oscar folded his legs under his slight body.

"Yes, during my monthly ritual." Jeremiah looked at Oscar, his face portraying his pain. "I've made offerings to the *orisa* as well," he said.

"Will she not listen to you?" Oscar gave Jeremiah a sympathetic look.

"Communication is non-existent." Jeremiah looked hopeless.

"It sounds like you may have to resort to more profound measures in this matter, then. This is a situation that calls for more drastic action." Oscar put his hand on his chin, nodding his head apparently in deep thought.

"What should do I do?" Jeremiah asked, glad to hear that there was something else he could do.

"In situations of life or death, or in desperate situations such as yours, a live sacrifice is often what must be done."

"What does that mean?" Jeremiah was alarmed. "Do you mean kill something."

"People sacrifice animals all the time for human consumption. In Ifa, we sometimes sacrifice animals for consumption by the ancestral spirits. Generally a fowl; a hen or a pigeon." He smiled at the doubtful look on Jeremiah's face.

"Where can I obtain live poultry?" Jeremiah thought back to

the days when he was a child in Newark. He often accompanied his father to the live poultry market that used to be on East Kinney Street. There they would purchase fresh killed chicken or turkey. He remembered watching the poultry handlers wring chicken's necks and sometimes Jeremiah would dream of headless chickens running around. The dreams had frightened him as a child.

"There are still places in Newark that sell live poultry. There's a place in the North Ward on Mount Prospect Avenue that I patronize from time to time," Oscar said.

"I wouldn't know how to go about performing the ritual," Jeremiah said.

"Only a *babalowa* is allowed to conduct this ritual." Oscar poured himself another cup of tea.

"Will you do it for me?" Jeremiah was desperate.

"If necessary I will conduct the ritual. I have some friends that are having an *egun* party tonight. *Egun* is the Yoruba word that refers to the ancestors. Sometimes they are called *egun gun*. Come to the party with me and perhaps you will be fortunate enough to experience the sacrifice of a live animal on behalf of those in attendance. Are you available?"

Jeremiah looked at his watch, not even 8PM. He had nothing better to do. "Why not?" he said.

Jeremiah and Oscar drove to the North Ward where the party was just beginning. He looked around at the guests. There were about fifty people crowded into the small house. They were mostly

Latinos and people of African descent; however, there were also a few Asians. Everyone was standing in the living room, but they were facing the adjoining dining room. Jeremiah moved closer to the dining room to get a better look at the happenings. He was handed an *egun gun* beaded bracelet to put on his wrist, which he did. Someone gave him a sheet of paper with the lyrics of the Yoruba songs that the guests were singing.

Aumba awaori, Aumba waori
Awa osun, Awa oma, leri oma iyawo
Ara onu caA? we

While the guests sang Yoruba songs, a man performed a ritualistic dance and another prepared to make the sacrifice. The sacrifice of two hens was made. The blood drained into a tub placed on the floor just for the occasion. Another man that was referred to as the *Oba* appeared to be the symbolic object of the offering. Jeremiah watched in amazement as the *Oba* eventually went into a trance. He walked into the living room among the guests taking their hands and giving them messages from their ancestral spirits. When the *Oba* got to Jeremiah he said, "Your mother sends you a message from the spirit world. She wants you to know that she is sending your father to help you."

"Come to the altar and give your burdens to God." Reverend Doggett appealed to his congregation. "The Lord wants to help you, relieve you of your burdens, bring your problems to the altar," he repeated over and over as the choir sang.

> "It's me, It's me, It's me oh Lord
> Standing in the need of Prayer
> Not my brother, Not my mother, But it's me oh Lord
> Standing in the need of Prayer"

Betty took Aliyah's hand and led her to the altar. Aliyah looked back at Mandela and Nia sitting in the family pew with their uncle Jamal and aunt Sheniqua. They were watching her, waiting to see what she was going to do.

At the altar mother and daughter knelt side-by-side still holding hands. Aliyah bowed her head and said a silent prayer. *Dear Lord, I have always tried to follow the way that you have made for me. I have loved you above all and then my husband and my children. I have tried to abide by your heavenly rules and made every effort to be the kind of person that you want me to be. I have been a faithful wife, a loving mother, daughter, sister and friend. I have accepted your blessings and offered my prayers as thanks. I ask of you now not to forsake me. Please heal this wound in my heart caused by my husband's infidelity.*

Reverend Doggett asked the whole congregation to stand and

pray for those so burdened. "Those members of our flock who had the courage to come before you, shamelessly, admitting their weaknesses and failures and asking the Lord for forgiveness and guidance need your help, too. Let us send up a resounding prayer for them, one that the good Lord can't help but hear. 'Whenever two or more gather in his name asking for help, help is forthcoming,'" he said.

During the drive to her mother's condominium for dinner, Aliyah thought about the altar to her ancestors that she had created the night before. She had been so excited about creating her own altar. She had covered a small table with a white lace tablecloth and put three white candles on her altar. She added framed pictures of her father and grandparents. She also put a crystal vase that her mother had given her years ago on the table. The vase had belonged to her maternal grandmother. Aliyah placed a few silk flowers in the vase. She added a string of pearls that once belonged to her paternal grandmother, and a pair of cuff links that once belonged to her paternal grandfather.

When she had finished her creation she placed a glass of cool water on the altar, lit the candles, and called out the names of those ancestors whose names she knew, three times.

Then she repeated the words that Oya had taught her. "My loving ancestors please accept this glass of cool water for your thirst and comfort and this candle to give you light and energy." Then she had asked her ancestors to help resolve her marital situation.

As usual Betty fixed a delicious dinner for her family. She had already fried chicken before leaving for church. Macaroni and cheese was ready to go into the oven. There was a pot of collared greens simmering in smoked turkey wings. Handmade rolls, already browned to a golden tan, just needed to be heated. There were string beans and a shrimp casserole. For dessert there was a delicious upside down toasted almond pound cake.

After Jamal said the blessing, from his father's former seat at the head of the table, the family dug into the food as though they were starving. Mandela sat in his booster seat and Nia sat in her high chair. Betty sat beaming in the chair opposite her son.

"We are all so blessed," Betty said. "It's different having Sunday dinner without Bill sitting at the head of the table, but having everyone together is still wonderful," she said.

"I'm sitting at the head of the table today," Jamal said, "but I hear that this may change soon." He smiled at his mother.

"What's that supposed to mean?" Betty asked.

"I hear that you're dating," he said.

"Who told you that?" Betty looked at Sheniqua.

"I didn't know it was supposed to be a secret." Sheniqua had met Gordon when she dropped by her mother-in-law's house unexpectedly one day.

"It's not really a secret," Betty said. "I was just waiting for the right time to invite Gordon over to meet the whole family. I wanted to wait until---," she hesitated.

"Wait for what Mom?" Aliyah asked. "Were you waiting for me and Jeremiah to get back together? That may never happen. But at least I've been able to give you back your space. Having that attorney put Jeremiah out of the house was a good decision."

"What do you mean put Jeremiah out of the house?" Jamal looked alarmed.

"I went to a lawyer last week and asked him to put Jeremiah out," Aliyah said.

"But Jeremiah volunteered to move out before you even went to see the lawyer," Jamal said. "Why did you have to get a lawyer involved? You want to parade Jeremiah in front of a court, conducted by white men, to have him thrown out of his home?" Jamal was furious.

"When did Jeremiah volunteer to move out on his own?" Aliyah asked.

"A while ago," Jamal said. "I guess I forgot to tell you. But it's not right the way you are treating him Aliyah. He deserves a chance to explain his situation. Even Dad thinks so."

"What does Dad have to do with this?" Aliyah asked.

"I woke up this morning and remembered that Dad visited me in a dream. It's the first time I have ever dreamed about him. He asked me to convince you to talk to Jeremiah." Jamal gave her a serious look.

"I don't believe you," Aliyah said. You're just taking his side over mine. Why didn't you tell me that Jeremiah volunteered to move out of the house before now?"

"I told you I forgot. So much has been happening it just slipped my mind."

"He told me about it, Aliyah," Sheniqua said. "It happened before you saw Jeremiah at the theater."

"I didn't think about it again until Dad came to me this morning in the dream," Jamal said very convincingly.

When Aliyah left her mother's house she went directly to the gallery. It was getting late, well past nine o'clock. The children were sleeping in the back seat of the car. She was nervous about seeing Jeremiah again after so much time had lapsed, but the thought of reconciliation filled her with anticipation. Jamal and Betty had both convinced her that she owed it to the children and herself to at least talk to Jeremiah before going to see a lawyer again. She finally agreed with them, especially when Jamal convinced her that it was something their father wanted, too.

When she pulled up to the gallery, Aliyah removed her cell phone from her purse. She thought it best to call Jeremiah first and ask him to come downstairs since the children were sleeping. Just as she was about to push the send button to speed dial his number she noticed the red sports car pulling up two cars in front of her. *Miss Melody,* she said to herself. Aliyah quickly ended the call before Jeremiah's telephone rang. She watched as Miss Melody got out of the car and walked up to the door leading to the gallery. She had a very seductive walk. She wore a short, dark, tight skirt with a white sweater. She was carrying an ice bucket with what looked like a bottle of wine in it.

Jeremiah took his time answering the door. Miss Melody looked as though she was getting impatient, but she smiled broadly when the door finally opened. Aliyah didn't see Jeremiah, as Miss Melody appeared to barge through the door before it was barely open.

The door closed behind them. Aliyah sat in the car watching the closed door for what appeared to be a long time. For a brief moment she entertained the idea of barging in herself. *I have every right to,* she thought. *After all I am still his wife.* She looked in the back seat at her sleeping children and said out loud, "And these are his children."

After sitting in the car for about twenty minutes Aliyah finally started the engine to the SUV and drove away. When it really came down to it she had to admit that she was afraid. Afraid that her husband would tell her to her face that he didn't love her anymore. Afraid that if she confronted him in the presence of Miss Melody he would choose her over his wife. When had she become so insecure? Aliyah didn't know the answer to that question, but she knew it was a fact, a fact that disturbed her, and one that she just couldn't deal with.

Chapter 20

Jeremiah slept late Sunday morning. He'd had a restless night. He dreamed that his mother visited him. He hadn't dreamt about his mother since the days following her death when he was only fifteen years old. Back then he dreamed of her every night. She constantly talked to him about taking care of his younger sister, getting an education, and listening to his father and grandmother. The dream last night was similar. She was telling him to listen to his father. He'd awakened that morning feeling his mother's presence. When he looked across the room at her portrait, the eyes still appeared sad. Her spirit was there; he knew it. *Perhaps the egun gun sacrifice was working,* he thought.

The gallery didn't open until noon and he hadn't planned to work, it was his day off. He wanted to take a shower, but put the notion out of his head. He would have to go over to the Newark YMCA, on Broad Street, not far from the studio, in order to do that. He settled on washing up in the basin and brushing his teeth. He then practiced his yoga, meditated, and rearranged the studio to make more living space. Feeling hungry he fixed himself a cup of hot Ovaltine and sipped it while eating a piece of anisette toast from a package.

At three o'clock he put on his sweat suit and walked to the "Y." In the weight room the guys were talking about racism. Jeremiah listened, not making any contribution to the conversation himself.

"Do you remember what the former Secretary of Education said about aborting black babies to cut down on crime?" a weight lifter asked.

"Yeah, I remember. It was wrong to say aborting black babies would eliminate crime," a short squat man said, panting heavily.

"That was bad, but it revealed what the general sentiment of this country is," another weightlifter said.

"That's as bad as saying that aborting all white babies would eliminate racism in the world. Racism is the axis of evil we all need to work towards eliminating, know what I mean?" the short, squat man said.

All this talk about aborting babies is wrong. Jeremiah thought to himself. *Maybe its time that Black people begin to think about repatriating Africa. It seems that we are not wanted in America. With so many educated Africans leaving the continent and coming here, maybe educated African-Americans should consider going back to the motherland to counteract the brain drain that is being created.*

It was after six o'clock when Jeremiah returned to the studio. He had stopped downstairs at the Jazz Garden and picked up a take-out dinner of mostly vegetables, cabbage and okra, with tomatoes and corn. Cook had slipped a baked chicken leg in with his dinner as well as a piece of cornbread. Jeremiah changed into a T-shirt and a pair of loose fitting cotton pants with a drawstring waistband. He turned on the small television set he had taken from the storeroom and made himself comfortable on the divan.

After eating his dinner Jeremiah took out his copy of Walter Mosley's book, *What Next,* and read for a while with the baseball game playing in the background. He wondered what Aliyah was doing and when he would see the kids again. He soon dozed off. A constant loud sound awakened him. The buzzer in the gallery was sounding off indicating that someone was ringing the bell. Jeremiah looked at his watch; it was almost ten o'clock. *Who could be calling on him at this hour? Who even knew that he was there?* The studio was dark; the lights in the gallery had been turned off hours ago.

When he got downstairs he could see through the small window in the door that it was Miss Melody. Unbeknown to him Aliyah and his sleeping children were in her parked car right outside. He had barely opened the door when Miss Melody pushed past him, and entered the small foyer at the bottom of the steps.

"What brings you here," he asked, noticing the ice bucket and bottle of champagne in her hand.

"You wouldn't stay after the performance to celebrate my success with me, so I thought I would just bring the celebration to you." She waved the bottle of champagne in front of his face.

"How'd you know I was here?" Jeremiah asked as Miss Melody made her way up to the gallery.

"You know how fast word gets out around here. People saw you moving your things in. I would have come sooner, but I've been working so hard. I have performances every night of the week and a matinee on Wednesday. My understudy finally gave me a break tonight. I'm working my buns off, but I love it so much."

"Look, Melody, I'm happy for you, really I am. But, it's late, and I have to get ready for work tomorrow."

"Don't throw me out yet, Jeremiah," she said with a hurt little girl expression on her face. "Look I brought a bottle of champagne." She waved the bottle in his face again.

"I don't like champagne," he said. "Besides, like you said people around here don't miss a thing. I don't want any more rumors starting."

"People are going to talk regardless. They should mind their own business." She walked through the gallery and started up the stairs to his studio.

Jeremiah grabbed her arm to prevent her from going any further. "Look, Melody, he said again, I want you to go."

"Why can't we just have a toast to my success, Jeremiah? I owe it all to you. If you hadn't helped me I never would have gotten the part. Why can't we just have one little toast?"

Jeremiah gave her a doubtful look, but then said, "Okay, one little toast and then you have to leave." He released her arm and watched her scramble up the steps.

Once in the studio Miss Melody made herself right at home. She set the ice bucket on the desk and walked around looking at how Jeremiah had rearranged things.

"How long are you going to live up here?" she asked incredulously. "This place doesn't even have a shower." She crinkled her nose.

"I'm going to be here as long as necessary. I shower at the "Y.""

"Why don't you get your own apartment, or do you expect to get back with Aliyah?" Miss Melody looked in the small cabinet for some glasses.

"I hope to get back with my family. I want to get back with them." Jeremiah took some plastic cups out of his desk drawer.

"Plastic cups?" Miss Melody frowned. "We can't drink champagne out of plastic cups. This is good champagne. Don't you have any real glasses? Champagne flutes would be nice."

"I told you I don't like champagne. Why would I have champagne flutes up here? It's plastic or nothing." He put two plastic cups on the desk.

"Okay, plastic it is." She handed him the champagne bottle to pop the cork. "You'll like this champagne. It's one of the best. Almost fifty dollars a bottle."

"I don't like champagne even if it cost a thousand dollars a bottle." Jeremiah popped the cork and sat down on the stool at his art table.

Miss Melody poured the champagne into the plastic cups. She walked the short distance from the desk to the table and handed Jeremiah one of the cups. "I don't know how you can make a toast without taking a sip," she said.

"Okay, here's to your success, Melody. I hope this is just the beginning for you. May you become the biggest, brightest, and happiest star in the galaxy." He touched his cup to hers and took a small sip before setting the cup down on the table.

"Thanks Jeremiah." Miss Melody smiled at him, took a sip of her champagne, and then set her cup down on the table next to his. In one quick movement she put her arms around his neck and kissed his lips.

Jeremiah tried to pry himself from her grasp, but she held on. She moved her shapely body between his legs as he sat on the stool. She smelled nice and felt nice, too. Despite his love for his wife, his longing for his wife, and his desire to be back with his family Jeremiah felt his manhood rising. Miss Melody kissed his face; she tightened her arms around his neck. He tried again to push her away. This time he managed to put some space between them. He tried to stand up but quickly noticed that the thin, cotton, loose fitting pants he had on revealed a gigantic erection that strained to free itself. The worst part of all was that, Miss Melody, she noticed it, too, and decided to seize the moment.

———————————

Takeoff from Newark Airport was delayed for almost two hours on Tuesday morning. Sitting in the presidential suite at Continental Airlines terminal waiting to board the plane, Aliyah thought about Sunday night. She'd had a difficult time falling asleep herself after putting the children to bed and watching them drift off. She couldn't put Jeremiah and Miss Melody out of her mind. She imagined them entwined in each other's arms as they lay on the divan that Jeremiah kept in his studio. It had been a long time since she had felt his arms around her, and she longed for his touch.

On Monday Aliyah had asked Jean to call Jeremiah to let him know that she would be out of town for a couple of days and that the children would be staying with her mother. Jean let him know that he could visit the children if he wished. He didn't ask to speak to Aliyah, but he asked Jean to wish her a safe trip.

Monday night Aliyah had gone to bed early. She had an early morning flight to Atlanta for the award ceremony. She had no difficulty falling asleep perhaps due to the fatigue she was feeling from working so hard throughout the day. Nevertheless, she fell into a deep slumber almost as soon as her head hit the pillow. Almost immediately she started to dream. Her father had come to pay her a visit. It wasn't the first time that her father had visited her in a dream, but this time was different.

In the dream Aliyah was a little girl. Her puppy had been run over by a car. Her father picked the puppy up, wrapped him in a blanket and took him away. Aliyah had cried and cried. When her father returned home he didn't have the puppy. He tried to tell her that the puppy was in the hospital. Aliyah couldn't fathom a hospital for puppies. She didn't believe her father. She thought he was making it up to make her feel better. She cried and cried.

A week later her father came home with her puppy. The puppy was bandaged around the middle, but he was alive. She remembered how she had smiled and smiled, and how her father told her he would never lie to her. That she must always trust him.

Aliyah was startled out of her thoughts by the announcement of the boarding of her plane. She quickly gathered her carry on bag and made her way to the gate. For the third or fourth time since the dream she wondered what her father was trying to tell her. Maybe he wanted her to listen to what her brother had told her. Jamal had said his father wanted her to talk to Jeremiah. *Is that what he wants me to do? How can I talk to him if he's always so busy with Miss Melody? Maybe my offering to the ancestors will work. Maybe they will help me.*

Atlanta was exciting. Aliyah could feel the energy as soon as she deplaned and took a taxi to the Marriot Marquis. She had one of the better suites reserved in her name. The city was bustling with attendees for various conferences and conventions. Aliyah welcomed the excitement of being away from home in a lively city such as Atlanta. The award ceremony wasn't scheduled until later that evening, but she had come early enough to prepare an acceptance speech just in case *Enigma* was the winner for editorial excellence.

After writing a rough draft of her acceptance speech, Aliyah showered, dressed and left the room to have lunch in a popular restaurant at the Hilton, just across the street. She wasn't particularly happy to be dining alone in a distant city but she was used to it. It gave her an opportunity to people watch and listen in on conversations about what was happening in the publishing world. She enjoyed listening to different perspectives.

She followed the hostess to an inconspicuous table in the main dining room where she could see everything going on in the restaurant without being obtrusive herself. She loved studying people when they were unaware that they were being observed. As soon as the waitress left she scoped the restaurant for people that she could study. She honed in on a table of women directly in front of her. They were dressed to kill in designer outfits and talking up a blue streak about the award that was to be bestowed on some lucky magazine for best fashion. Although Aliyah was interested in fashion, it was not something that she liked to dwell on. She let her eyes rove on.

Several tables to her right sat three men and two women. Aliyah thought she recognized one of the men so she leaned in for a closer view. Sure enough it was someone she knew, Mark Griffin, a photojournalist she used to date before she met Jeremiah. He was still as handsome as ever. He still wore his hair in locks only they were longer now, shoulder length. She watched him for a while. He was so animated explaining something to the others. The excitement in his mannerisms suggested that it must be something very important. She let her eyes move on.

To her far left she spotted an interracial couple that appeared deeply in love. They were holding hands and staring into each other's eyes. A second look told Aliyah that it was Dotty and Derek. She watched them for several minutes. Dotty, all smiles, was listening, as Derek appeared to be absorbed in what he was saying. Aliyah sat back in her seat, she didn't want them to see her. She knew that Dotty would, out of courtesy, invite her to join them at their table, and that, she didn't want to do.

Aliyah let her eyes wander back to the table where Mark was sitting. This time she was surprised to find that Mark had spotted her too. He smiled when their eyes met. Aliyah was glad that she was sitting so far from him and that he couldn't see her blush. She couldn't help but smile back. Probably a mistake because Mark got up and started walking towards her secluded table.

"Aliyah it's so wonderful to see you again," Mark greeted her when he reached the table. "How have you been?" He stood at her table, smiling broadly.

"I'm great, Mark." Her smile matched his.

"You won't believe this, but I was hoping that I would run into you. As soon as I heard that *Enigma* was one of the nominees I was hopeful that you would attend. You look great." He gave her a thorough going over. "How long has it been, seven, eight years?"

"Something like that," Aliyah said, checking him out, too. Mark was a good-looking man, tall, dark, and handsome. The same sex appeal that Aliyah remembered from almost a decade ago emanated in exuberance from him now.

"Are you still married with kids?" He gave her a look that hinted he hoped it wasn't true.

"Still married, still with kids," Aliyah said.

"Are you happy?" His eyes searched her face. Mark could always read her like a book.

Avoiding his question and his look, Aliyah asked, "What about you?"

"Never married, no kids." He shrugged his shoulders, but kept his smile. "How long will you be staying in Atlanta?" Mark shifted feet, waiting for an invitation to sit down.

"I'm leaving tomorrow morning, and you?"

"I'll be here for a few more days. I have a couple of interviews set up for later in the week. Have you eaten yet?" He looked hopeful.

"I'm still waiting to give the waiter my order," Aliyah said. "Looks like the service here is not that great."

"Well, they're pretty busy with all the conferences going on.

There must be at least three or four conferences going on this week as well as the awards ceremony. Is it okay if I join you for lunch? I'm starving." Mark gave her a sexy smile.

"What about your friends?" Aliyah asked.

"They're not really friends just business associates that I've become acquainted with over the years. I just ran into them today, it wasn't planned. I'd much rather catch up on what's been happening in your life." He took the seat across from her.

"Well, there isn't much to tell." Aliyah avoided making eye contact. You must know that I'm the editor-in-chief for *Enigma Magazine* now."

"Yes, I know that. As a matter of fact that's the reason I attributed to my not getting any assignments from *Enigma*. I figured you were still upset with me because of the way we broke up."

"That's ridiculous. When I became editor-in-chief I wanted to explore and find my own people. As I recall you got a few assignments after Joe Simmons retired. You worked with my assistant, Dotty Caprio."

"That's true. But I didn't get very many assignments from her, though. I think I saw Ms. Caprio here in Atlanta, today."

"Yes, she's sitting over there." Aliyah gestured to indicate where Dotty was sitting but noticed that Dotty and Derek were no longer in the restaurant. "They must have left," she said just as the waiter came to take their orders.

Throughout lunch Mark was his old charming self. He made Aliyah laugh with stories of his adventures all over the world taking pictures and bringing exciting stories back home. Aliyah shared some stories of her own about her recent travels to West Africa gathering information about issues pertaining to women of African descent.

"I see you're still interested in targeting the African-American readership," Mark said, and then smiled.

"Yes, Mark. That's my mission in life I guess. I would like to believe, as you apparently do, that America is just one big happy country with no biases or prejudices and certainly no racism. I believe the events of Hurricane Katrina convinced a lot of Americans, especially African-Americans that black America fares a lot worse than white America due to the evils of racism. If you don't see that now then there is no hope for you." She folded her napkin and put it on the table.

"I know that Aliyah. I know that people of African descent are discriminated against around the world. But really, Aliyah, what can we do about it?"

"Well Mark, as journalists we can do one of two things as I see it. We can ignore it as you apparently have chosen to do, or we can expose it. I understand that 'ignorance is bliss' and that many African-Americans would rather be blissful than suffer the consequences of exposure. As for me, I would rather suffer the consequences. You once told me that I would never be able to work for a white magazine with my views, and that I would never make the kind of money that I could make if I worked for a white magazine, but I'm happy doing what I do. I hope you are, too." Aliyah opened her purse to get her credit card.

"I've changed, Aliyah. Read some of the stories that I wrote about Hurricane Katrina and look at the pictures that I took before you pass judgment on me. Lunch is my treat." Mark grabbed the bill that the waiter brought to the table. "Will I see you later," he asked, sensing that Aliyah was ready to leave?

"Win or lose *Enigma* will be hosting a party in our hospitality suite after the ceremony. Please come as my guest." She walked towards the door. "Oh, thanks for lunch," she said over her shoulder.

The party in the hospitality suite turned out to be a real lively celebration. *Enigma* had managed to capture three of the most prestigious awards including the one for editorial excellence. The publishers were delighted and gave her full credit for making it all possible. Dotty was in her glory because *Enigma* had also received recognition for its fashion creativity, an area she had always paid particular attention to. The champagne was flowing freely and everyone appeared to be having a wonderful time.

After two hours in the hospitality suite, Aliyah was ready to go back to her room. By the time she made her way across the large room, receiving congratulations and toasting with everyone she encountered on the way, she was feeling a little giddy. She hadn't been paying attention and had gone way beyond her two-glass maximum of champagne. One of the first people she ran into on the other side of the room was Mark Griffin. He had been paying attention to her champagne consumption, and was well aware of her reaction to too much of the bubbly liquid.

"Hi Mark," she said, greeting him warmly with a big smile. "Glad you could make it."

"I wouldn't have missed it." Mark smiled back at her. "You look wonderful," he said, checking her out from head to toe.

Aliyah couldn't help but notice the gleam in Mark's eye. She liked knowing that she could still put that gleam in a man's eye. "Do you like my new dress?" She twirled around, something totally out of character for her, showing off her elegant, off the shoulder, clingy, party dress.

"Yes," Mark said reaching out to grab her before she stumbled. "You always looked good in red. Let me walk you to your room." He held her arm.

Aliyah let Mark lead her to the elevator, grateful that she had a strong arm to hold onto. As they waited for the elevator she remembered that it was on an elevator that she'd had her first encounter with Mark. She recalled the story for him. By the time the elevator reached her floor she and Mark were in stitches laughing about that first encounter.

"We had some good times together, Aliyah," Mark said as they walked down the corridor leading to her suite. "Too bad it ended."

He gave her a remorseful look.

"It ended because you cheated on me, Mark."

"I didn't mean to," he said. "Why couldn't you have forgiven me?"

"Is that all you men think? You think that you can cheat and then be forgiven and that's the end of it. Why do men cheat in the first place?"

"Because we're stupid. We never know what we have until we lose it. I'm so sorry I lost you." His eyes looked all soft and sexy.

They both heard Aliyah's telephone ringing as they approached the door. Mark watched as she fumbled with the key trying to open the door. He gently took the key from her hand and opened the door. Aliyah ran to get the telephone, but it stopped ringing just as she was about to pick up the receiver. *Who could that have been?* she wondered.

Before Aliyah could turn around she felt Mark's breath on her neck. She froze where she stood. Encouraged Mark put his arms around her waist. He kissed her hair. Aliyah felt herself relaxing from his touch.

Chapter 21

Jeremiah was shocked when he entered the Jazz Garden for dinner on Wednesday evening. Sitting at one of the back tables, finishing up their meal was none other than his father and his mother-in-law. He stood there staring incredulously until they noticed him. Mr. Jones beckoned his son to the table.

"It's wonderful to see you again, Son," Mr. Jones said, giving Jeremiah a big hug. "How are you?"

"I'm just shocked to see you here. Why didn't you call to let me know you were coming?"

"I've been trying to call you since yesterday morning, New York time. Why haven't you been answering your cell phone? I tried to reach you at home, no answer there either. Finally I decided to call Betty. She just picked me up at the airport a couple of hours ago.

"Since yesterday?" Jeremiah was still incredulous. "What was the urgency that you just jumped on a plane and traveled to New Jersey all the way from Senegal without letting me know you were coming?"

"I can't explain it to you now, Son, I just had this compelling need to see you and my grandchildren. Somehow I knew you were in trouble and that you needed me here. From what Betty has been telling me I'm glad I came."

Jeremiah looked at his mother-in-law who gave him a weak smile.

"We're leaving now," Jeremiah senior informed his son. Betty is taking me to her house to visit my grandchildren. You go ahead with your business. I'll catch up with you a little later on." He left a few bills on the table for the tip, grabbed Betty's arm and walked toward the door, leaving a dumbfounded Jeremiah staring at their backs.

What's going on? Jeremiah wondered as he made his way to the bar where he decided he would eat his dinner. *The strangest things are happening.* He let his mind go back to Sunday night when Miss Melody had almost succeeded in seducing him in his studio.

Jeremiah still wondered how far things would have gone with Miss Melody if the portrait of his mother had not fallen, making a loud crashing noise, startling him and Miss Melody out of their wits. Jeremiah had looked about the room frantically to find out what had caused the noise. When he noticed the portrait on the floor he had crossed the room to investigate, followed by a thoroughly disappointed Miss Melody.

Jeremiah had looked around the studio as if someone deliberately caused the portrait to fall. He was sure that it had been well secured to the wall. The portrait had landed in such a way that his mother's eyes appeared to be staring right at him. The eyes were angry now.

"What are looking for?" Miss Melody had asked from behind him.

"I don't know," Jeremiah had said. "How could the picture just fall like that?" he had asked himself aloud. "This is really weird. She must be in here," he said, referring to his mother's spirit.

"Who must be here?" Miss Melody had looked at him with a weird expression on her face. "Your wife must have super natural powers if you think that she had something to do with this. Let's go sit on the divan," she had said, reaching for his hand.

"You've got to go." Jeremiah had grabbed her arm and rushed her towards the stairs.

"That woman must really have a hold on you," Miss Melody had said as Jeremiah practically shoved her out the door.

Eating his last fork full of green beans, Jeremiah wondered what was going to happen next. He knew that the spirit of his ancestors, his mother's in particular, was involved in the incident at the gallery as well as his father's hasty decision to come to Newark. The thought that his mother had come to his aid made Jeremiah smile to himself. Things may have been out of his control, but he knew now that his ancestral spirits had the situation well under control.

When he left the club Jeremiah returned to his studio where he put the finishing touches on the painting for his mother-in-law. He'd planned to have the painting ready in time for her birthday, only two days away. Just as he put his brushes and paints away the telephone rang. It was his father asking him to come back down to the club and have a drink with him. Jeremiah looked at the wall clock, *9PM already,* he thought.

"The children are wonderful," Mr. Jones said after his son was seated at the table. They sat at a small table for two against the wall of the club, isolated enough to give them the privacy they needed. "Mandela was so glad to see me again. He asked me when we were going fishing again." The older man chuckled. "Nia is so beautiful, just like her mother. Son, you have a beautiful family. I know how much you must miss them. Why didn't you tell me about the separation?"

"I didn't think it would last this long," Jeremiah said, looking into his father's face. "I really didn't know it would last this long," he said again, shaking his head, still in disbelief.

"I thought something was wrong by the way Aliyah behaved in Senegal," Mr. Jones said. "She was so quiet and appeared to be carrying a heavy burden, but she would not talk about it. She walked the beach everyday, and I thought she might have been crying. I didn't want to pry, though."

"I knew she was unhappy, Dad. But she would never tell me what the problem was. Believe me I had no clue until she returned from Africa." He looked down at his hands.

"Well, thank God your mother told me to come here. I plan to get to the bottom of this mess. I will not have my grandchildren raised in a broken home environment."

"Mother told you to come?" Jeremiah looked up in amazement. "When and how?"

"She has come to visit me in my dreams every night for the past two weeks. She said I must come to help you. I haven't dreamed about her in a long time. I knew I had to come even though you hadn't said a word."

"You're not going to believe this, but I knew you were coming," Jeremiah said. "I asked the ancestors for help and here you are. What are you going to do?"

"I am going to open the lines of communication between you and your wife. Nothing can be resolved unless there is communication. Tell me the truth, Son, are you having an affair with this woman, Miss Melody?"

"No, Dad. I'm not having an affair with her." He looked into his father's eyes.

"Jeremiah, you have never lied to me. I know that you are not lying now. So tell me why were you kissing Miss Melody in your studio?"

Jeremiah told his father about the mistaken kiss.

"What about the earring in your bedroom?"

He told his father about the rehearsals for the Sassy role, and how Miss Melody lost her earring as she snooped through the house.

"Well, Son, I'm satisfied with your explanations. We just have to get Aliyah to listen now. I'm going to spend the night with your sister, Naomi, but I will be visiting Aliyah tomorrow. She has agreed to talk to me. I telephoned her in Atlanta, and she said that she would be home sometime this evening. I will call you after I have spoken to her." Mr. Jones got up to leave.

"Won't you need a ride to Naomi's house?" Jeremiah asked.

"No, Son, I've rented a car. I still remember my way around Newark."

When Jeremiah got back up to his studio he had a big smile on his face. After talking to his father he was confident that somehow things were going to come together. He didn't know how or when, but he knew that the ancestral spirits were busy making things happen that would reunite him with his family.

He lay on the divan thinking about Aliyah, wondering when he would be able to hold her in his arms again in their king size bed. He knew that they had a lot to talk about before things could be right between them again. He thought about what he would say and anticipated her response. Then he thought about making love to his wife again, and how much he had missed her touch. Finally he fell asleep with that same smile on his face.

The flight to Newark had been delayed for unknown reasons. Aliyah sat in the presidential lounge of Continental Airlines in Atlanta for over two hours waiting to board the plane that would take her home. She really didn't mind the delay. She had a lot on her mind and wanted to think things out. Strange things were happening and the only explanation she could think of was that her offering to the ancestors was working.

The first indication she had that the ancestral spirits were at work helping to resolve her marital situation was when Jamal said that their father had visited him in a dream and told him to encourage her to talk to Jeremiah. That had been strange, but even stranger was the phone call that had come just as she was about to succumb to the charms of Mark Griffin right in her hotel suite.

Aliyah wanted to believe that she would not have succumbed to Mark's charms, but as she recalled the events of the previous night she was not so sure. She'd left Mark standing in the doorway of her hotel suite when she ran to answer the ringing telephone, only to have it stop ringing just as she reached for it. Mark, who had come into the room behind her caught her completely off guard when he put his arms around her as she stood with her back to him wondering who had called.

Aliyah recalled the consolation she had felt at his touch. She could feel his breath on her hair and then his lips on her neck.

It was really a good feeling. It had been so long since she had felt the comfort of a man's arms around her. She had been under such stress the last few months. She was feeling relaxed from the champagne she had consumed at the party. That, along with the strong arms and the hard body, was enough to break down her defenses and cause her to become aroused at Mark's touch. Mark was the comfort that she needed at the moment and if the telephone hadn't rang again she didn't know where her feelings might have taken her.

The telephone call had been from her father-in-law. He was at the Senegal Airport about to board a plane to Newark. He had been trying to reach her and Jeremiah without success. Finally he had called her mother in desperation. Betty had given him Aliyah's hotel number and he had called there. He thought he dialed the wrong number the first time and tried again. He was glad that he did. He just wanted her to know that he was coming to Newark to visit her and the kids. They made a date to have dinner together on Thursday evening. He wanted to talk to her.

Aliyah had been stunned by the telephone call. *What was that all about?* she wondered. After she had hung up the telephone Mark had reached for her again, only her mood had changed. She quickly ushered him out of her room. The look of surprise and disappointment on Mark's face almost made her laugh. She was so grateful that her father-in-law had called. He had prevented her from making a serious mistake; one she knew she would have regretted for the rest of her life. Surely the ancestors were responsible for the phone call coming as it did, just in the nick of time.

The plane ride to Newark was only a couple of hours long. Aliyah tried to read. She loved Octavia Butler's books and had purchased *Fledgling* in Atlanta to read at the airport; only she had too much on her mind to really concentrate on reading. Wondering what was going to happen next consumed her thoughts. *How can the ancestors resolve this? How can they make Jeremiah's infidelity go away?*

Aliyah took a taxi from the airport to the brownstone. The cab driver had an attitude. He was upset that his fare would be low due to the short distance from the airport to her home in downtown Newark. He would have preferred getting a passenger that was going to Baskinridge or Princeton NJ or some other more remote place from the airport. *Too bad,* she thought. She had gotten used to the attitude of Newark Airport cabdrivers whenever she took a cab home, which was seldom. How did they think Newarkers were supposed to get home from the airport?

The house was quiet when she came in. The kids were still in South Orange with her mother. Jean was going to bring them home in the morning. Aliyah walked into the kitchen and turned on the teakettle. She sank into the kitchen chair and thought about Jeremiah. Oh how she missed him at times like this. In the past whenever she would return home from a business trip he would pick her up at the airport, and they would stop off for a bite to eat or a glass of wine. They would grin into each other's face, so glad to be back together after a two or three day separation.

The humming of the teakettle brought her back to the present. After she brewed herself a cup of strong chamomile tea that she took upstairs to her bedroom, she kicked off her shoes, and sat in the chair near the window, overlooking the street. Aliyah took a sip of the tea and looked out at the street. It was a nice street, lined with colonial style street lamps and well-maintained brownstone homes. Clay pots of various sizes holding late blooming begonias and geraniums and colorful fall chrysanthemums sat on almost all the front stoops. Aliyah wondered what had brought her father-in-law to town so suddenly, and what did he want to talk to her about?

She had been sitting in the chair for over an hour when the telephone rang. *Who can this be?* she wondered as she picked up the handset.

"Hi Sweetheart," her mother's voice came through the receiver. "When did you get in?"

"A couple of hours ago. How are the kids?"

"Wonderful," Betty said. "They were so excited to see their grandfather. He just left a little while ago. We had a nice talk." She let out a long sigh.

"What did you talk about?" Aliyah was curious.

"You and Jeremiah, what else." Betty let out another sigh.

"Well, what did he have to say?"

"I think I'll wait and let him talk to you in person. He told me that he's going to see you tomorrow. Just listen to him sweetheart, he's only trying to help."

"How can he help mother?" Aliyah was doubtful.

"I've been dreaming a lot about your father lately, Aliyah. I thought it might be because I was feeling guilty. Now I'm not so sure it was for that reason."

"What do you mean, Mother. Why would you be feeling guilty."

"You know, because I've been dating Gordon. But in my dreams your father is very reassuring. He keeps telling me that everything is going to be all right. I think he's talking about you and Jeremiah. Promise me that when your father-in-law talks to you tomorrow you will have an open mind and an open heart."

"You know I will mother, but I don't know how he can change the fact that Jeremiah was unfaithful to me."

"Maybe he wasn't, sweetheart, maybe he wasn't."

"What do you mean by that?" Aliyah sat up in her chair.

"Just keep an open mind when you talk to your father-in-law," Betty repeated."

Jean came in bright and early with the children the next morning. Aliyah could hear them running through the house looking for her.

"Mommy, Mommy," Mandela called out. "Mommy where are you?"

"Up here," Aliyah answered, moving to the top of the steps

waiting to scoop up her beautiful children.

"Hi Mommy," Mandela said, giving her a big hug and a smile.

"Ha Mahmy," Nia tried to imitate her brother.

Aliyah grabbed them both by the hand and led them into the nursery.

"Grandpa came to see me at Grandma's house," Mandela said excitedly.

"I know," Aliyah told him. "He's coming to see us later on today."

"He's coming to our house?" Mandela looked at her with wide eyes.

"Yes, he'll be here for dinner."

"I want to show him my piano." Mandela ran to get the keyboard Jeremiah had recently bought him. "I want to show him what I can play."

The Morning went by quickly. Aliyah worked up in her office for a good portion of the day, but she quit at 3:30 to start dinner. Her father-in-law was coming at 5:30. Jean had taken Nia with her to pick Mandela up from school. She'd said they would be stopping off at the library on the way home, giving Aliyah a couple of hours alone. She checked to make sure that she had all the ingredients she needed to make Joloff Rice, a Senegalese dish that was eaten everyday by most of the people of Senegal. Mr. Jones was accustomed to the dish, and Aliyah wanted to surprise him with her culinary skills.

By five o'clock the Joloff Rice had been prepared. Aliyah was at the sink washing red leaf lettuce for a salad when Jean came in with the children.

"Where's grandpa?" Mandela asked. "You said he was coming."

"He'll be here soon." Aliyah continued tearing up lettuce, watching as Jean took the children upstairs to get them washed for dinner. *What did her mother mean when she had said that maybe Jeremiah hadn't been unfaithful?*

At exactly 5:30 the doorbell rang. Aliyah, still in her apron, went to answer the door. Before she could get the door open Mandela ran up behind her yelling, "Grandpa, Grandpa."

"Hello, hello, hello," Mr. Jones said as soon as the door opened.

"Hello, hello, hello," Mandela said, grabbing his grandfather around his legs holding on tightly.

Mr. Jones reached down and scooped him up with one arm, and put the other arm around his daughter-in-law giving her a kiss on the cheek.

"Hello," a smiling Aliyah said, giving him a hug and leading him into the house.

Jean appeared holding Nia who wanted to get in on the excitement. "Lo, lo, lo," Nia said, causing everyone to laugh.

As Jean made her exit for the evening, Aliyah and her father-in-law made their way to the kitchen.

"Something smells familiar." Mr. Jones made a sniffing noise with his nose.

"Simone taught me how to make Joloff Rice while I was in Senegal. I hope you enjoy mine as much as you enjoy it at home." She gave him a worried smile.

"Thank you for going to so much trouble, my dear. I always knew my son had a gem for a wife."

After they sat down to eat at the kitchen table, at Mr. Jones' insistence, they made small talk to include the children. Aliyah could hardly contain herself. She was dying to find out what her father-in-law had to say to her. There were a couple of times during dinner when she slipped and asked something relating to the nature of his visit, only to have him respond with, "That can wait until later, my dear, or not in front of the children."

After dinner while Aliyah tidied up the kitchen, her father-in-law took the children upstairs to hear Mandela play his keyboard. *What could he possible say that would make a difference?* she wondered as she filled plastic containers with leftovers, and stacked dirty dishes in the dishwasher.

By the time she finished in the kitchen and went upstairs Nia was asleep on her grandfathers lap and Mandela was listening to a story his grandfather was telling him. Aliyah listened at the door for a while. The story was about Jeremiah Jr. when he was a little boy. Aliyah smiled to herself. *This is what family is supposed to be all about. Passing down the history of one generation to the next. How fortunate my children are to have a grandfather who is willing to do that.*

314

While Aliyah got the children ready for bed, her father-in-law waited downstairs for her. When she came into the living room, she noticed that he had made himself comfortable on the sofa, and had poured them two glasses of sherry.

"Sit down." He gestured to a chair and handed her one of the glasses.

"Am I going to need this?" Aliyah took the glass of sherry from his hand and settled back in the chair.

"I think it will be good for you to be relaxed while we talk. I don't want you to think that I'm meddling in your business, but I want you to know that when my children or grandchildren are unhappy I consider that to be my business. You, my dear, are one of my children."

"Thanks for being concerned about me."

"I suspected a problem when you were in Senegal. I had hoped it would work out in due time. Then, when I didn't hear from Jeremiah, I thought everything had worked out. I was surprised when Jeremiah's mother appeared in my dreams and insisted that I come to Newark to help him." He took a sip of his sherry, but kept his eyes on her.

"His mother?" Aliyah was incredulous. "How did she know?"

"Her spirit is very much alive," he said. "From what Jeremiah has been telling me he summoned her spirit to help him get his family back together."

"Oh," Aliyah said. "He wants to get back together?"

"Most definitely." Mr. Jones moved to the edge of the sofa to make better eye contact. "He never wanted his family to be apart."

"He should have thought about that before he cheated on me," Aliyah said sarcastically, tears beginning to form in her eyes.

"But, my dear, he never cheated on you, he loves you too much for that."

"Did he tell you that? If he did, then he is a liar. I saw him with my own eyes."

"What did you see?" Mr. Jones took another sip of his sherry and leaned forward in his chair.

"I saw his kissing Miss Melody." Aliyah looked at her father-in-law, unashamed that tears were now running down her face.

"That was a mistake," he said.

"How could it have been a mistake?"

He told her the story that his son had told him about the circumstances surrounding the kiss in Jeremiah's studio. "Is it so hard to believe that he thought you had changed your mind and come to the studio to surprise him?" Without waiting for a response he continued to speak. "Apparently not, because you did just that, arriving only a few seconds after Miss Melody surprised him. My son told me that she was even wearing your scent."

"Oh," was all that Aliyah could say. She supposed that could have happened. Maybe she should have stuck around a little longer and not run away like a frightened little rabbit. "Well that might explain the kiss, but did he tell you about the earring in my

316

bedroom?" She gave her father-in-law a look that defied him to do so.

"Did you know that he was helping Miss Melody rehearse for the role of Sassy in the Broadway musical?"

"No." Aliyah was all ears, now.

"Well he helped her get the part." Mr. Jones sat back in the chair. "The day that she lost her earring in your house was the same morning of her audition for the part. That's the reason for her being in your house. As for her earring in your bedroom, well---" he explained the circumstances to her.

"What about the newspaper article?" Aliyah was still a little doubtful.

"Jeremiah had no control over that," Mr. Jones said in defense of his son. "The newspaper article was wrong." Mr. Jones finished the last of his sherry, then got up to leave. "I have given you a lot to think about, my dear. I hope that the next time I see you, you will have weighed the evidence and come to the same conclusion that I have. Jeremiah is not a liar. He has never lied to me or to you. He loves you. Now you listen to him the next time he wants to talk to you about this." He let himself out of the house while Aliyah sat in the chair dumbfounded.

Chapter
22

The YMCA on Broad Street in downtown Newark was a well-utilized building. The clientele came from all walks of life. Some of the most-well-to-do residents of the city and out-of-towners working in the city frequented the gym and swam regularly in the pool. College students from Rutgers University, Seton Hall Law School, University of Medicine and Dentistry of New Jersey and New Jersey Institute of Technology occupied rooms on some of the lower floors while they waited for dormitory space to become available. Rooms at the top of the building were occupied by some of the neediest residents of the city, the homeless.

Jeremiah had become a daily visitor to the "Y" since his separation from his family. He used the weight room and occasionally took a dip in the pool, but his main purpose for going to the "Y" was to shower. Generally after he finished dinner at the

Jazz Garden he would walk over to the "Y", complete his workout, shower, and then head back to his studio.

Tonight as he walked across Broad Street, making his way back to his studio, he noticed the clearness of the sky. There was a full moon casting plenty of light on the already well-lit downtown area. Trees, not fully shed of their leaves, cast a shadowy, ominous look on the pavement. Generally the streets were deserted this time of night, but Jeremiah had begun to notice in his nightly walks back and forth to the "Y" that the streets were becoming livelier. Downtown Newark was beginning to flourish once again after dark. There were new clubs and restaurants opening on a regular basis. People working in the city no longer hesitated to stop off after work to have dinner or drinks with friends. The construction of the new sports arena was in full swing, promising to spur even more activity in the area.

As he turned the corner onto New Street, Jeremiah noticed a young man panhandling a couple of young women walking towards a parking lot. One of the women reached into her purse to give the young man a bill. Jeremiah stopped and waited until she closed her purse. He stood and watched as the women continued their walk into the lot, and the man walked off in the opposite direction. Jeremiah then continued walking towards Halsey Street satisfied that the women would be safe.

Newarkers were an eclectic group, encompassing the young and the old, white, black and brown people. The city had its share of vice, but it was also full of goodness. There was an abundance of ignorance and poverty, but some of the wisest and wealthiest people in the State lived in Newark. Although the crime rate had been steadily dropping in the city, Jeremiah knew that children, women, and the elderly were still prey to some of the most unscrupulous types that would take advantage of the most vulnerable.

Once settled in the studio, Jeremiah lay on the divan listening to the radio play some of his favorite music. He wondered if his father had met with Aliyah yet. He quickly glanced at the clock on the wall and saw that it was almost nine o'clock. He had confided in his father all that he knew about Aliyah's suspicions. His father now knew as much as Jeremiah knew himself. *Can he convince Aliyah that I'm innocent?* he wondered.

At nine-fifteen the telephone rang. Jeremiah got up to answer it knowing that it could only be his father.

"Hello, Son," the older man said.

"Hi." Jeremiah was full of anticipation.

"I'm downstairs in the club. Do you want me to come up or will you come down."

"Come upstairs," Jeremiah said. He didn't want to discuss his marriage in the club.

Once upstairs Mr. Jones looked around at Jeremiah's living quarters.

"So, this is what you have been reduced to?" he asked.

"It appears that way for awhile anyway." Jeremiah pulled up a chair for his father before making himself comfortable on the divan.

"I just left your children. They're the most adorable children I have ever seen," Mr. Jones said still checking out the studio. "I can imagine how you must feel not being with them."

"It's tough," Jeremiah said anxious to know what happened. "But, I spend plenty of time with them. It's just different having to take them out all the time. I don't want them to visit me here, as you can see this place is not adequate for children. If things are not going to work out with Aliyah, then I'll have to find an apartment."

"I don't think it will come to that, Son; but what I don't understand is how things got to this point."

"Why don't you think it will come to that? Has Aliyah said something to you?"

"No. But I left her with plenty to think about. She's a very unhappy woman."

"She should be. She brought this all on me, the children, and herself. At first I was hurt and disappointed. Lately I've been angry with her. This was all so unnecessary." Jeremiah looked at his father hoping for understanding.

"I understand how you feel, Son." Mr. Jones gave Jeremiah a sympathetic look. "But you do want a reconciliation, don't you?"

"I don't know, Dad. This marriage thing is so hard. Just when I thought everything was perfect, it all blows up in my face. I know

I can't go through this again. I definitely don't want a marriage that is not based on trust and respect."

"Communication is the key, Son. If there is no communication, then there is not trust. How did things get so far with the two of you not even talking to each other?"

"I don't know. I wanted to talk, but she just shut down. How am I supposed to know what she is thinking if she doesn't communicate it to me? I know my wife pretty well, Dad, but I can't be expected to read her mind."

"Then tell her that, Son."

"When am I supposed to do that, Dad? She hasn't called me in Lord knows how long, and she refuses to take calls from me. If she has something to say to me about the kids she speaks through the children's nanny, or her lawyer, her secretary, her mother, or her brother, anyone, except me. I'm sick of this." Jeremiah stood up and paced the room.

"Sometimes it's better to speak through others," Mr. Jones said. "You get a different perspective. In this case a mediator was necessary. Aliyah was too angry and too hurt to trust herself to speak to you. Don't worry, Son, between her mother and me we will have you communicating again soon. Aliyah has heard your version of the story now. She just has to digest it."

"Well I'm angry and hurt, too, you know."

"Yes, I know that, Son. Why do you think I am here? Your mother told me to come and I came. Things are going to get better now. Trust me. It's Betty's birthday. I understand that Jamal and Sheniqua are having a birthday dinner in her honor at their home this weekend; she invited me. You'll come, too, won't you?" Mr. Jones gave his son a pleading look.

"No one invited me," Jeremiah said.

"I'm sure they'll want you there. You can come as my guest. You've got to start communicating with your wife. This will be a perfect time."

"I'm sorry, Dad. I didn't mean to imply that I'm not grateful for your help. If it wasn't for you and Jamal I wouldn't have anyone on my side. I was feeling really alone and lonely before you came. Thanks for coming to my rescue."

Mr. Jones reached out to give his son a hug. "You can always count on me, Son. Even after I'm gone from this earth. You know how to contact my spirit just like you contacted your mother. We will always be there for you." He sighed. "I'm tired now, Son. I think I'll go back to your sister's house and get some rest."

"How is Naomi?" Jeremiah asked as he walked his father to the door.

"She's wonderful, and so are the children. When was the last time you looked in on them?"

"About two weeks ago," Jeremiah said. "I know I don't see them enough, but the gallery has been keeping me pretty busy, and Naomi has been pretty busy herself. Maybe we can all get together before you leave. How long will you be staying?"

"As long as I am needed." Father and son hugged again before the older man departed.

After his father left for Naomi's house, Jeremiah turned the volume on the radio back up and made himself comfortable on the divan. He wondered what Aliyah was thinking now that she had heard his side of the story from his father. *Does she believe me? Is she remorseful? Will she call me?*

After a restful nights sleep, Jeremiah woke up early the next morning. He'd left the skylights open and the sun was streaming through, giving the room a hazy appearance. Flickers of light danced off the walls creating a beautiful kaleidoscope of colors dancing around the studio. Soft jazz emanated from the radio that he had neglected to turn off. Jeremiah's eyes moved about the room until they rested on the portrait of his mother. Her eyes were smiling at him now.

He jumped out of bed, did a few stretching exercises on the floor and then turned on the teakettle to make himself a cup of hot Ovaltine. He had dreamed throughout the night. The dreams were mostly of his mother. She was with him as he walked with his children through a forest. She seemed to be guiding them someplace. Wherever they were going everyone seemed happy. Noticeably absent from the dream, though, was Aliyah. *What's to become of us?* he wondered.

At nine o'clock Jeremiah called the brownstone. Jean answered he telephone. Aliyah had already left for her Manhattan office, she told him. "Yes," Jeremiah could drop by to pick up the children as long as he got Mandela to his preschool class by noon. Jean was very accommodating.

Jeremiah carefully removed the birthday gift he had painted for his mother-in-law from the easel. It was a beautiful painting if he said so himself. After wrapping it in brown paper and carefully securing it with masking tape, he dressed and went to pick up his children. It was nine-fifteen when he rang the bell at the brownstone. How strange he felt ringing the bell to what had once been his home. He still had his key, but he had never tried to use it since he had relinquished the house to Aliyah. *How many weeks ago was that? Was it months now? Would the key still work? Had she changed the locks on the door?* He wondered as he stood on the stoop waiting to see his children.

The smile came on his face automatically as soon as the door opened and Mandela gave him a high five and a "Hi Dad." Nia had on a dress and looked so adorable Jeremiah picked her up and wanted to gobble her up. "Stop, stop," she giggled.

"You look happy." Jean gave him a smile.

"Seeing my kids always makes me happy," Jeremiah said, hustling the kids to the car.

"Don't forget Mandela has to be in school by noon." Jean reminded him.

"Don't worry, he'll be there."

When they left the house Jeremiah drove directly to Nealz'

Benz with his children and the painting. He didn't know if his mother-in-law would be there, he hoped so, but if not he would leave the painting with Jamal. When he entered the dealership with the kids, each holding onto one of his hands, the first person he saw was his mother-in-law. She was dressed in a stylish black business suit with a smart mint green scarf tucked around the neckline creating a striking contrast.

"Hello my darlings," Betty said, coming over to give both of the kids a kiss. "And how are you?" she asked Jeremiah."

"I'm fine." Jeremiah smiled at her. "I didn't know if you would be here, but I took a chance and came anyway."

"I have a board meeting in an hour," Betty said. I wanted to get here a little early to talk to Jamal. He's already upstairs in the board room, come on up."

"You and the kids go on up," Jeremiah said. "I have a birthday gift for you in the car. I'll go and get it."

When Jeremiah entered the boardroom, Jamal greeted him with a warm embrace and a big smile. "Man, it's great to see you," he said.

"It's good to see you again, too."

"What's this?" Jamal took the package from Jeremiah; it was rather large, at least three and half feet by two and a half feet.

"It's a birthday gift for your mother."

"What can it be?" Betty came over with the children to look at the package.

"Looks like a painting to me." Jamal laughed.

"Oh I know that, but a painting of who or what?" Betty examined the package curiously.

"Why don't you open it?" Jeremiah said.

"No," Jamal said. "Let's wait and unveil it at the birthday dinner. You are coming aren't you, Jeremiah?"

"I don't know," Jeremiah said. "When is it?"

"Saturday night at seven," Jamal said. "Why don't you invite your sister and her family, too? The whole family will be there, including your father."

"I don't want to make anyone uncomfortable," Jeremiah said.

"You're a part of our family," Jamal said. "As far as I'm concerned you will always be a part of this family." He picked up Nia, and hugged her to him. You're the one responsible for giving these beautiful children to us. We love you, man."

"Yes," Betty said. "We're a family and it's time that we started acting like one again. Please come to my birthday celebration, Jeremiah." Betty's eyes pleaded with him.

"Okay, I'll come, Jeremiah said. I want to see the look on your face when you open your gift." He smiled at Betty.

"Then we'll have the unveiling at the party." Jamal smiled happily.

"Sounds like a plan to me," Jeremiah said, gathering up his children to leave so that Jamal and his mother could talk business before the other board members began to arrive.

Sleep did not come easy for Aliyah after her father-in-law departed for the evening, leaving her full of doubts, doubts about her own conclusions. *Could I have been wrong?* she wondered. She tossed and turned all night dreaming intermittently. Her dreams were of her ancestors. In the dreams her father had held her as he said to her "Sweetheart you've got to learn how to listen. You're a smart girl and you know a lot, but you don't know everything. If you don't learn when to listen you'll miss out on a lot."

Aliyah's grandmother also visited her in the night. In the dream she, too, cautioned her granddaughter about jumping to conclusions. She had said "Child I know I told you to close one eye after you got married, but I never told you to close your ears. Listen to your husband. Open your ears and open your heart."

Early the next morning Aliyah left the house to go into Manhattan. The train ride was a blur to her. All she remembered was staring out the window while scenes of Jeremiah occupied her mind. She saw Jeremiah in his studio holding Miss Melody in his arms. Aliyah remembered that Jeremiah had asked her to join him for lunch that day. Although she had declined his invitation, perhaps he thought she had changed her mind and come to the studio anyway. *Could the kiss have been a mistake?*

What about the day she saw him in the club lifting Miss Melody onto the piano? She remembered a scene very similar to that in

329

the musical she had attended with her mother. Could they have been rehearsing? Was that the reason Miss Melody had been in her house? Maybe Jeremiah hadn't made love to Miss Melody in their bed. Was that just an assumption on her part? Why hadn't he told her about the rehearsals? *When did I give him an opportunity?* she had to ask herself. She had stopped communicating with him after her suspicions first surfaced. *That was a mistake,* Aliyah concluded.

As the train pulled into New York's Pennsylvania Station, she walked robotically to the nearest exit consumed with thoughts of the previous months. Every since her birthday party she had been suspicious and unwilling to communicate with her husband. *What was she so afraid of? Losing him,* Aliyah admitted to herself. She was so afraid of losing him that she was inadvertently doing just that.

Her father-in-law was right. Jeremiah wasn't a liar; he had never lied to her. Yet she had called him a liar and she had cut off communication and pushed him out of her life. Maybe she thought that by leaving him as she did she could be the one to dump him before he had a chance to dump her.

When Aliyah arrived at her office building she was so consumed with her own thoughts that she barely noticed Dotty waiting for the elevator along side her. They exchanged pleasant "good mornings," but they both went back to their private thoughts, riding up to the eighteenth floor in silence.

"See you in a few minutes," Dotty said as they both moved in separate directions towards their respective offices after exiting the elevator.

"Okay," Aliyah said, forcing herself to refocus her attention. "I need you to help set-up for the meeting," she said over her shoulder to Dotty's back.

The department meeting was scheduled for ten o'clock and it was already nine. Aliyah wanted to get the layout for the coming edition of *Enigma* on the conference table for a final review before it went to press. Twenty minutes after their chance encounter in the elevator, Dotty met Aliyah in the conference room to begin the set-up.

Both Aliyah and Dotty moved about the room quietly consumed with their own thoughts as they placed documents at each seat around the conference table, and other documents in the center of the table as well as on display tables that were especially set up for the meeting. Aliyah checked the set up for her Power Point presentation totally oblivious to Dotty's presence. It wasn't until she heard Dotty sigh once or twice that she turned her attention to her.

"Are you all right?" she asked Dotty.

"No," Dotty said. "No I'm not all right, but I'm trying to keep everything together for the meeting. I will get through this." She sighed again.

"You want to talk about it?" Aliyah secretly hoped that Dotty didn't.

"Do you want to listen?" Dotty asked, giving Aliyah a pathetic look.

"What's wrong?" Aliyah became concerned now. Dotty was a special friend and she didn't want to be rude.

"Derek went back to his wife," Dotty said close to tears.

"What? When did this happen? I just saw the two of you in Atlanta and you looked so happy together."

"I guess the trip to Atlanta was his goodbye gift to me," Dotty said sarcastically. "Two days after we got back he told me that he was moving back home. 'It was a mistake to leave,' he said. I'm the one that made the mistake, not him. Why do I keep doing this to myself?"

"Is that the only explanation he offered?" Aliyah was sympathetic.

"He didn't have to say anymore, Aliyah." Dotty sighed again. "I knew all along that it was bound to happen. Derek wanted his family and me. He liked having both of us; that's what he really loved. He went back not only to his wife, but his kids, their friends, their life. When it came down to either her or me, he wanted her. He has a history with her. You know community property, social life and memories. He had nothing with me. He wasn't willing to start over and rebuild all of the things he had with her already.

Aliyah listened without making any comment. She shook her head thinking *what a jerk Derek is. He hurt so many people with his irresponsible behavior. He hurt his wife, his children and Dotty.*

Jeremiah is not like that. What was I thinking?

"I really love him though, Aliyah. He wants to continue seeing me, but he wants to stay with his family, too. I told him no, but I don't think I'm strong enough to resist him. I guess I was meant to be a mistress and not a wife." She gave another sigh just as the rest of the staff began to come into the conference room ending their very personal conversation.

The train ride back to Newark was not unlike the one into Manhattan. Aliyah was again consumed with thoughts of her marriage. Now that she had doubts concerning her suspicions she wondered how she could go about communicating her feelings to Jeremiah, he hadn't tried to call her in weeks.

For the first two weeks following her abrupt departure from the house Jeremiah had called her daily, sometimes three and four times a day, but she never took his calls. His calls had slowed down until finally he had stopped calling her altogether. She had thought that he was too busy with Miss Melody and had put thoughts of her out of his mind. After that one attempt to visit him at his studio, the night when Miss Melody visited him with a bottle of champagne, Aliyah hadn't tried again.

Have I pushed him into an affair with Miss Melody by my behavior? she thought. *Maybe nothing was going on when I left but has something developed since our separation?* she wondered. She couldn't blame Jeremiah if he had sought the comfort of another woman after his own wife had refused to even talk to him.

What a mess she had made of things. *How can I go about undoing this mess?*

It was only three o'clock when Aliyah put her key into the door of the brownstone. She was a little startled to see Jean and Nia ready to walk out of the door.

"We're going to pick up Mandela from his pre-school," Jean told her.

"Oh," Aliyah said. "Why don't you leave Nia with me. I'm going to change into my jogging suit and take a walk around the lake at Weequahic Park. I'll take Nia for a ride in her stroller.

"Good," Jean said. "Me and Mandela will stop at the supermarket for some fresh vegetables for dinner tonight. I'll meet you back here in an hour or so, okay?"

The foliage at Weequahic Park was absolutely beautiful in the fall. Aliyah was disappointed that the turning of the leaves had been so delayed due to the unusually dry summer and the lingering warm weather. Everything was turning brown instead of the usual reds, yellows and oranges. As she pulled into her usual parking lot she noticed the red sports car that she had come to hate. No one was in the car and she didn't see Miss Melody anywhere in sight. She quickly buckled Nia into her stroller and headed for the jogging path. The sun would be descending soon.

The lake looked so peaceful, still and tranquil. Aliyah couldn't help but notice how Nia stared out over the water as quiet as the lake itself. All they heard were the squawking of birds and the rustling of dry leaves on the path as the stroller rode over them. Aliyah walked briskly pushing the stroller along the smooth paved path. She said hello to an old man sitting on the banks of the lake fishing. A little further ahead she spotted a lone female with her back to the path standing on the bank of the lake smoking a cigarette. *Miss Melody,* Aliyah thought as she pushed the stroller on.

Just as she and Nia passed Miss Melody Aliyah heard a voice from behind her.

"Aliyah."

Aliyah stopped and turned around slowly. She looked right into Miss Melody's face, but she didn't say anything. Miss Melody had a pretty light brown face. She had a flawless complexion with lips that were painted a soft pink. Her hair was curled loosely and fluffed around her face. *Must be a wig,* Aliyah thought. She looked a lot like a young version of Sarah Vaugh. She was wearing tan slacks and a matching tan sweater with a brown cape like jacket thrown loosely over her shoulders. They stared at each other for almost a minute before Miss Melody spoke again.

"You're a fool," she said not batting an eye. "Did you hear me, Aliyah? You're a fool if you let him go." Her voice was loud and crystal clear.

"I've been a fool." Aliyah's voice was just as loud and just as clear. "But not anymore." She turned around and picked up her pace pushing the stroller in front of her.

After putting the children to bed Aliyah lay on her own bed trying to work up the nerve to call Jeremiah. *Suppose he won't take my call? What will I do then?* Just as she reached for the telephone it rang, startling her for a minute. She hoped it was Jeremiah calling her.

"Hello," she said sweetly into the telephone.

"Hi Sweetheart," her mother's voice came through the receiver.

"Hi, Mom," Aliyah relaxed a little. "What's up?"

"Just calling to say hi and to remind you that my birthday dinner is tomorrow night. You will be there won't you?"

"Mom, have I ever missed your birthday?"

"No you haven't. But don't I always call to remind you?"

"It's not necessary you know?"

"I know. But I wanted to tell you to wear something extra special tomorrow night."

"Why? Just family is going to be there, right?"

"That's true, but there will be a guest."

"Who?"

"Well Gordon for one. And then there will be Mr. Jones."

"You invited my father-in-law?"

"Yes. And his daughter and her family."

"Oh, Mom. Why did you do that? I think they'll be uncomfortable without Jeremiah there, don't you think?"

"But he's coming, too, that's why I asked you to wear something special."

"You're kidding?" Aliyah jumped off the bed. "When did this happen."

"This morning when he and the kids came by the dealership to bring me my birthday present. Jamal and I invited him to the party tomorrow night."

"And what did he say?" Aliyah was pacing the floor by this time.

"He said yes, of course."

"Oh!" Aliyah said excitedly. "He'll be there tomorrow night? What will I wear?" She ran to her closet.

"Wear something sexy. Something that Jeremiah likes to see you in."

"I've got to go now, Mom. I've got to start getting ready for the party."

"But the party isn't until tomorrow night," Betty said.

"I know."

Chapter 23

Jamal and Sheniqua lived in a brand new colonial style home on a quiet tree-lined street in Newark's WestWard. Jamal had purchased the lot shortly before they were married. The house that previously sat on the lot had been destroyed by fire. Once it was razed they had a house built to their own specifications. The replacement house was Sheniqua's dream home. It sat back quite a distance from the street, and had a large front lawn. There was a large oval driveway and a flagstone walkway that led to the front door.

Aliyah arrived at exactly six-thirty with Mandela and Nia in tow. Her eyes scanned the driveway checking out all of the parked cars. Dr. Gordon's Lexus was there. Behind the Lexus was a silver SUV that she recognized as belonging to Jeremiah's sister, Naomi. Parked closest to the house was a van with the name of the caterer that Sheniqua was using painted in bold lettering on the sides.

Where is Jeremiah's car? Aliyah wondered. It appeared that all of the invited guests were there except for him. Aliyah's heart sank a little. *Maybe he changed his mind,* she thought as she carried Nia up the walkway while Mandela ran ahead of them.

Sheniqua opened the door while the doorbell was still chiming. Aliyah entered into a huge entrance hall with beautiful marble flooring and exquisite light fixtures. She could hear laughter coming from the living room. A housekeeper, hired for the evening, came to collect their wraps. Aliyah checked herself out in the hall mirror; she looked glamorous. After trying on every dress in her closet she had finally settled on the black knit that Jeremiah loved. The walks around the lake at Weequahic Park had paid off. The walks and the stress she had been under for the past few months, that is. Exercise and stress were a sure way to lose weight she concluded. The dress that was too tight to wear for her fortieth birthday party fit perfectly now.

Sheniqua escorted them into the living room where Betty and the rest of the family were gathered. Aliyah's eyes moved around the room taking in the smiling faces of all of the people that she loved, except for one. Jeremiah was not there.

Mandela and Nia were delighted to see their older cousins, Naomi's two children, Noah and Rachel. The four of them squealed in delight. Their grandfather who relished in the delight of his grandchildren joined them.

"This is the first time that I have had all four of my

grandchildren together in one room," he said.

"I know the joy you must be feeling," Betty said. "You are truly blessed. Soon I will have another grandchild to add to my joy." She gave Sheniqua's swollen stomach a gentle pat.

Aliyah made her way around the room exchanging warm greetings with her brother, sister-in-law, brother-in-law, father-in-law and finally to her mother and Dr. Gordon.

"You look wonderful!" Dr. Gordon said, giving her a gentle hug.

"Thank you," Aliyah said. "I'm so glad you could be with us this year to celebrate Mother's birthday."

"The pleasure is all mine." Dr. Gordon revealed a genuine smile of appreciation.

Someone from the catering company came by with a tray of delicious looking hors d'oeuvres. Aliyah put a couple on her cocktail napkin and reached for a glass of champagne from a tray that another one of the caterers was carrying. She wanted to ask about Jeremiah, but for some reason she couldn't. Finally her eyes found the painting, still wrapped in brown paper, sitting on an easel in front of the unlit fireplace.

"What's that?" she asked her mother.

Betty's eyes followed hers to the painting. "It's my present from Jeremiah. I'm waiting for him to arrive so he can unveil it."

"What time is he expected?" Aliyah asked.

"Jamal told him to come at seven." Both Betty and Aliyah

looked at their watches at the same time that the doorbell rang. Aliyah's heart began to race. She hadn't felt this excited about seeing Jeremiah since before they were married. Betty, sensing her daughter's anxiety, reached for her hand.

"Stay calm," she whispered to Aliyah.

"I'll try," Aliyah whispered back.

This time it was Jamal that went to open the door. Aliyah heard laughter coming from the entrance hall. The sound of Jeremiah's laugh made her tremble. She hadn't heard his voice, let alone his laughter, in months. She held her mother's hand tightly for a few seconds before letting go.

All eyes were on Jeremiah when he and Jamal entered. Jeremiah's eyes went first to the children who ran towards him.

"Daddy, Daddy," Mandela sang out.

"Dah Dah, Dah Dah," Nia squealed.

"Uncle Jay," Noah and Rachel both said.

With the children holding onto him Jeremiah made his way across the room to his mother-in-law.

"Happy Birthday," he said, giving her a hug and a kiss on the cheek.

"I'm so glad you're here." Betty hugged him back. "Jeremiah I would like for you to Meet Dr. Michael Gordon. Gordon is a very special friend of mine."

"Pleased to meet you." Jeremiah's eyes revealed a mischievous twinkle when he smiled. After shaking Dr. Gordon's hand he made his way around the room greeting and hugging the other family members, first his father, then his sister and brother-in-law, then Sheniqua. Finally he was standing in front of his wife.

"Hello, Aliyah," he said courteously, without giving her a hug.

"Hello," Aliyah said, feeling very uncomfortable.

Much to Aliyah's relief Jamal came and took Jeremiah's arm leading him toward the fireplace. "We've been waiting for you to unveil the painting," Jamal said. "Everybody's starving and we want to go into the dining room where a spectacular meal has been prepared in honor of Mother's birthday."

Jeremiah carefully removed the brown wrapping from the painting and stood back for all to see. The silence that followed was deafening. Aliyah was the first one to speak. "It's absolutely beautiful," she said in amazement.

He had managed to capture the essence of his late father-in-law on a piece of canvas. Bill's eyes had the sparkle that was always present. Even when he was sick and dying the sparkle had remained in his eyes. He had a hint of a smile; his lips were slightly curled at the corners but not quite enough to reveal his teeth. His hair, completely gray at the temples and sprinkled with gray evenly over his entire head gave him a distinguished look.

Betty appeared to be in shock. "Jeremiah you have outdone yourself," she finally said. "You have captured the essence of my beloved Bill on this canvas. You could not have given me a better present." Her eyes were filled with tears.

"I can't believe it," Jamal said. "You've brought my father to life in this portrait."

Sheniqua stood staring at the portrait with her mouth open.

"Who is it?" Mandela asked.

"It's your grandfather," Jeremiah said, picking him up so that he could get a better view.

"I thought that was my grandfather," Mandela pointed to Jeremiah Sr. with a puzzled look on his face.

"That's your other grandfather," Jeremiah said as everyone laughed. "I thought the portrait would make a wonderful addition to the new board room at Nealz' Benz."

"I have the perfect spot for it," Betty said still staring at the portrait.

"Okay," Jamal said after everyone had had a chance to recover from the initial shock of seeing Bill's lifelike portrait. "Let's all retreat to the dining room." He picked up the portrait and easel to take into the dining room with them.

The dining room table was exquisitely set with many of Sheniqua and Jamal's wedding gifts. There was lovely bone china and beautiful silver flatware. Expensive crystal stemware and serving bowls also graced the table. The centerpiece was a magnificent silver candelabrum. It created an aura of flickering light giving off a dazzling sparkle that reflected off the china and glasses. Everyone busied themselves looking for nametags to determine where they should sit.

"I relinquish my seat at the head of the table to my most graceful mother-in-law who is the matriarch of this family and whose birthday it is we celebrate tonight," Sheniqua said, pulling out the chair for Betty.

"And I relinquish my seat at the head of the table to Mr. Jeremiah Jones, Sr., who I consider the patriarch of this family whenever he is present in my home," Jamal said, pulling out the chair for Mr. Jones.

"I am honored," Mr. Jones said, taking his seat.

"So am I," Betty said.

Sheniqua and Jamal sat to the right and left of Betty, while Aliyah and Jeremiah sat to the right and left of Mr. Jones, directly across from each other. Jeremiah seated Mandela next to him while Aliyah seated Nia in the high chair next to her. The others followed suit and seated themselves. After everyone was seated Jamal asked Mr. Jones to bless the table.

"Let's all join hands in the spirit of family and unity," Mr. Jones said before beginning the grace. Everyone listened intently as Mr. Jones thanked God for bringing the Neal and Jones family together again in celebration. While eyes were still tightly shut and heads bowed he concluded the grace. "I want everyone around this table to know that the Jones family is an honorable and respectful family and that we understand the importance of conducting ourselves in an honorable and respectful manner at all times. My son, Jeremiah Jones, Jr. did not have sex with that woman," he said before saying "Amen."

Aliyah looked up in shock. Jeremiah raised his eyebrows, amazed at his father's audacity. Jamal laughed out loud. "Oh no he didn't say that," Sheniqua said. Betty smiled and Naomi chuckled.

"Let's eat now," Mr. Jones said rather nonchalantly as though he had not said anything out of the ordinary.

Throughout the meal Aliyah avoided looking at Jeremiah. She busied herself feeding Nia. She made small talk with her father-in-law and her-sister in law. She laughed at stories her father-in-law told, and at the stories Dr. Gordon told. She listened to the stories of her brother and brother-in-law. She toasted her mother with the rest of the family.

After the family sang happy birthday to Betty, Stevie Wonder style, and the birthday cake had been cut and eaten, Jamal announced that cordials would be served in the living room. As everyone got up to leave the room Betty took Nia out of the highchair and carried her out of the room. Mr. Jones, Sr. took Mandela by the hand and led him out of the room. Neither Aliyah nor Jeremiah moved with the rest of the family, they remained seated at the dining room table. They sat quietly listening to the chatter of everyone as they made their way to the living room. Finally there was silence. Jeremiah got out of his seat and walked up to the portrait of his father-in-law. Aliyah came up behind him.

"You know my father was right in what he said." Jeremiah finally said, turning to face her.

"I believe that now," Aliyah said. "I'm sorry, Jeremiah. I should have trusted you. Can you forgive me?" She looked Jeremiah in the eyes.

"I don't know. You hurt me, Aliyah."

"But I was in just as much pain as you were Jeremiah. It hurt me to believe that you were sleeping with Miss Melody."

"You brought that pain on yourself, Aliyah. Why would you think that I would risk what we had by having an affair with Miss Melody?"

"I don't know. All the evidence was there. It all seemed to add up." Her eyes begged for forgiveness.

"You just didn't trust me, and you wouldn't even let me explain to you how wrong you were." Jeremiah shook his head in disbelief. "I thought I knew you better than that. I never thought you would behave like that. Now I wonder if I know you at all."

"I'm sorry," she said again. "Give me another chance and I promise I will make you forget this and make everything go back to the way we were before all of this happened." The desperation in her voice was obvious.

"No," Jeremiah said. "I don't want to go back there. Back there you didn't trust me, you wouldn't confide in me. You wouldn't tell me what was troubling you or what you were thinking."

"I won't do that again, I promise." Her eyes filled with tears.

Ignoring her tears, Jeremiah turned his back to her and looked at the portrait again. His father-in-law had been a man of good character. He always spoke his mind. One never had to guess what

Bill Neal was thinking. Jeremiah had always liked that trait in him. You always knew where you stood with Bill. *Why isn't Aliyah more like that?* he wondered.

"You know that communication is the key to a healthy relationship, Aliyah," he said, turning to face her again. "If we decide to get back together we will have to go forward, not backward. No more distrust. You will have to confide in me whatever you are feeling. Can you do that?"

"Yes," she said in all earnestness. "I can do that. I will do that for us."

Jeremiah looked at her as though trying to read her thoughts. He saw the pain in her face and the hope in her eyes, but beyond that he saw the love that she had for him and for the family they had created together. Seeing this look of love in the woman he loved so much caused the slightest hint of a smile to appear at the right corner of his mouth. It was all that she needed.

Aliyah flung herself into Jeremiah's arms, and he pulled her close to him. He kissed her eyes tasting the salty tears that were now running freely down her face. His lips found hers and she released all the passion that had been sealed up in her heart for longer than she cared to remember.

"They're kissing, they're kissing." The voice of eleven-year old Noah came from somewhere in the house. Next came the pitter-patter of little feet running in and out of the dining room. Jeremiah and Aliyah were oblivious to all that was going on around them. "They're kissing, they're kissing," four little voices were saying in unison running about the house.

When they finally came out of the dining room, Jeremiah holding Aliyah's hand, everyone was standing outside the door. The applause and laughter that followed was heartwarming.

"I'm taking my wife home," Jeremiah said, heading toward the front door. A dreamy looking Aliyah followed her husband.

"This is the best birthday present of all." Betty smiled, deliriously happy.

"Don't worry about the children," Naomi said. "We'll take them home with us."

Mr. Jones smiled at the prospect of having his grandkids together overnight. All four of the children jumped up and down, gleeful that they would be spending the night together with their grandpa.

"Yes, take her home," Jamal laughed. "She needs a good spanking," he said playfully.

Entering the brownstone, Jeremiah headed toward the basement. "Why don't you go upstairs and get comfortable," he said to Aliyah. "I'll be up in a few minutes."

"Oh no!" Aliyah said, knowing where her husband was headed. "You come upstairs with me. I have something to show you."

On the third floor in front of her ancestral altar Aliyah and Jeremiah lit the white candle. Aliyah poured a glass of cool water. Together they thanked the ancestors for bringing them back together.

"Thank you mother for sending Dad to the rescue," Jeremiah said.

"Thank you Dad and Grandma for your words of wisdom to me, to Mom, and to Jamal. I needed to hear all the things you had to say.

"Thank all of the ancestral spirits for using their influence with God to help us get back on the right track," Jeremiah said.

After making their first offering to the ancestors as a couple, Aliyah and Jeremiah retired to the master bedroom where they ended one of the most blissful days of their marriage.

Epilogue

For their fifth wedding anniversary Jeremiah made good on his promise to take Aliyah to Ghana for a second honeymoon. The first honeymoon had been spent at the brownstone. They both agreed that their fifth wedding anniversary would be the perfect time to renew their wedding vows. The motherland would be the perfect place. Everyone they loved was invited to Ghana to witness the ceremony.

Leaving the hotel in Accra, the capital city of Ghana, five Land Rovers, each with a driver, carried the procession to the site. Betty and Gordon along with Jeremiah Sr. and his wife, Simone, rode in the second car. Jamal and Sheniqua with their son, little Bill Neal, along with Jeremiah's sister, Naomi, her husband, Phillip, and their children, Noah and Rachel, rode in the third car. Jean and her husband, Claudia, Kwami and Ebony rode in the fourth car. Kanmi and Oya with their two children, Mwangi and Yori along with Jeremiah's spiritual advisor and babalowa rode in the fifth car. The lead car carried Jeremiah and Aliyah with their children. What a sight it was to see this caravan making its way over the Ghanaian terrain heading to "God's tree" in Aburi Gardens.

Each car carried a tightly woven sisal basket with a picnic lunch, a bottle of champagne, and a kente tablecloth. When they arrived at the site, the picnic tables had already been set up under the extended branches of "God's tree." Close to the trunk of the tree was a gazebo decked with lovely white Orchids, Calla Lilies and Gardenias. A golden arch graced the entrance to the gazebo, and a golden runner led to the altar.

Musicians, already in place, began playing as soon as the happy couple exited the car. Aliyah was dressed in a white organdy dress, and Jeremiah wore white slacks with an open collared white shirt. They, along with their children and followed by their guests, made their way to the gazebo. Once everyone was in his or her proper place the babalowa started the ceremony. It was a perfect day for a perfect wedding. All ears strained to hear the beautiful couple recite their wedding vows:

"I vow to be a faithful, loyal, and devoted partner to my spouse;
I vow to be trusting, always giving the benefit of any doubt to my spouse;
I vow to love my spouse unconditionally,
'Til Death Do Us Part."